2182 kHz

2182 kHz

A NOVEL

DAVID MASIEL

RANDOM HOUSE

NEW YORK

Copyright © 2002 by David R. Masiel

All rights reserved under International and Pan-American Copyright
Conventions. Published in the United States by Random House, Inc.,
New York, and simultaneously in Canada by Random House of Canada
Limited, Toronto.

RANDOM HOUSE and colophon are registered trademarks of
Random House, Inc.

Grateful acknowledgment is made to Faber and Faber Limited for permission to
reprint seven lines from "The Wasteland" from *Collected Poems 1909–1962* by
T. S. Eliot. Copyright © T. S. Eliot. Reprinted by the kind permission of Faber
and Faber Limited.

Library of Congress Cataloging-in-Publication Data
Masiel, David.
2182 kHz : a novel / David Masiel
p. cm.
ISBN 0-375-50606-3 (alk. paper)
1. Merchant mariners—Fiction.   2. Seattle (Wash.)—Fiction.   3. Arctic
regions—Fiction.   4. Rescue work—Fiction.   5. Scientists—Fiction.
6. Alaska—Fiction.   I. Title.
PS3613.A8 C48 2002   813'.6—dc21   2001041878

Random House website address: www.atrandom.com

Printed in the United States of America on acid-free paper

9 8 7 6 5 4 3 2
FIRST EDITION

Book design by Joseph Rutt

For Dawn

Who is the third who walks always beside you?
When I count there are only you and I together
But when I look ahead up the white road
There is always another one walking beside you
Gliding wrapt in a brown mantle, hooded
I do not know whether a man or a woman
—But who is that on the other side of you?

—T. S. Eliot, "The Waste Land"

PART ONE

Distant Early Warning

Flush and Sprint

I n ten seasons working the arctic offshore, Henry Seine had never encountered anything quite so disgusting as the shitpile. He realized its presence one icebound morning in May, while on his way to the head to soak his hands in hot water. He ducked fast up the windward side of the camp barge, where a north wind beat down off the polar pack and threatened to make freezer-burned steak out of one side of his face.

The camp barge lay in frozen anchorage at the trailing end of a gravel causeway that stretched twenty-five miles into the Arctic Ocean. Out here, the windward side of anything was no place to stop and gawk, but Seine couldn't help himself. Behind him the camp barge superstructure loomed like a three-story trailer park. Before him the main gangway sloped thirty feet from the barge edge to the gravel below, spanning a narrow lagoon. There on the ice, looking like a pile of frozen mud laced with toilet tissue, lay five days' accumulation of human sewage.

It appealed only slightly to Seine's morbid sense of humor that he had survived 138 days on a winter drill rig, trying to keep the Big Man from stepping on his neck, only to find himself two months later choking on a pile of frozen shit.

The Pile had emerged because Al George had grown tired of trying to fix the broken sewage processor and because the entire crew had grown tired of the Dry Way. Just a week before, each toilet stall had come equipped with a five-gallon bucket and a roll of tall kitchen trash bags. Crewmen would sit on the plastic rim, empty themselves out, tie off the bag, and carry it to the garbage Dumpster on their way to work each morning. Carrying a bag of your own crap was part of the daily routine.

On this particular morning, Seine seemed to be the only worker in camp who wondered what the hell their customers would think of it all. He wondered this partly because a group of them—four Exxon managers—were currently approaching the main gangway, and partly because the Big Man was doing what he called a Flush and Sprint.

Arctic nomenclature had a tortured kind of bluntness to it, and the Flush and Sprint was just that. It began with a Flush, exploding from somewhere in the bowels of the camp barge, and ended with the Sprint: the Big Man, all 6-8, 280 pounds of him, hauling ass around the corner and skidding to a stop just in time to see his own turd pile overboard. The sewage steamed there until it froze over, which in the climate of May took all of about fifteen seconds.

"Why don't you just take a dump right in front of people?" Seine said.

"Why do you not mind your own business?" said the Big Man in his methodically Big Accent, his great Slavic eyes staring dully down at Seine.

Seine nodded in the direction of the Exxon managers, who paused at the base of the gangway, logos emblazoned atop their white hard hats. Their eyes darted from the Pile to the Big Man as if no amount of corporate training could have possibly prepared them for a moment such as this. When the Big Man saw their reaction, the color drained from his face.

Seine had spent the winter working for the Big Man on an exploratory rig at Cross Island—an Exxon rig, in fact—and he knew firsthand how important managerial perceptions were to him. Learning to read the Big Man's moods while doing hard labor fifty miles offshore in the frozen dark was a simple matter of survival. Now Seine watched the Big Man move his lips in a vain attempt to form words out of the primordial mush that filled his mouth. He searched for English that eluded him in direct proportion to the pressure of the moment, and there was no mistaking the pressure of having taken a dump in front of four oil company white hats. "It—it is always good to know where your shit has gone! It was once a part of you!" he announced, as if this would actually explain something. Then he growled under his breath, "It is better than the Dry Way, Mr. Seine."

Seine had no argument there. With the Dry Way not only did you know where your shit went, you had to take it there personally. So he closed his mouth, turned on a heel, and ran to the camp barge head to soak the feeling back into his hands.

Since the season of his twenty-second birthday, Seine had led a migratory existence, coming north each spring and flying south each fall in a great circle of profit and loss. The bulk of that profit was gained in the service of Biller Ocean Transport, which had earned its reputation as well as a considerable fortune using oceangoing tugs and barges to haul heavy equipment into the North Slope oilfields.

Fourteen years before, during the frozen debacle of '75, harbor tugs and dredgers spent an icebound October stuffing cargo barges into a shoal-ridden dock on the east end of Prudhoe Bay. Even the dredgers couldn't keep a channel open, not with ten months of ice scouring the shallow tundra shore. So the following winter the oil companies built a causeway, a raised gravel road that ran offshore into the deeper waters of the Beaufort Sea. From the air this causeway looked like a giant neuron, a tendril of gray meandering north to nowhere. Finally it turned east and flared like a terminal bulb before stopping abruptly at a sheet-steel dock face known as North Dock. And there lay Biller's camp, fifteen flat steel barges buried in snow, clinging to the last strip of connected land before a two-thousand-mile stretch of frozen ocean. Anything beyond here was strictly for dogsleds and crazy people.

On the morning of the Pile, Seine's belly surged for having skipped breakfast, thanks to sewage-induced loss of appetite. In his room on the second level, he pulled insulated coveralls over jeans and sweatshirt and felt a familiar squeeze inside himself. He hated things like shitpiles. He hated the hubris they implied. He kept imagining how the Pile would smell after it thawed.

He felt like doing a flush and sprint of his own: flush his job down the toilet and sprint off across the polar pack. The only thing that kept him from it was a $250,000 construction loan coming due on his house in Washington State, and the overriding reality that sprinting across the polar pack would freeze his lungs.

Geared up for a frigid twelve hours outside, Seine grabbed a snow shovel from the equipment van and made his way through the labyrinth of the 200-foot camp barge. He crossed a grated steel catwalk connecting fore and aft housing units, fought a crosswind that howled through the second-level vans, and ducked down a blocky wooden staircase to the heart of the main deck. The main gangway lay to his north. He heard a toilet flush. He swung south past the rear of the double-wide galley van and squeezed along a leeward passage between a reefer van and a stout wooden structure housing the desalinator, better known as the watermaker. The camp barge rose in chaos all around him, born by no plan but the inspiration of sudden need, which involved mostly the seasonal housing of longshoremen, tugboat crews, and barge laborers. To Seine it looked like a windblown shanty town grafted onto a bloated houseboat.

As he made his way through the barge, Seine stuffed his free hand into his jacket pocket, where his numbed fingertips flicked the edge of a letter he'd been writing to his wife, Heather. He'd been writing it for three weeks now and still hadn't quite made his point even though he'd received three more letters from her in the interim.

He stepped across a narrow gangplank that connected the camp barge to the adjacent equipment barge and started south. He hiked over drifted snow into a section of camp called the String, utility barges shoved bow first into the gravel causeway, lined up side by side like cars in a snowed-in parking lot. Seine hiked from barge to barge out a narrow snow trail that he himself had shoveled. The drifts here were far too deep to shovel away completely, so he merely leveled the snow on top, and set down wooden planking so the Wolf could walk the length of camp without getting snow in his boots.

Seine had shoveled through endless days washed out by the terrible whiteness of arctic ice and punctuated by the throbbing numbness of carpal tunnel syndrome. The rubble of shore-fast ice appeared like broken porcelain stretching to a pale horizon, where it merged with a cirrus sky to eradicate all shadows. Working here was like being encased in a giant white bubble. The only things of color were the camp itself and the thin ribbon of gravel that was their only link to shore.

Underneath the snowdrifts lay the equipment of arctic shipping: coils of line, steel cables, forklifts, diesel generator sets, welding machines, and stacked drums of gasoline and diesel fuel. Where the string barges were shoved into the causeway, massive anchor chains were secured to the barges and tied to cables that ran down into the frozen gravel, where they were shackled to deadmen, odd tangles of welded steel like great winged dragons buried deep in the causeway gravel to keep the entire camp from blowing away on a gale.

The most important cargo on the string barges was the Mosquito Fleet, six harbor tugs that overwintered each year on the flat long decks. As Seine walked, he counted the wheelhouses and radio antennae that stuck out of the blizzard drifts like steel cabins in an industrial wilderness, and contemplated digging each one out.

At trail's end he began work, shoveling through the crusted drifts— one, two, three—stabbing and flinging snow downwind with the flat shovel. From out of the south, the pale headlights of a truck meandered out the causeway toward camp: a Chevy Blazer full of more Exxon white hats. The vehicle floated north like a black ghost out of a white fog. When it reached camp, four smudges emerged, vanished into the twisted snarl of the camp barge, and climbed topside to the Com Shack, the lone dispatch and observation room that hovered over camp like a guardhouse over a prison.

Seine stopped shoveling, pulled out the letter, and looked over the section he'd written last night after composing it in his head all day. He glanced over his shoulder and saw at this distance—almost three hundred yards—the silhouette of the Wolf pacing among a crowd of oil executives crowded into the Com Shack, gesturing, pointing toward an invisible horizon, where later this season they would build an island fifty miles to the northwest, make land for the singular purpose of drilling for oil.

In his mind Seine continued his letter: *Dear Heather,* he thought, and imagined feeling his hands well enough to grip a pen, imagined feeling the turn of his wife's waist. *I am currently engaged in digging a half-mile swath out of the snowdrifts that have buried our camp. I shovel snow 12/7. No days off. I hope you like the house and that you're sleeping well. I am up at all hours. My hands throb. Day lasts all night. Every day is Monday.*

He gave up on the letter, then, and counted his money. Now he saw green instead of white, green like trees torn down and pulped out to make money. He kept a running total, accurate to the hour since his arrival on Cross Island in January. Cross was a natural island of flat gravel with a wooden cross sticking up twenty feet out of the north end, carved with the initials of whalers and explorers going back a hundred years. Seine had arrived on Cross Island ten days before New Sun, temperature a straight 62 degrees below zero (forget windchill), and since that moment had made $32,765.29. With good luck and strong hands, he'd make twice that much before the season was finished. Then he'd go south, find his wife, migrate to the tropics, and curl up into a warm winter.

At afternoon break, the crew sat around with coffee and cigarettes while Seine complained about the Big Man's perverse fascination with the function of toilets. "It's not enough that people foul the temperate zones, now we have to foul the arctic," he snarled.

"Not *this* again," said Mr. Hanson, the camp welder.

Mr. Hanson was a gifted welder but a meek guy, a onetime metalshop teacher from Tacoma who'd been working in camp longer than anybody but the Wolf. Reportedly, one day during his second year on the Slope a former student of his came to work in camp, and from then on nobody called him anything but Mr. Hanson. Seine had always liked Mr. Hanson, even if he didn't know his first name, but now he pointed an accusing finger. "Don't you think our customers might be sort of *offended* by a pile of shit right by the gangway?"

"A flush and what?" said Al George, the gnomish barge engineer. Al looked like an oily version of Santa Claus and, since he refused to wear ear protection on the job, picked up only about half of all conversation.

"And sprint," said Seine. "Don't look at me, that's what *he* calls it."

"That is enough," said the Big Man, looking up from a bowl of Cheerios. "It is my shit, I can follow it outside if I choose."

"Fecal freak," said Buffy Errol. "I know your kind."

The Big Man lifted his eyes toward the Buff. "It is too cold outside for you to call me things that I am not."

"You make me quiver with fear," said the Buff, and shoved a cream cheese tart into his mouth.

"Can we please talk about something else?" said Mr. Hanson.

"Well I'm sorry if you don't like talking about shit," Seine said. "Maybe you prefer drinking it, since it's four feet from the water intake."

The entire crew winced.

"Now wait a minute there," said Al George, holding a stubby filterless cigarette in his mouth. "You could pump raw sewage into that watermaker all day long and get nothing but pure water for your morning coffee."

All at once the crew gazed down at their morning coffee. Then they set their cups on the table, and every last one of them got up and left the galley.

"Just shut up about it, Seine," said Buffy Errol on his way out. "Nobody gives a shit about shit."

"Until they're swimming in it," Seine said.

The last man left was the Big Man. He methodically poured his leftover cereal milk into the garbage can while simultaneously giving Henry Seine his death stare.

Outside the galley, Seine ducked through the various wind tunnels and fought his way to the head. Before the line of sinks and the long mirror and the slash of fluorescent lighting, he ran hot water over his hands and flexed his knuckles and massaged the pits of his palms. His hands seemed to embody the paradox of his life in the north: numb on the outside, painful on the inside. Carpal tunnel joined with arthritis to awaken him nightly with a stabbing pain in his palms like some kind of industrial stigmata. He felt his own heartbeat at the base of his thumb, easing away as the stiffness melted into the hot water. He sighed relief, closed his eyes, and thought about all the ways that Mother Earth would come down on them. Part of him wished for it. Wished he could be there to see the expressions on their faces when they realized how shortsighted they had been. They would deserve it. But when he looked in the mirror, he saw only himself and a row of toilet stalls.

Topside, Seine pushed into his room, where he found the Buff peeing into a Styrofoam cup. "Four cupper," the Buff said, switching cups so fast he lost only a drop to the desktop.

"How about going to the head?" Seine yelled.

"How about shutting the door?" bellowed the Buff. "Haven't you noticed, it's fucking *cold* outside."

Seine shut the door.

The Buff was half Eskimo from his mother's side, half Irish from his father's, and full-blooded barbarian all on his own. His eyes were the merest of black slits across the upper half of his face, and his hair hung to his neck in a ragged mane of black. Aside from this and a Fu Manchu mustache, his face bore more physical resemblance to a block of concrete than anything else.

Almost everything about the Buff frightened Seine, including the claim that he'd been a member of Navy SEAL Team II during Vietnam. To prove this by nobody's standards but his own, he wore a wicked-looking row of Buddha-face tattoos on his right forearm. "One for each gook I gutted in the 'Nam," he'd say if anybody asked. But few did.

Now the Buff shook off into his last Styrofoam cup, leaving a good splash around the desktop, and asked Seine what the fuck his problem was.

"You're *pissing* on my desk."

The Buff's eyes narrowed into minuscule dots, like twin pencil points. He had a fat gnarled scar low on his neck that looked like he'd choked on a piece of meat once and dug it out with a serrated steak knife. When he got pissed it turned bright purple and he fingered it whenever he was thinking of something unpleasant, which as far as Seine could tell was pretty much all the time. "If you don't chill the fuck out, *I'm* gonna be your main problem," he said.

Seine rolled his eyes and retreated out the heavy steel door, turned north up the catwalk, and ran into the Big Man's chest. This was definitely not his day.

The Big Man peered down. "*Sayne,*" he snarled. Seine had worked with the Big Man since 1980, and he knew this form of address to be a bad sign. The Big Man held up a Big Finger in front of Seine's chapped face. "I have been talking to the Wolf and we have discussed all of the ways in which you would be better off if you shut your mouth more often."

"Thanks for discussing my well-being."

"You and I are quite different, Seine. You are idealist, I am pragmatist. You are political hire, I am in-spite-of-political hire."

The Big Man meant Seine had contacts in the Company and he himself was a poor immigrant. The Big Man had defected to the United States from the Ukraine during the height of the Cold War. In the late '70s, he had been a popular oilfield laborer, due mainly to his willingness to drive belly-dumps at insane speeds along winter ice roads, and his ability to dead-lift 450-pound tugboat propeller shafts without any help. In the arctic, everybody loved a strong man, and there was nobody stronger than the Big Man.

"Now you listen to me, *Sayne*. In this country I have only one thing: my relationships with people I work for. That is how defector from communism can make one hundred thousand dollars a year, *Sayne*. Without relationships I do not work, and without work I must go back—" He couldn't bring himself to say it. "I do not mean for you to fuck up my life with your talk. You did it last winter with all that Russian spy bullshit, and now this. You complain too much and you talk too much."

All winter on Cross Island the Big Man had ridden herd on Seine like a horseless Cossack. At North Dock working for Biller they were nominal equals, but on the rig working for Exxon the Big Man was something called a pusher—a rig foreman—and he took his title to heart. Seine had meant the Russian spy business to be a joke. He didn't expect anybody to actually believe him, but he had underestimated the average rig worker, and it took the Big Man a cold month to quash the rumor entirely.

Now Seine considered his situation while facing the Big Man's oversized arms. The Big Man said, "I think real problem is your wife has sent you additional Dear Jonathan letter. Am I right? Ah?"

The Big Man's mentioning Heather made Seine want to tear his own beard out. But it was May and he needed all the facial hair he could get, so he decided that no reaction was the best reaction.

"It is no shame," said the Big Man. "We all get such letters, sooner or later, jah? Perhaps it is time for you to go home."

Seine felt his scalp itch. A shout boiled out of him: "This is how I make my *living*!"

"Then perhaps you should stop thinking quite so much. It is dangerous for a man of your psychological frailties to imagine perfection."

"Oh, *God*—get away from me!" Seine slipped past, rattling the cat-walk all the way up to the Com Shack, where he'd take up the matter of sewage with the only person who could do anything about it.

As GM of Arctic Operations for Biller, Robert Irons ran the camp at North Dock as well as all company operations along Alaska's north-ern coast. They called him the Wolf, or the Arctic Wolf, and he pretty nearly resembled his namesake. In his sixtieth year, his eyes squinted as a matter of windblown reflex, his lips snarled even at rest, and his entire face told of a wintry existence of violent need and torn flesh. The worst part was his nose, or lack of it. It had frozen off during the legendary and horrible fall of 1982, when a southern storm brought hurricane-force winds that tore the barges loose from their moorings and blew them 200 miles into the polar pack. The Wolf and a skeletal crew of three (including the Big Man and Buffy Errol) broke ice for two weeks retrieving them. In the process the Wolf gained his reputa-tion but lost his nose.

Compared to frozen body parts, frozen shit was a petty concern at best. For one thing, the Wolf was in the midst of a corporate struggle to keep the new CEO from doing away with his entire operation.

"Tell ya what, Seine, since this Pile puts such a burr in your balls, how about you clean it up," he said.

"All right, I will. Provided you take care of the source of the prob-lem," Seine said.

Irons frowned. "Seine. The source of the problem is people taking a dump every morning."

"I mean get Al George to fix the sewage processor."

"It's *frozen*, Seine," the Wolf growled. "The ocean, the lagoon, the shit, the processor. Everything is *frozen*. It's either straight pipe over-board or the Dry Way, and we got customers in camp; we can't be run-ning around crapping in plastic bags. It ain't *civilized*."

The Wolf was deadpan, even with a hole in the middle of his face. Seine couldn't think of a good comeback, which disappointed him. All the way down the catwalk stairs, he supposed that somehow the Wolf really did think the shitpile was civilized.

On the main deck, Seine passed the expediter, who had just come back from Deadhorse, forty miles to the south. He carried a pouch of mail up the gangway. As Seine moved past, he held out yet another letter from Heather. Seine took the envelope and stuffed it into his jacket pocket. He leaped across the narrow gap between the camp barge and the equipment barge and pulled open the Pinup Van.

The Pinup Van sat among a two-story row of storage vans and contained, in addition to shovels, pickaroons, and axes, about a hundred or so centerfolds and clipped pictures of naked women dating back to 1973. When Seine had first come to work in camp in 1980, the Pinup Van had been called the Cunt Van. The name bugged him from the first. Then one day an idea came to him, one whose logic and simplicity the others couldn't fail to appreciate: he simply started calling it the Pinup Van. "There aren't any *cunts* in there," he said.

Within a season everybody called it the Pinup Van, all except Al George and Arne Olleson, both of whom were older than time and beyond change.

Inside, Seine opened the letter in the dim light. *Dear Henry,* he read. *I know you mean well. You're probably up there right now trying to stay warm, working hard thinking that's the thing to do for us, but it's time you understand how cold it is down here too.*

Heather was always clever that way. She always got the best of him in arguments, turned him with words that always eluded him. Seine read on while he moved in a daze to the rear of the Pinup Van, where he paused long enough to pull out a flat shovel, a fire ax, and five clear Hefty trash bags. He dragged the tools toward the van door. Heather's letter explained how their life had turned into cyclical extremes of separation and reunion, a marital pogo stick. *When you're home, it's great, but before I know it, you're gone. And for too long.*

"I'm gone trying to pay for our house!" he shouted, toward a picture of Miss September 1985.

The letter went on: *And each time you come back, I have a little more bad feeling left over from your being gone. The truth is, Henry, my feelings have changed in so many ways. You know I've been uncertain. And in that state, anything can happen. So I guess this letter is to tell you that something has happened. The truth is, I've met someone.*

Seine stopped reading. He folded the letter about fifteen times and stuffed the tight square wad into his jacket pocket. He pushed through the van door and into the blow. By the time he stepped out onto the ice of the frozen lagoon, he felt like somebody had hit him over the head with the flat shovel and chopped him in half with the fire ax. Up on the barge edge, Irons stood over him with both hands stuffed into the pockets of his arctic parka, wearing a victory smirk. "Make sure you put a little spit polish on her!" Irons cackled.

Seine tried not to lose his mind over this, thinking it all paid the same, and if Biller wanted to shell out two and a half grand a week for shoveling shit, then the joke was on them, even if the place *was* costing him his marriage.

It took him all of five minutes. He used the fire ax to chop the frozen pile into five manageable chunks. Then he used the flat shovel to scrape the pieces up and stuff them into the trash bags. Then he climbed up the gangway and heaved them into the camp's garbage bin with a rattling *bong.* The sound had just receded when he heard a flush, and a second later more sewage came slipping out, splattering to the ice. Seine stared long and low at it, then all at once swung the flat shovel against the side of the steel bin, a clanging sound that made Irons grimace.

"*Fuck it!*" Seine shouted. "*Fuck it, Fuck it, Fuck it!* Dig a ditch, fill it up! This is a *waste!*"

Irons frowned. He supposed there was some kind of analogy in there, but damned if he knew what it was.

The crew gathered to watch Seine beat the shovel on the side of the Dumpster. On the fifth blow he bent the flat blade straight back, and on the sixth the blade flew off entirely. It arched downwind and clattered into a windy corridor between living units.

A snarl wrinkled Irons's already distorted face. Seine had been a fine worker once, the most efficient, the most fluid, the smoothest deckhand he'd ever seen—an athlete on board ship, an artist at tossing a line onto a cleat. Irons wasn't sure what had happened to him, he only knew he wanted him gone before the CEO came through camp. He couldn't bring himself to fire one of his old hands, but he had no problem making Seine's life more miserable than it already was. Maybe he'd quit on his own. So Irons decided right then to give him every shit job in camp until the ice broke up, and after that send him someplace *really* maddening.

Someplace like the gravel haul.

Gravel Haul

That summer Seine spent sixty-four days on the gravel haul, going back and forth on a one-hundred-mile round trip offshore aboard a tug called *Kimberly D. Biller,* while the letters from Heather poured in like buckets of ice water. He had assumed that the letter revealing her infidelity would be the last, the crowning achievement, the adulterous crescendo. But somehow she felt a need to continue justifying what she'd done. Either that or she was just trying to get a reaction.

The *Kimberly D.* was shaped like a sixty-foot cracker box. She was known as a "triple-screw"—because her engine room housed three Caterpillar turbodiesels connected to three screw-type propellers. The engines screamed from the engine room. Normal conversation while under way was next to impossible; at the same time, privacy was completely absent. The entire crew slept bunkhouse style in the middle deck and went around shouting at one another just to be heard.

Kimmy D. was no tugboat at all but a pusher boat that wired up behind a flat empty barge and shoved it river-style toward the gravel loading station, an immense system of conveyor belts that in the reflection of still summertime water looked like a mechanical cockroach lying sideways on the sand. *Kimmy D.* pushed past the conveyors, gravel raining down into three cone-shaped hills, and then shoved off for the north through sporadic ice fields to a spot fifty miles offshore, where Exxon wanted to build a gravel island they had already christened Muktuk.

In this way, Seine not only helped build Muktuk Island, he actually became the first person to set foot on it. By then it was late summer, or at least Seine thought so. The passage of time grew more vague the longer he worked on the water. He worked a watch schedule of six on, six off, so that half the time he went to sleep and woke up only to discover it was the same day. His mental state deteriorated accordingly, a state complicated by the fact that Seine and the entire crew of the *Kimberly D.* were stoned a good portion of the time.

The skipper's name was James Mann, but everybody called him Hang Mann. Seine thought the nickname a joke, but it turned out the guy actually answered to it. Of all the skippers in the company, Hang Mann had the lowest crash rate, a statistical truth made all the more remarkable because he also had the *highest* number of *Cannabis indica* plants growing hydroponically in his Seattle basement. The year of the Muktuk Island job, he brought one entire harvest north in prerolled Rastafarian blunts, which he smoked pretty much incessantly.

Though a stoner in fact, Hang Mann regarded himself as a gentleman towboater. He wore an array of button-down Izod sweaters, ranging from navy blue to pale pink. His blue jeans were always pressed and perfectly faded, and on his feet he wore white-white Nikes. Over his eyes he wore a two-hundred-dollar pair of Ray Bans, and while running a tugboat he listened to Jimmy Buffett, the Beach Boys, or Boz Scaggs. He let Seine steer all the way to the dump site while he bobbed his head and sang and played drums on the wheelhouse con-

sole. *"We were always sweethearts, different in our way,"* he sang, and then
said, "You're a natural, Seine Man. You gotta get your operator's license." Then he'd add, "Dock's in sight. Time to burn one."

The dock wasn't really a dock at all but a bullet-shaped icebreaker
barge called *Arctic Odyssey.* Anchor wires led off the *Odyssey*'s four
quarters, winched tightly over the precise location of Muktuk Island.
On the so-called docking side, double layers of heavy equipment tires
were chained in place as fenders. On *Odyssey*'s deck two stout cranes
loomed, their skeletal booms hanging out over the barge edge waiting
like vultures for the gravel barges to come alongside.

Hang Mann would duck below the wheelhouse console and fire up
a joint while the radio chattered and Seine stood above him, steering.
"I hear they're gonna bring dogs, man," Hang Mann said from a
crouch. "They'll sniff out my weed," and he handed the joint up to
Seine.

Seine took the joint and inhaled the heavy sweet smoke of the *indica,* holding it as he stared at the line of the polar pack. It loomed
a few miles north, distorted by refraction into apparent cliffs, like
snowy palisades.

Hang Mann had killer weed. It got Seine so stoned he wasn't entirely sure he could do his job without being crushed or knocked overboard. He turned the wheel over to Hang Mann and pointed to the
cranes. "Once I was working with a crew of Indonesians," Seine said.
"Off-loading cargo in the hold of a steamer off Singapore, and a load
from a crane just like that flattened two of them."

"Whose fault was it?" Hang Mann asked.

"Fault? I don't know. Bad load. I tried to tell them."

Hang Mann nodded grimly. "Yours, huh?"

"I didn't say that. I said I tried to tell them."

"Guilt's a wicked thing. What you gotta do now is shove that paranoia aside, Insane Man."

Seine's job involved climbing over the bow railing of the *Kimmy D.* and boarding the gravel barge. It stretched ahead of him, three peaked mountains aligned down the deck's centerline, their gravel slopes reaching nearly to the edges of the barge on all sides. Seine stepped to the outboard and made his way carefully to the bow to put up a lonely bow line. From the opposite side, the two massive clamshells flew in for the kill.

Seine wondered if he could have done more for those Indonesian stevedores, but decided he might be better off focusing on doing more for himself right now. The cranes attacked the gravel mountains and dragged the barge and the *Kimmy D.* alongside. The barge pitched and rocked all over as the clamshells scraped it clean with frightening speed.

Seine got as far away from the cranes as he could, which wasn't far enough for his taste. He crouched behind the H-bitt on the outboard bow. Used for tying off the heaviest of barge lines, H-bitts stuck up at the corners like midget goal posts. By holding to the crossbeam, Seine could squat down without fear of being pitched overboard. The entire expanse of the Arctic Ocean seemed to hover and hum around him, his heart pounding like a claw hammer in his chest.

For most of the sixty-four days spent in a seagoing circle, the crew did nothing but steer and mop and paint and wash windows and get stoned.

Seine wrote to Heather. His letter had evolved from a simple reply into something more closely resembling an epistolary novel. It had multiple dated entries and was a diary of his activities and mental evolution while in the north, so that she could appreciate the isolation and pain involved in making ten grand a month. He reminded her of their youthful dream of traveling the world together. But she had wanted a house. So he had agreed to the construction of a split-level behemoth nestled amid cedar trees on Bainbridge Island. *My hand is forced,* he wrote. *Don't you see? You want me and you want the house. I can't give you both!*

He had begun referring to it as Braindamage Island.

He tried and failed to explain his need to stay in the present. Within the daily grind, survival meant living inside the small rhythms of time, looking no further forward than two fifteen-minute coffee breaks, a half-hour lunch, dinner, and finally welcome sleep. Five A.M. came early, a 6 A.M. to 6 P.M. minimum that ran him gradually into the ground. In an average season including all overtime he would work 15.6 hours per day, 7 days per week.

The Big Man was right, he was not psychologically strong. When he allowed himself dreams of her, the emptiness flowed through his every vein, made his blood ache and his organs weep. He saw them lounging on some beach in Costa Rica. He saw them wriggling their toes into white sand only to regain consciousness and find himself trudging in pac boots through gray gravel. In the letter he included a ledger, a precise act of accounting. At that moment he had made $52,491.84 for a year now two-thirds gone. He continued his running total. He said the word *money* to himself, repeated it, chanted it, counted the numbers that represented it, and felt himself going gently mad.

But something else haunted him. As he wrote, he became aware that the house and the money and her desires for both weren't the only reasons for his annual flight north. He came for some other need all his own, one he couldn't pin down or name. This need hovered like a shade, lurking at the corners of vision, almost out of mind. Something about his long-dead father, maybe.

Every night he stood wheel watch, kept the single-sideband radio tuned to 2182 kHz, the vague hissings of the international distress channel leaving him empty and lost. He imagined people out there, alone as he was, adrift in an oceanic rut, their bows digging in, their decks awash.

Every day, usually stoned, he wrote to her. When he was satisfied that he had probably written too much, he folded the pages into an envelope, addressed it, stamped it, and stuffed it into the outgoing mailbag. Then he waited five days for the mail boat to swing by.

When it finally did, Seine had just smoked a whole Hang Mann joint on his own. His entire body hummed a tune. He focused on the way the mail boat's blue paint glowed in the arctic twilight, on the way sweat beaded on the upper lip of the deckhand. He accepted the incoming mail, thanked the sailor, and watched the mail boat motor off, noticing the pattern of bubbling water rushing off her stern, hearing the groan of main engines under the constant buzz of the generator. Then he went inside the galley and opened the pouch. It contained two postcards for the engineer, a CARE package for the captain, and five Dear John letters for Henry Seine. He read them straight through in chronological order, each more angry and definitive than the last. The final one ended like this: *Since I haven't heard from you I can only conclude that you feel as I do—that our marriage is over. On August 5th I filed divorce papers at the Jefferson County courthouse.* She signed the letter *Love Your Wife Heather.* He was uncertain if she had intended to leave the commas out, or if she just didn't know how to punctuate a Dear John letter.

When he finished, he wished for a telephone, or ship-to-shore radio, or *some* way of expressing to Heather his alternating feelings of panic and acquiescence. But this was a harbor boat operating in distant seas—it had no ship-to-shore; in fact, it never *went* to shore but had all supplies and mail delivered to it. Then he caught sight of the outgoing mail pouch. It sat on the counter by the coffee machine and included, among other communications, a forty-one-page tome addressed to his wife. Seine let out a frustrated howl that not a soul could hear over the din of the main engines.

He took the bulging envelope from the outgoing pouch and walked it topside, where he briefly contemplated throwing it out the wheelhouse window. But something kept him from it. Clutching the envelope in one hand like a book, he walked to his bunk in the middle deck, lifted the mattress, and shoved it in.

Muktuk Island finally rose out of the sea, a slushy gravel peak. Not quite as romantic as the formation of Hawaii, but still pretty damned impressive. A day later, they craned a bulldozer onto the newly formed island to start working the gravel into a flat pad for an oil rig. But no sooner did they release the hook than the bulldozer sank out of sight, swallowed whole by the soft wet gravel of the infant island.

Seine actually witnessed this, which was how he ended up being the first person to walk on Muktuk Island. He stood in the wheelhouse with Hang Mann and the mate, Jack Badecker, all three of them whacked out of their minds. Hang Mann was telling Seine to forget all about his wife, that they'd all been there, they'd all lost a wife or two along the way, it was the curse of being a merchantman. "Go towboating, man, forget her. Jump a line-haul and head for Africa or someplace. Then find a broad who can stand the life and hang with her."

Seine was imagining Costa Rica as the radio call came, asking the *Kimberly D.* to send a man onto the island to find the bulldozer and apply a crane hook to it. Seine was appointed, since he was the deckhand, and since Jack Badecker had absolutely no desire to do it himself. Around his neck, Seine wore a hand-held radio. In his hands he carried a shovel. In one pocket of his Carhartt jacket he carried

Heather's last letter. In the other he carried two of Hang Mann's joints.

On the foredeck, the towboat's push knees rose up like wedges. He climbed around the stairlike incline of one knee and stepped off the blunt bow to the surface of the island. He was buoyed emotionally by the chance that he might die an accidental and tragic death. He hoped such a death would make his wife miss him terribly. He wanted more than anything for Heather to wake up one morning alongside the Someone She Had Met and regret deeply her decision to leave her husband, only to find he had died accidentally and tragically.

Once he was ten or twenty feet from the tugboat's bow, Seine forgot all about his marital problems. For one thing, the actual possibility of being swallowed by a gravel island had a way of focusing the mind. For another, an Exxon corporate helicopter swung around him in slow, surreal circles. He could count the rotations of the chopper blade. The white hats inside leaned toward the windows and snapped photographs and laughed, and one of them was actually applauding. Seine thought for a second the applause was for him, and he almost bowed, then thought better of it. He was pretty well baked by then, probably best not to act like it.

Walking on a newborn gravel island was like slogging through wet concrete. It occurred to him that if he ever started sinking he wouldn't stop until he hit the ocean floor. He stepped as flat-footed as he could, put his weight on his forward leg, and felt it sink. When it stopped at about mid-calf, he sighed in relief and hauled his back foot out with a sucking sound. In this way it took him fifteen minutes to make the hundred or so feet to where the bulldozer had disappeared. There he started digging with the spade. He heard someone over a loudhailer complain about his not wearing a hard hat, which made him think about Marco Barn. He shoveled as fast as he could, sinking a few inches himself with every shovelful he hauled out. Everybody watched him: the crane operators, the circling helicopter pilot, the applauding white hats, the stoned towboaters. About a foot down he encountered a steel bar painted Caterpillar yellow. He hooked a towline to it and then turned, surveying a spot where no man had ever walked. And that's when he started to laugh. He thought about Heather's Dear John letters and figured few people ever got to walk where nobody else had. This was true in sex as it was in everything else.

Then the island decided to swallow him anyway. As the bulldozer rose out of the gravel, Seine sunk down in its place. The round stones of river gravel, polished by currents, slid and rolled out from beneath the weight of his feet. He felt himself going down. He tried grabbing the bulldozer, but the deck winch of the *Kimmy D.* had already dragged it twenty feet off. He tried walking, but that made him sink farther until finally he couldn't move. Gravel slurry pressed at his chest, but oddly he didn't panic. Instead, he savored the conviction that he'd go down in arctic history. Not only would Heather miss him, but he'd be remembered in legend as the Man Who Was Eaten by an Island.

The chopper thumped low and Seine felt the hook hit him directly on top of the head. Not as hard as the padeye that once scrambled Marco Barn's brain, but hard enough through his wool cap to wake him from his suicidal reverie. He reached up, slid gloved fingers around the base of the hook, and hung on for his life. He felt a slurping sensation when the chopper pulled him out, not unlike birth, he thought, wet suction holding him back and then letting him go all at once. The chopper dragged him fifty feet to the edge of the island, where he took hold of the taut winch wire and shinnied upside down to the afterdeck of the *Kimmy D.* Hang Mann and the crew were laughing hysterically as he hauled himself aboard. After that they called him Gravel Man.

Overhead, the white hats smiled and applauded some more as the chopper swung off to the south and disappeared. Hang Mann slapped his back, while Seine laughed and tasted gravel grit in his teeth. He had never felt happier in his life. And then he realized all at once that he wasn't swallowed up anymore, not by Muktuk Island, not by the Wolf and his random mindfucks, not by a house on Braindamage Island, not by Heather and the letter he carried in his pocket. He could do as Hang Mann suggested and hop a line-haul, head south for white sand beaches, find a woman who could stand him, and together bathe in warm rain.

So a week later he found a stout harbor tug in need of a hand, a company boat slated to run coastwise around Alaska and down the Inside Passage for Seattle. It was this choice that led him to sail south with a lunatic skipper that everybody called the Chemist.

THREE

A Tug Called *Fearless*

The Chemist made Hang Mann look like a normal guy. He didn't smoke weed while running a tugboat—he didn't have to. After fifteen minutes on board, Seine figured life inside the Chemist's brain was adventure enough all by itself.

Fearless lay a mile off the low tundra shore at Point Oliktok, tied off to the side of a cargo barge called *Early Warning* and lying nose to nose with her sister ship, a tug called *Terror*. As Seine motored alongside in a Zodiac rubber raft, a low-slung fog obscured the upper portions of both vessels. As the name *Fearless* came in view, Seine scanned up a narrow steel tower rising thirty feet above deck, where the tug's wheelhouse looked like a tree fort in a coconut palm. Seine got dizzy just looking at it.

Fearless inspired nothing if not disorientation. He came aboard thinking he was replacing the deckhand, a surly character who had walked off at Barter Island 150 miles east. But it seemed everybody on board thought Seine was there to replace the mate, who wasn't surly at all but apparently walked off at the same time and for the same reason: to get away from the constant verbal haranguing of the Chemist.

The assumption that Seine was the new mate began with the engineer, an affable guy in his mid-forties by the name of Terje Narvik.

Narvik had once worked for the Wolf at North Dock. He remembered Seine skippering the day boat *Whale,* running supplies and ballast pumps around camp, and so assumed Seine had his officer's license. Narvik was lanky and absurdly strong, with a wavering, clipped accent formed by his Norwegian youth combined with twenty-five years sailing American ocean tugs and watching John Wayne movies. There were times Seine couldn't tell if he was from Oslo or Oklahoma. But he was a good-natured sort, who unlike the Big Man didn't actually know his own strength, a trait that made him both more likable and more dangerous. He helped Seine aboard, unconsciously flinging his forty-pound seabag onto the afterdeck like a sack of rice. Then he shook Seine's hand as if trying to tear his arm from its socket, and talked about the departed crewmen. "They paid their own way home from goddamned Kaktovik! That's two grand apiece! Can you believe that kinda shit, boy? Unbelievable!"

Seine stood on the side deck and pondered the legacy of two crewmen jumping ship in the middle of absolutely nowhere. What was the Chemist really like?

"You go talk to him, boy, he's gonna wanna meet his new mate. Now you be warned, he's a freak, but he's one helluva boatman."

Inside the deckhouse, Seine found the able-bodied seaman, a fat dark-eyed kid named Joe Deperod. Deperod sat at the mess table adjoining the galley, holding a Styrofoam cup in each hand. He lifted his chin toward Seine, said one word, "Deperod," and then didn't open his mouth again except to drink coffee out of one Styrofoam cup and spit Copenhagen juice into the other. By the look on his face, Seine wondered if he hadn't mixed them up. He kept the tobacco puffed in his lower lip even after the cook brought him lunch, a steaming bowl of Campbell's soup.

The cook's name was Cliff, and he looked like he'd recently fallen off one. His left leg was shorter than the right, giving him a shuffling, drag-ass gait. He wore a cook's apron over a pinstriped sailor shirt, which he left unbuttoned far enough to reveal a thick purple worm scar, thanks to open-heart surgery the previous winter. Still, he greeted Seine through a haze of tobacco smoke, inhaling so hard on a filterless Pall Mall that the scar swelled until Seine thought it might pop open right in front of him.

Seine scanned the galley deck and noticed how filthy the boat was. Hang Mann wouldn't have waited for the mate or the deckhand to quit, he would have fired them both for not sweeping the decks. "When's the last time anybody did the sanitary?" Seine asked, and got no reply beyond the squirting sound of tobacco spit.

While Seine chalked up the crewmen's departure to some combination of incompetence and sloth, Cliff the cook launched into a defense of his skipper. "The Company's gonna see it different, I know, but them guys leaving ain't his fault. Them two were wacky from the start, and he tried to bring 'em in line. Now he's feeling betrayed, I know," he whispered in a Brooklyn accent.

"The Chemist?"

"The Chemist, sure. He's smart, but he's got feelings like anybody else."

"He's weird," said Deperod.

"Sure, but who of us ain't?" said Cliff, then leaned close to Seine. "At Point Lay he pierced his—his—" and made a fingering gesture toward his chest.

"His nipple?" Seine offered.

"That's right! I didn't wanna say it. His nipples. Both of them! Numbed them with pack ice and run a sail needle right through!"

Deperod let out a grunt, dug a wad of Copenhagen out of his lower lip with his tongue, and accidentally spit it into his coffee. "Shit!" he said, peering down into the cup.

Seine climbed the long internal ladder topside. It was a narrow, dimly lit chute that spiraled upward. He didn't know Deperod at all, but he remembered a story he'd heard about Cliff going blind on a transatlantic run to Lisbon. Caused by some infection to his optic nerve, the blindness caused Cliff to mistake a bag of popcorn for a bag of split peas. Serving popcorn soup while passing the Canary Islands was the joke of Cliff's professional life, even though he was the only one who broke a tooth on it.

As Seine climbed higher, he heard industrial music rake out of the wheelhouse, like somebody dragging steel I-beams over concrete. He mounted the last ten steps out of darkness and into the arctic light, a mottled 10 P.M. glow of broken fog and blue sky over a scattered ice field.

The Chemist sat in a raised captain's chair, thin as a spindle, a long dash of black from his jet-dyed hair and belted leather jacket to his steel-toed fire-jumper work boots. The only break came at the glowing white of his face, where a row of silver rings punctuated the cartilage of his upper ear. He looked thirty but dressed like he'd never gotten over a high school obsession with black leather and Sid Vicious.

The Chemist finally turned, flicking the ash from a filterless cigarette. His eyes hid behind round, blood-red glasses. "Mr. Mate, I presume?"

Under normal circumstances Seine would never have pretended to be something he wasn't, but after nearly being swallowed up by Muktuk Island, he felt himself soaring through a fog thinking *what the hell?* "Sure," he said. "I'm Seine. Good to meet you."

The Chemist gave a perfunctory nod. "Seine, indeed. I've heard of you. I used to run the *Whale* nights out of North Dock, before I got this gig."

"I remember. My first year. You're Auric, right?"

"Call me Chemist. Everybody does." The Chemist spun open a can of Copenhagen and stuffed his cheek full. Then he spit into a cup, lit another cigarette, and slugged down a shot of coffee. Then he professed to have no idea why they called him Chemist. "So tell me. Do you have any tattoos?"

"No," said Seine. "I'm not into needles."

"What a shame."

The Chemist loved tattoos, though he himself didn't have any. The prettier the person, he said, the more tattoos they ought to have, and since he himself was ugly, he needed none. He despised unbroken perfection, loathed aesthetic symmetry. He liked people who limped, which was why he liked Cliff the Cook, and ugly people, which was another reason he liked Cliff the Cook. He liked Irons because Irons had only half a nose, and he somehow managed to make Irons like *him* despite using words like "aesthetic symmetry."

Seine said he had inherited the Chemist's job skippering the *Whale*, whereupon the Chemist's eyes lit up. "You? I loved that little tub of shit! Does she still have a pink boom?"

"A pink boom?"

"On the deck crane. So when you telescope it out it looks like a Great Dane with a hard-on."

"No," Seine said. "No pink boom."

"Too bad. That was a *statement*."

Of what, Seine was uncertain. He hadn't interacted with the Chemist at all that first year, only saw him passing on his way to and from the camp barge. The Chemist was best known for his obsession with a woman he had never met. Her name was Cynthia, and she was the former girlfriend of Marco Barn as well as the scantily attired subject of a photograph that Marco kept on the wall by his bed. Marco and the Chemist were roommates that year, and by season's end the

Chemist had written Cynthia two long love poems, both highly liter-
ate and erotically detailed. Instead of writing back, the girl wrote to
Marco asking who his weirdo roommate was and could he please stop
sending such strange letters.

As they bid farewell to *Terror* and took the barge called *Early Warning* in tow, Seine had the occasion to notice the Chemist's reading ma-
terials, and they were certainly not the norm for towboaters, who
rarely ventured beyond genre Westerns and cheap pornography. The
Chemist on the other hand read obsessively from a duct-taped copy of
Finnegans Wake, crying out, "It ends with *the*, Seine!" as if this should
have immediate significance to somebody who had once majored in
economics. When it clearly didn't, the Chemist screamed, "What I'm
trying to *say*, Seine, is that the entire book's a *circle*!"

"Oh," said Seine. "I get it now."

"Like hell you do."

When the Chemist wasn't reading inaccessible literature he was listening to inaccessible music, mostly gutter punk and an early industrial band called Throbbing Gristle, which sounded to Seine like a
sampling of noise from a construction site. When Seine asked why he
listened to it, the Chemist replied that it sounded like the inside of his
brain, which came as no shock to Seine after listening to him read
aloud from *Finnegans Wake* all the way to Lonely, Alaska.

The barge called *Early Warning* was so named for the cargo run it
served, the line of Distant Early Warning radar stations that dotted
the western and arctic coasts of Alaska. The next in that line came at
Lonely, where tug and barge lay offshore awaiting backhaul items.
The Chemist awakened Seine from an off-watch sleep, whispering
that the best part of the DEW-line run was that all DEW stations had
a bar. "This is Last Booze, Seine. Then we have to go home. We have to
return to our women and make them want us again."

Seine was pretty well convinced he had no hope of doing that, but he went ashore anyway, mostly to deaden that part of his brain that thought he might. Secretly he wanted to find a telephone so he could call Heather and tell her how five Dear John letters all at once seemed like overkill.

Like all the DEW stations, Lonely DEW was built during the Cold War to inform the United States of imminent destruction by Soviet missile. Despite outward resolve, Seine still fought an internal Cold War of his own, swinging between the policy extremes of forgiveness on the one hand and Mutual Assured Destruction on the other, wherein Dear John letters and their replies would fill the role of intercontinental ballistic missiles. He knew deep down that he had already absorbed a fatal first strike, but couldn't resist the thought of lobbing back a few hand grenades and then drinking himself into a coma.

With the rest of the crew asleep, Seine and the Chemist made their way to shore on a bright evening, the Chemist driving the tug's small metal skiff through an ice field. Halfway there the fog thickened and turned to whiteout. Seine looked up to see blue sky hovering above, but straight ahead he couldn't see his hand. It was like swimming in an ocean of milk.

Seine called aft to where the Chemist gunned the outboard full out. "Maybe we should head back!"

"Don't turn weak dick on me now! Do you want a libation or don't you?" the Chemist said.

The question was purely rhetorical, for the Chemist had no intention of stopping. He sniffed the air, claiming he could smell land, then gunned the outboard into the whiteout. Seine thought *Oh Jesus* and blinked half a dozen times fast, trying to clear his vision. But the cold fog brought tears, and he had to duck his head to keep from freezing his eyeballs. They struck an ice floe and jerked left, the engine winding out as they caught air. Seine grabbed the gunwales on both sides and then abruptly felt the bottom go *shhhhhhush* up the sandy shore, launching him over the bow, where he landed in the soft tundra. "You don't drive a tugboat that way, I hope."

"Indubitably so! And you had better be ready for it, Seine!" cried the Chemist with a happy laugh. "I was taught to navigate by an Aleut from Adak," he added, and bounced out of the skiff, disappearing into the bright mist. "Onward!" he barked.

Over the tundra shore, the fog lifted to where Seine could see ten feet. He blinked and tried to follow, starting up a soft trail that cut through the tundra, calling, "Auric! Where'd you go?"

"I'm here!"

"Where's here?"

"Here is here!" And then a sidesplitting cackle drifted out of nothingness. Sound played tricks in a whiteout, and Seine couldn't quite tell where his voice had come from. He turned left and found a gravel road where a roaring truck appeared suddenly before him. He dove and found himself rolling down a gravel embankment as the truck thundered past. "Jesus!" he called. "You see that?"

But he got no reply. There was no one and nothing to witness. He climbed back up to the road and walked until gradually he became aware of dusk falling, and finally darkness. Uncertain, he stopped and listened intently while the whiteout turned to gray and then to black. Finally he spotted the milky headlights of a truck, giving him some warning before it blew past in a flash. But in the afterglow Seine saw the outline of a structure. Thank goodness, he thought, the DEW station.

When he came up closer he saw it wasn't the DEW station at all but a simple plywood shack out in the middle of nowhere. He had no idea how it got there. When he stepped inside he found a long wooden bench, on the middle of which sat a Touch-Tone telephone. He felt like a character in some absurdist drama. He picked up the phone and actually found a dial tone. He laughed out loud and dialed his home phone, the number for their erstwhile dream house. The phone rang four times, and then a man answered. "Who's this?" Seine asked.

"Who wants to know?" said the man.

"Is Heather there? This is her husband calling from Alaska."

"I'm Larry," said the man.

"Well, thanks for telling me, *Larry*. How about you put Heather on?"

"Fuck off," said Larry, and hung up.

Seine called back four more times, and each time someone picked up the phone and then hung it up again without saying anything. He stepped outside and screamed into the arctic night, his voice flipping off in the cold air and freezing, falling to the ground, where it shattered like glass.

He wasn't sure long how he'd stood there before another truck came by. It could have been ten minutes or ten seconds. He flagged it down and nearly shouted with exasperation, "I'm trying to find the goddamned DEW station!"

"No problem, buddy," said the driver. "I'll give you a ride. Didn't you know? It's *happy* hour!"

Radar operators and truck drivers crowded the tiny DEW station bar, which wasn't a lot bigger than the plywood telephone shack. Seine found the Chemist working on his third scotch. "Don't tell me, you got lost in the fog," he said, evidently perturbed.

"Yeah, that's it," said Seine, and ordered a shot and a beer. "Lost in fog."

"Pfffft," said the Chemist. He drank with an irritated, curling

mouth, and Seine knew right off he was a mean drunk. "I won't toler-
ate a mate who gets lost in the fog, you know. Especially as I have
built-in radar, thanks to Gordo the Aleut. I can see you don't believe
me."

"Sure, why not. An Aleut named Gordo. I'll believe anything." Seine
had no doubt that the Chemist was convinced of his own prowess as a
navigator, but after yet another fast scotch the guy didn't look like he
could navigate his way to the bathroom. Seine watched his fingers
massage his cigarette. Black electrical tape encircled his left wrist.
"What's that?" Seine asked. "Are you in mourning?"

The Chemist turned the wrist, regarding his own band of black
tape. "It's just something I do."

"But why, that's the question."

"The answer is no one's business. I put it on September 21, 1979,
and I haven't taken it off since. Except to shower and replace it
afresh."

Seine might have been more curious if he could have stopped
thinking about Heather and "Larry." Seine didn't have the patience
for mystery. In fact, about then he didn't have much patience for the
Chemist. "The truth is, I went to call my wife," Seine said.

"Ahhh. So judging from your disposition, let me guess: your wife's
a raving bitch," the Chemist said.

Seine didn't answer right away. Part of him wanted to ram his fist
right through the Chemist's smug little smile, but finally he just said,
"No, she's not."

"Figures. I bet you got laid in high school too. I bet you were *popular*." The Chemist turned back to his scotch. "I, on the other hand, was
beaten senseless every day of the seventh grade. By a pack of logger
jocks. They delighted in stealing my glasses and hiding them in the
bushes."

"Maybe that's where you developed your navigational abilities," Seine said.

"I'd pay a year's salary for just one of them to sign aboard my vessel. In the words of Perry Smith, *Oh, what a sweet scene!*"

"Who's Perry Smith?"

"A multiple murderer. Are you illiterate?"

"Yes," Seine said, and slammed back the whiskey, then added, "We've known each other since tenth grade."

"The wife? I knew it—sweethearts. How *grand*."

"Now we have 'conflicting needs.' Also, she's 'met someone.' "

The Chemist looked horrified. "What on earth does *that* mean?"

"I think the first part means we aren't in love anymore. The last part seems self-explanatory."

"At least yours isn't haunting you. *My* lover's right behind us."

Seine turned around. The truck driver who gave him the ride in was talking to an obese woman of forty-five who drank martinis straight up while discussing the irony of being blinded by staring into a radarscope for eight hours a day.

"Her?"

"Not behind us *now*, moron," said the Chemist. "I mean she's fifteen miles behind us on a tugboat called *Vigilant*. In fact I was thinking if we laid over here long enough they might walk in. She's sailing with Macky. He loves the DEW-line bars."

The Chemist looked at the doorway as if expecting his beloved to walk through the door. It was entirely possible, Seine thought; he only knew Heather wasn't.

The Chemist held his smoke in the corner of his mouth, smoke furling around his face as he pulled his wallet out to show a picture. "That's her."

Seine saw only her eyes. "She's beautiful."

"You're a fucking *master* of the obvious, Seine."

The Chemist snapped his wallet shut and slipped it back into his hip pocket. Then he jabbed out the smoke as if shoving it into somebody's eye. "She breaks my heart," he said morosely.

"Does she. What does she do?"

"It's what she *doesn't* do."

"And what is that?"

"She doesn't love me back."

"I'm sorry," Seine said.

The Chemist stared out over the top of those blood-red glasses and squinted. "Well, good! Between your pity and the fact that you married your high school sweetheart, I feel all peachy inside."

Except for making him more belligerent, drunkenness seemed to have no effect on the Chemist. It certainly didn't alter his ability to navigate. He marched the same thin-legged way through the black fog of night as he had through the white fog of day, straight to where they'd beached the skiff. Seine couldn't have found it if he'd looked all night. "How do you *do* that?"

"I told you, Seine. Don't make me repeat myself just because I'm drunk. If you prove yourself feckless, I'll have to tie you to the yardarms."

Seine didn't know what *feckless* meant, but he was glad tugboats didn't have yardarms. He decided the Chemist was dangerous in more ways than one, despite his navigational abilities. "I hope you're careful, that's all I'm going to say," Seine said. "I don't like people dying around me."

"Oh, you don't, do you? Why is *that*?" the Chemist said, climbing into the skiff.

"Because they have."

"And you think it's *you* who killed them?" He lit off the outboard and they motored offshore.

"I guess in every instance there was a moment. When I felt I could have chosen—maybe differently."

"And you chose to survive. What a shock. Henry Seine lives out one hundred thousand years of natural selection! There are points in life, Seine, where you just *do* things, you know? You don't ask, you don't wonder, you just *do*."

And they motored into the fallen dark.

False Pass

The Chemist was an anarchist in political ideology and a fascist in personal relationships. "Do things!" was his favorite order. In fact, the Chemist didn't think he should *have* to issue orders. "Do things!" meant a lot more than just keep yourself occupied. It meant "You should know enough about your job to define *things* all on your own." As they rounded Point Barrow and entered the Chukchi Sea, Seine decided it meant *read my mind.*

The Chemist called the northwestern horn of Alaska the Hog's Head, though to Seine's knowledge he was the only one. He said from a map it looked just like a pig, which was true. The ruffled razorback of the North Slope led upward over the ears at Barrow and down the dished forehead to Point Lay, then flared out toward the flat snout of Point Hope.

Fearless sailed for three days with the photograph of the Chemist's love taped to the wheelhouse glass. They squeezed past ice into the Chukchi Sea and darted past the rising promontory of Cape Mountain in the Bering Strait, all the while the Chemist cajoling his beloved's image as if praying to some pagan icon, only to turn abruptly and point a finger at her, deriding her for being "heartless and whorelike." Seine steered through frost smoke rising off the

Bering Sea like steam, the woman's image staring at him. He found himself studying that photo and her almond eyes until he'd memorized them.

"She won't come to the radio now!" the Chemist cried, as they navigated past the bluffs of Cape Nome. "She's *ignoring* me!" He was listening to a Throbbing Gristle song called "Maggot Death." "I write her love poetry and she *ignores* it," he said.

With his eyes Seine traced the angle of her upper leg as she sat on an H-bitt somewhere in southeastern Alaska, head tilted, smile slight, her long black hair swinging over her shoulder in a loose rope that fell so long it ran right out the bottom of the picture. "Maybe the poems aren't any good," Seine suggested.

"My poetry is *brilliant*! Not simplistic tripe, but original, with metrical patterns appropriate to circumstance. As if that means anything to an Econ-cretin like you."

Seine steered and watched the woman in the window. He thought he might have seen her before but couldn't place where, on some dock somewhere, passing by, a vague figure not unlike the Chemist himself. Something occurred to Seine. "Is she really your lover?" he asked.

"What the fuck do you *think*, Seine?"

Seine saw a homicidal moment flare in the Chemist's face, but he calmed as quickly as he angered. Then he took off his glasses, rubbing his eyes. "All right. In truth, we *were*. In truth, she's left me. Satisfied?"

Seine thought of "Larry" answering his telephone on Braindamage Island and wished that Heather had just left, had one day disappeared. At least then he wouldn't have to face the reality of actually meeting the two of them. Now he couldn't think of a thing to say to the Chemist except, "Sorry."

And the Chemist couldn't think of a thing to say except, "Go piss yourself!"

Despite disliking Seine rather intensely, the Chemist seemed to want his company, not only in the wheelhouse, where they worked, but in the DEW-line bars, where they drank. At Nome they drank until dawn and waited for the Chemist's love. When she didn't show, they started south again. After only five minutes running south into Norton Sound, the Chemist found by radio and radar that his love-on-a-tugboat was no longer fifteen miles behind them but fifteen miles *ahead* of them. Seine thought the Chemist would pitch himself out the wheelhouse window when he finally figured it out.

"Beastly *shit!*" yelled the Chemist.

"It's all right, man," Seine said, taking the wheel so they wouldn't run into the side of an island. "What's the difference? It's a big sea out there. You need to talk to her, call her."

"I will never catch up now!" The Chemist held his head for five minutes, then grabbed the radio, calling for Macky. "Whatta ya want, Bill?" said Macky.

"I want to talk to Julia, that's what I want."

There was a moment of static before Macky said, "Why don't you give it a rest?"

"She's supposed to be running cook-deckhand, isn't she? That would entail wheel watch, I should think, unless you're giving her *preferential* treatment!"

"Now why would I do that?" Macky said with a chuckle, as if the Chemist's already overactive imagination needed further baiting.

"Someone should do something to you, Macky."

"And you're just the one to do it, huh? Big bad guy like you? I'm just giving you a hard time, Auric. Of course she stands wheel watch."

"Then call me when she's there. I need to talk to her, it's *important*."

Then he threw the radio mike to the countertop and moved to the window and slid it down to let a rush of frigid air inside the wheelhouse. The wind tore at his hair. His screams flew into a spelling cheer: "N-U-T-H-I-N-G, yer *nuthin',* you're *nuthin',* yo' momma says yer *nuthin'!*"

Seine considered this a trifle unbalanced, but he kept his mouth shut and concentrated on steering a course. Behind him the Chemist threw the window closed and reached for the boom box volume, where he cranked the Sex Pistols and thrashed his head for half a minute to Johnny Rotten screaming his way through "Anarchy in the U.K."

Watching the Chemist's neck snap back and forth in a blur gave Seine a headache. He held to the wheel and felt the roll of the vessel underneath and started thinking ahead to where he might be able to jump ship.

The Chemist abruptly stopped his thrashing head dance and turned to the chart table as if he'd finally cleared his mind. The chart table sat dead center, directly behind the wheel and forward of the hatch leading down the internal ladder. The Chemist started pulling charts from the racks beneath, until he found the master chart for southwestern: Bering Sea, Aleutian Islands, and Gulf of Alaska. He laid it down flat on the table and bent over it with compass and parallels and started feverishly plotting a course. Using a pen, he wrote numbers on the back of his hand. His pale face and the two red blots of his glasses hovered low under the chart light. Darkness fell.

Seine could see him in the reflection of the wheelhouse glass, while *Fearless* entered the reality of the Bering Sea. The sea swell deepened as the Chemist kept with his manic plotting and replotting of courses. They made their way south of St. Lawrence Island. Winds came from the northeast at thirty knots and *Fearless* ran on a following sea for an hour, steaming downwind before the wind shifted. Still the Chemist was hunched over the chart table.

Seine craned his head to catch a glimpse of what he was plotting, but the Chemist covered the chart like a schoolboy and stared him off. "When I'm finished."

The wheelhouse had started to rock side to side, heeling five degrees in each direction as the wind raked their starboard stern quarter, getting them into an uncomfortable trough. "Can't I come east ten degrees, at least?" Seine asked. "Get a better angle on this trough?"

The Chemist said, "Fly *away*!"

Seine steered with one hand and flipped open a tattered copy of the *U.S. Coast Pilot,* where it said this about the Bering: "The weather over the Bering Sea is generally bad, except in the winter months, when it is consistently terrible."

Seine had no trouble believing this. He decided to *do things*, so he came east ten degrees and hoped the wind would change direction again before the Chemist noticed. In the meantime they were on a course that, if left unaltered, would run them aground on the north side of Nunivak Island.

"There!" the Chemist finally said, standing upright and nodding with pride.

"Where?" Seine asked.

"Don't be a smart-ass, Seine. Here! This is the new course. I want full power at all times on *this course*." Then he looked up at the gyro-compass and saw the change of heading. "What are you *doing*?"

"Things!" Seine announced. Then he smiled.

The Chemist shoved past him and stepped to the wheel, where he swung the rudder back ten degrees. "Are you trying to run us aground?"

Seine didn't even attempt an explanation. He gave up the wheel and checked over the new course instead. Precisely drawn pencil lines led through the Aleutians and then took an apparent straight shot across the Gulf of Alaska for Seattle. An outside crossing. Seine frowned. And there wasn't just the one course, but two. He'd labeled one *Fearless* and the other *Vigilant.*

"I don't get this."

"What a shock. Now be a good mate and do what the captain asks.

That is, if you really *are* a mate." He eyed Seine with raised eyebrows, like a teacher who'd caught a disfavored student cheating on a test.

Seine traced the line of the first leg—labeled *Vigilant*—as it passed through the Aleutians at the normal spot, to the west of Unimak Island. But the second line, labeled *Fearless,* ran to the east of Unimak, through shallow waters known to every towboater operating in Alaskan waters. "This shows a course through False Pass," Seine said.

"And that would be significant *because* . . . ?"

Seine held one hand to the chart table for balance. He looked back toward the looming dark shape of the barge *Early Warning,* trailing them a thousand feet back on a short towline. "Because it can't be navigated in a vessel this size?"

"Oh, bat shit. It *can* be done on a rising tide. By my calcs, if we haul ass we'll hit False Pass on just such a tide on the morning of the seventeenth. You don't think I can do it? Watch me."

"What's the point? So we get home a day earlier?"

"I'll tell you the point. Because while *they* go another eighty miles south to slip through Unimak Pass, I'm gonna slip to the east and make up not one but two days' sail. So then I'll be in the lead again."

"The lead?"

"That's right."

"So this is a race now?"

"You are astoundingly quick on the uptake, Seine."

"Who is *they*?"

"Who do you think! *Vigilant!* Macky. *Julia.*"

The Chemist looked away and lit a cigarette, holding the smoke so long Seine thought he might never breathe air again. "That's crazy," Seine said.

"Oh, *crazy.* You have opinions on things about which you know nothing. And that is something up with which I will not put. Do you

know who said that? Quick, quick, quick. BAHHHHH! Winston
Churchill."

"Right," Seine said, and went below for coffee.

At the galley table Terje Narvik filled out his engineer's log. The
seas had leveled off on a quartering wind, and Narvik wanted to know
what was the big hurry.

"Wants to get home before *Vigilant*."

"What the hell for?"

"Not sure, exactly. Maybe it's a bet. Or a dare. Or maybe love. Hard
to tell with the Chemist."

"High-strung little bastard, ain't he? I told you he was. But he
knows what he's doing."

"You think?"

"Sure. This is our tenth run together."

Seine thumped the bottom of his coffee mug onto the rubber web-
bing that covered the table. "He wants to run False Pass."

"He probably will, then. I seen that kid land a five-hundred-foot car
barge at Terminal 116 on a goddamned towline. He thinks he can do
anything."

Seine returned topside, climbing the swaying tower ladder, feeling
the arc grow wider the higher he climbed into the metal chute. At first
he heard a tape of the Violent Femmes singing, *"Please please please do
not go-ohhh—"* and then he heard the Chemist talking on the radio
in earnest, personal tones. "Won't you just wait for me so we can
talk? Please? Won't you? I should think you'd at least want to *talk*.
Please—"

Seine cringed and backed down the internal stairway, slinking
away really, not wanting the Chemist to know he'd heard the truth in
his voice, the weakness in his heart. He'd heard the same voice from
himself before, and knew well the desperation that caused it.

*   *   *

The Alaska Peninsula sprouted from the state's underbelly and ran in a southwesterly crescent, trailing off into the long tail of the Aleutian Islands. False Pass lay at the geographical separation between the islands and the mainland and, under the best of circumstances, was a squeeze for any vessel drawing more than eight feet. As they approached the north entrance, the barge *Early Warning* drew eight feet and the tug *Fearless* drew twelve.

From the Bering Sea, light stations marked both sides of the entrance, a sandy mudflat called Bechevin Bay, the inside channel marked on one side by a lighted buoy and the other by a bell buoy. On deck, Seine found Narvik pumping fuel from port to starboard tanks. "What the hell are you doing?" he asked.

The bell buoy bonged through the gray morning as they approached the entrance, driving between the barren humps of rocky land. "He's gonna heel her over like a sailboat! You feel it? She's going!" said Narvik.

The boat moved gradually into a starboard list, the deck beneath Seine's feet tilting. From topside Seine could hear the faint ring of music from the wheelhouse. As he craned his neck to see, a window slid open and Jethro Tull's "Aqualung" flew out from above like a cacophonous bird, the Chemist's pale face sticking out to peer down on them, singing *"Snot running down his nose!"* before he shouted "You're *nuthin'*!" and ducked back inside.

"Tell me he's always like this; that way I don't have to think he's losing his mind on my watch."

"Oh, yeah, he always was a freak, I told ya. Watch this. You feel it?"

Seine felt it; the heeling grew more pronounced. Overhead, the Chemist stuck his head out again. "Kick 'em in the right knee, kick 'em in the left knee, kick 'em in the weanie, touchdown, touchdown. R-E-C-T-U-M: rectum rectum we really *wrecked 'em!*"

Seine thought he'd met some strange characters since he'd started working on the water at age thirteen, but no one quite like this. He supposed the Chemist was a product of the age—a punk rock towboater careening through a mad ocean. The boat listed farther and then flopped all at once to a 45-degree angle, where it found a new stable center of gravity. Seine reached out to hold to the deckhouse railing.

"I thought Hang Mann was weird," he said.

"They're all weird," said Narvik, as they motored on their side between the marker buoys into Bechevin Bay, drawing only four feet of water.

They cut east into the Isanotski Strait proper. There, Unimak Island rose up off the water, and at the Chemist's order Narvik pumped all the fuel back to port to even out her trim. The Chemist called Seine over the loudhailer, yelling over and over, "Deckhand, oh, *deckhand!*"

Seine climbed topside, where he found the Chemist playing air guitar and dancing through the wheelhouse. "You need me for something?" Seine asked.

"Need?" The Chemist thrashed his arms and shook his head until his glasses fell off. He groped for them, put them back on, and stood upright. "I just wanted to see the look on your face! I saw Ted Turner do that over a coral reef in the America's Cup, but nobody does it in a hundred-ton towboat but *me!*"

"It was pretty impressive, I admit," Seine said.

"*Yeowwwwwwww!*" screamed the Chemist. "So now you know who is the *superior.*" His smile was bright and grand at what he clearly regarded as Seine's admission of inferiority. He turned the wheel over with instructions to hug the Unimak side of the Strait, where the shore dropped off steeply and there was no danger of running aground. They passed the burned-out cannery at False Pass, with its ferry landing, and some residential shacks clinging to a sand flat before a brown hillside awaiting winter. No place to jump ship, Seine thought; it might be next spring before he got out.

"Now be careful of currents and winds off the Peninsula there—see that?" The Chemist smiled. "Wicked winds, flying down from the highlands!"

"I believe you," Seine said.

"*Now* you believe me! Now you believe!" said the Chemist, slapping Seine on the back and howling and throwing the window open. "You're *nuthing!*"

But this time the wind caught his glasses and tore them from his head. Seine turned from the wheel in time to see the Chemist grasp futilely for the blood-red glasses as they fell away from the wheelhouse window and tumbled, sailed, caught air, and *soared* out into the churn of the wheel wash. "*All stop!*" the Chemist yelled, but Seine didn't act quickly enough. The glasses floated an instant and then were sucked under, ground back to sand. "*Goddamnit!*" said the Chemist. "Goddamn you for not stopping!"

Seine looked into the gray reach, felt the bow pound against a wave, sea spray fanning upward and back, raining onto the deckhouse below. The seas seemed remote from way up here, even as the wheelhouse rocked. Beyond the bow, the swollen gulf stretched to forever. In the reflection of the chart-table light, he saw the Chemist grope his way to his stool, muttering about incompetence, looking up and squinting toward storm clouds that ran in a black band along the horizon.

Free Radicals

A leftover from his days studying chemistry at the University of Washington, a free radical was the Chemist's own term for a rogue wave, the one in a hundred that rose twice as high as the average. In the Gulf they were known to reach eighty feet or more in a routine gale, washing shipping containers off cargo decks seventy-five feet up.

Fearless turned east-northeast and ran coastwise before angling through the Shumagin Islands, the Chemist squinting the entire way, shoving his face inches from the gyrocompass and nautical charts just to read them. They towed the *Early Warning* past the humped islets called the Haystacks, and ran the gauntlet of the Shelikof Strait, a battered venturi of wind and current between the Alaska Peninsula and Kodiak Island. They took weather straight on now, with *Vigilant* falling in behind as the Chemist had predicted. He gloated over the momentary victory and proclaimed his willingness to take a normal course toward the Inside Passage so long as *Vigilant* stayed behind him where she belonged.

Running the Shelikof was like running headlong into a jackhammer, butting heads with a northeaster and the prevailing current combined. They slammed short waves, releasing, slamming, releasing in a snapping motion that drove them more mad than seasick. The

Chemist's mood settled into blind determination, perched in his captain's chair for eighteen hours out of every twenty-four. When he
wasn't steering or navigating, he slept on the wheelhouse settee with a
wool blanket pulled around his thin shoulders.

Four days later they broke east into the Gulf of Alaska on a straight
course across toward the entrance to the Inside Passage at Cape
Spencer. On the evening of the fifth day, Seine steered east by south
as the Chemist awakened behind him and said groggily, "Where?
Where's *Vigilant*?"

"Same position, nine miles back. She's made up some ground,"
Seine said.

The Chemist's chin bobbed up and down as if constantly saying
yes-yes-yes to some voice in his own head. He stepped in front of Seine,
knocking into him more than he ought to have, making Seine wonder
how well he could see. Then he ordered Seine below to pay out more
tow wire. "Do you notice the shift, Seine? Ever since we've been outside, we're out of rhythm. I can feel the pull of the barge in my sleep.
Good tow is a matter of rhythm. We want barge and boat going up
and down in unison. Got it, man?"

Seine got it. "Do you have another pair of glasses?"

The Chemist squinted into the dim reach. "No. But I don't need
glasses to sail across open ocean. Just take care of that tow gear."

As Seine moved to the top of the stairs, the Chemist reached for the
radio. "Macky old bean," he said. "Julia there?"

"No, Auric, she's not."

"You gonna tell me about the Kuskokwim?"

"What's your problem, man? Why don't you quit with that? Leave
her alone."

And Seine went down rather than listen, the mention of the
Kuskokwim jogging something in his memory, a story he'd heard

somewhere, a twisted tale of merchantmen. He left the Chemist top-side to swirl around in his captain's chair.

On the main deck, Seine made his way aft from the galley, down a narrow hallway past the cook's quarters, and through an insulated door leading to the fiddley deck. The fiddley was a grated steel cat-walk deck, like a balcony overlooking the engine room below, where Terje Narvik checked fluid levels. Seine waved until he got his atten-tion, then motioned aft to indicate he was going outside. Narvik nodded, wiped his hands on a rag, and came up the open stairs to the fiddley. "Chemist wants us to pay out towline—get the barge in rhythm!" Seine had to shout even though they were only inches from each other.

Narvik nodded, and the two stepped out the rear door leading out-side to the open air of the winch room. The winch room wasn't a room at all but more like a deep alcove that housed the tow winch. It had no roof and no fourth wall leading astern, and the two side walls were formed by the exhaust stack housings.

Seine circled the massive drums and gears of the tow winch and held to the waist-high railing that ran around the entire deckhouse. As he rounded the tow winch to face the open afterdeck, the vessel slammed into the trough between waves. The boat thudded to a near standstill, then released and groaned up the face of the next wave.

With an awkward, lunging motion, Seine shifted his grip from the house railing to the fat tow wire, which ran off the tow winch at shoul-der height. He held to the curling striations of the wire cable and stepped aft toward the stern railing. The tow wire angled downward toward the deck until it reached a two-foot length of chain called the hold-down. The hold-down did just what it sounded like: held the tow wire down. Hanging tight to the stern rail, Seine traced its path. From the hold-down, the wire ran off the back of the boat and over the railing, where a flat length of rubber tire was wired in place to prevent the tow wire from chafing in half. There, the wire ran between two tow pins, sticking up from the stern railing like the arms of a referee signaling touchdown.

Seine stood there observing the towing assembly while simultaneously clinging to it to keep from being washed overboard.

He knew there was no avoiding some level of swing and lift from the barge. The seas were heavy, and the barge outweighed the tug by tenfold. It was about like using a dirt bike to tow a dump truck over a motocross course. Seine could feel the pull. It meant the barge was back there, swinging hard in the storm. He felt upward tension on the wire. The hold-down chain came taut with a jerk.

The tow wire pivoted left and right between the tow pins. No danger there. Pulling on the very stern caused some yaw but did nothing to compromise the boat's stability. But if the hold-down were lost, the tow wire would lift out from between the tow pins and start to sweep, wider and wider, causing a hazard to anybody standing on the afterdeck and pulling sideways directly on the tow winch.

Since the tow winch was set almost dead amidships, a sideways pull from that angle could conceivably lever a boat over. Particularly in heavy seas. Particularly a top-heavy tug like *Fearless*.

Within about five seconds, Seine realized that the Chemist was right; they *were* out of rhythm. As the tug lifted, the barge fell and vice versa. He felt the pitch and yaw of *Fearless*, watched the hold-down chain slacken and come taut with a jerk. Back a half mile now, the barge *Early Warning* lifted on a wave, out of time.

Their goal was to get tug and barge going up and down together. Narvik ran the tow winch, releasing wire until the barge shrunk behind them. A plume of white water slammed the barge's bow. A moment later, Seine felt the pull. The hold-down chains—what tugmen

called a gob rope, probably because they had once been made of rope—
snapped taut as the tow wire lifted.

Through the driving rain he saw the swaying tower and the dimly
lit wheelhouse of *Fearless*. He motioned for Narvik to continue paying
out wire, holding on so he could feel the wire slip through his gloved
hand. Finally he felt the tension ease. Rhythm, Seine thought. Finally.
We're in rhythm. He waved a closed fist toward Narvik, who stopped
the winch and set the drum brake. A moment later, Narvik was duck-
ing back into the engine room door, and Seine stood alone in the torrent of the afterdeck.

As much as he didn't like hanging out five feet from a black ocean,
Seine wanted to check the gob rope directly. He looped one arm
around the tow wire for balance and flexed hard to keep from being
thrown overboard. He traced the circles of chain with a flashlight, in-
specting each link in turn. They appeared solid, without stresses or
cracks, so he pulled himself forward along the tow wire as if it were a
lifeline, circling the winch again and pushing through the fiddley
door to the dry warmth of the inside.

From the fiddley he could hear nothing besides the din of main engines, but he had tuned himself to the feel of the tug laboring through
heavy seas, the pitch, the swirling yaw, the halting forward motion of
the trough, before starting the climb again. And he could feel the
hold-down too, as a tiny pull just as they crested the next wave, and he
thought, *damn*.

He pushed back outside.

It began as a gentle tugging, a clinking he could feel but not hear,
but within ten minutes a vicious metallic crack bolted over the afterdeck. He looked behind, seeking the barge—how far off? And there,
next to where the tow wire led overboard, he saw his father, sitting on
the aft railing, turning toward him with a white-faced grin. Seine felt
a chill and let out a paralyzed whimper. But the hold-down chain

jerked tight again, and broke Seine out of his freeze. The old man was gone then, but inside himself Seine thought, What the hell; the old man, the old man was dead.

From behind the winch, protected by the three walls of the winch room, Seine engaged the drum and unreeled another two hundred feet of wire, until the barge was mostly out of view within the swells. Even from here, he could feel the stress on the hold-down ease, the way the driver of a speedboat can sense exactly where a water skier carves hard behind him. The wind speed picked up ten knots, and the seas rose another five feet, but Seine felt good about the rhythm, even as the wind twisted them in that corkscrew motion that makes the most seasoned salts want to lose their dinner.

Seine took a lungful of air. At least the old man was gone. He had plenty to think about without ghosts appearing to complicate things.

Off watch, middle deck, Seine soaked his hands for five minutes in hot water. In his room he pulled his bunk mattress down to the floor, stuffed survival suits and gear under the sides to create a U-shaped trough, and wedged himself in so he could sleep without getting his nose broken.

On his back he pondered his life and stared at the image of his father on the end of the bunk sitting with his legs dangling, immune to the toss of the seas, grinning down at his only son.

"What do you want from me?"

You need to think about where you are.

"Why are you here?"

I just told you. You need to think about what you know.

Seine rolled onto his side and closed his eyes. His old man had been a money man, a corner cutter. A crabber, he'd taken his only son as his first mate at age thirteen, taught him everything about crabbing anybody needed to know except how to survive doing it. When things got

bad on a towboat, Seine would remember back to those ungodly mid-
nights hauling four-hundred-pound crab pots out of the frozen Gulf
of Alaska and think, Thank God I'm not crabbing.

The old man's way of jacking profits was to haul as many crab pots
as possible. He'd pull ballast from internal tanks so he could stack as
many crab pots onto the afterdeck as he could fit. Young Henry never
did like it. One night he refused to help the old man. He was nineteen
and had just returned that summer from a year of college his father
didn't even want him to have. When the old man pulled ballast, Henry
protested. It happened in the dead of night, dockside at Port Angeles,
northwester screaming down the Strait. Henry explained about center
of gravity.

"Gonna whip some college on me, huh?"

"It's not safe."

"My boat, boy. I'll do as I always done it. Now toss off."

Henry shook his head. "I'm not doing it."

His father had stepped up, a good inch shorter than his son. The
old man stared Henry in the eye and said, "First what you wanna do is
get the fuck outa my wheelhouse, and next what you wanna do is get
the fuck offa my boat."

So Henry got the fuck out of his wheelhouse. He got the fuck off
the boat too. He stood on the dock and watched the old man pull out.
Watched the gaunt faces of the fishermen he sailed with, watched the
bitterest of faces the old man could muster as the tach lights reflected
off his stubble beard in the darkened wheelhouse, looking betrayed
even as he raised his middle finger and said, "Fuck you, son."

You haven't lived, Seine thought, until you've heard your father say
that.

An hour later the old man ran northwest out the Strait of Juan de
Fuca, headed for Alaskan waters. It was no great thing of a storm, a
routine boiler, but the Strait was a bad spot when incoming weather

hit outgoing tide to make standing waves. They bounced the high-gravity crabber. She wobbled, waved, gave a brief heave as if to right herself, and then turned turtle. In less than a minute, the boat went down with all hands.

Seine was uncertain if he slept or if he merely drifted in the null zone of near sleep, his head disconnected from his body and drifting one instant, then a rush of light and a voice the next: "Seine! On the after-deck, boy! We gotta hold down!"

He pulled himself to his feet, realizing he must have been asleep, for in the time he'd been horizontal the seas had shifted. He held to the upper bunk as the boat slammed into a wave, knocking him to his knees. He pulled himself up. The force of another face-on wave felt like they'd run hard aground, throwing Seine into the forward bulkhead. He righted himself, grabbed his rain suit. His head weighed fifty pounds. He managed his way out of his room and down to the main deck. "What's the problem?"

"That hold-down," said Narvik. "We're out of rhythm again. I tried two times to adjust and it ain't working. Chemist wants you topside."

Seine shook his head. His instinct was to *do things,* but it hit him that their best chance for making it through this might just be talking the Chemist into swinging coastwise for safe harbor.

It took him ten minutes to climb the swirling tube of steel, the ladder spiraling upward. If he slipped he'd take it on the chin for twenty feet down, so he reached up the railing with numbed hands sliding and gripping and drawing himself topside with every shred of remaining strength. He emerged into the wheelhouse to find the Chemist running ahead full power on both main engines, through dense wave cliffs and storm skies.

From up here, though, at least Seine could see. When the boat lifted on a wave, he caught sight of the barge behind them, taking windward seas over the bow.

"Where the hell have you been?" the Chemist shouted. "We got fifty knots now, quartering off our port bow. Weather report looks like shit and more shit between here and anything resembling solid ground."

"Where are we?" Seine asked. He held to the rear of the chart table, looking down to see the lighted surface glowing white, with a heavy-duty magnifying glass lying there alongside a compass and parallels.

"The Gulf of fucking Alaska!" the Chemist barked.

Seine scanned the bank of radios that hung from the ceiling, directly over the console. A digital LED shone on the face of the side-band, 2182 glowing like a silent beacon. Then a transmission came over a different radio, the short-range VHF crackling with the rush and roar of the tug *Vigilant.* "Roger that. We're nine miles behind you, *Fearless,* continuing present course but making no headway, repeat no headway, over."

The Chemist grabbed the mike and paused as if biting back an acid comment. Then he said calmly, "Yeah thanks for *nuthin',*" and tossed the mike down. It clattered across the console and bounced up on its spring cord, then flew into the wheelhouse glass and bobbed there like a spring-loaded marionette.

"We got a hold-down problem," Seine said. "The barge is stressing on the gob rope. Back off a quarter. We gotta get in rhythm."

"No shit we got a hold-down problem! You need to adjust the length of the tow wire, Seine. Changing speed will have no effect on rhythm, trust me."

"I've adjusted it three times and it's still out of phase. The seas are variable."

"And forward speed will have no effect on timing!"

"You know what happens if the hold-down goes."

"The hold-down won't go if you do your job."

Seine pointed to the chart. "I think you should swing north and go for Whittier. You ever made an outside crossing in this boat?"

"Yes! Albeit with a competent crew! She's uncomfortable, but she's solid. Now you take care of the deck gear, and I'll run the boat." The Chemist sat in his captain's chair, not quite looking at Seine but, like a blind man, only approximating his location. He appeared to Seine to have closed his eyes entirely.

"It's about the woman, isn't it?" Seine asked. "You're afraid she won't be there. So you gotta get there first."

The Chemist's eyelids fluttered and he rose up out of his chair and stared over the chart table. The swing and sway of the wheelhouse threw them around as if they were riding a treetop in a gale. "Seine. I need you to do your job, and amateur hour on the shrink couch isn't part of it. Do you know your job? Let me say it slowly, so even a logger jock can understand it. I am the captain. You are the mate. In fact, you aren't even the mate. You're an overpaid deckhand. That's right. I checked up on you. You don't even have an operator's license. So what the hell do you *know* about it? Answer? Nothing!"

Spit flew from his mouth as a wave dropped out from under them, the smash of the trough nearly throwing Seine back down the hole of the internal ladder. Jesus, he thought, where the hell am I?

His father stood next to him then. *What do you know?* he asked.

The wheelhouse oscillated in tilted circles, and at thirty feet tall, slamming the trough felt like the boat might just pitch forward and dive like a submarine. Even in a thirty-foot wheelhouse, Seine couldn't see over the peaks of the waves. In fact it wasn't even close. "These are fifty-foot seas," he said aloud.

He thought if he stayed topside he'd either strangle the Chemist or throw up all over him.

Making his way down was way worse than making his way up. He lost his footing halfway down and his heels thudded from step to step ten feet before he grabbed a handhold and caught himself.

In the galley, Cliff the Cook stood over the stove, simmering some kind of stew in a pot with the lid clamped down by bungee cord. "What are you doing, trying to scald yourself?" Seine asked.

"Beef stew, want some?"

"No I don't want any. We've got bigger problems."

"Ya gotta clear conscience, Henry? Cause ya can't sleep without a clear conscience."

"Sleep? Who the hell can *sleep?*"

Cliff smoked a Pall Mall while he cooked, staring at Seine, looking mush-mouthed. "I can always sleep. I gotta clear conscience."

Then Seine realized that Cliff had taken his dentures out. He had a clear conscience, Seine thought, but no teeth. As they stood there, Terje Narvik came running into the galley.

"I got what sounds like somebody dropping a load of bricks on my head down in that engine room!" Narvik said.

"Where's Deperod?" Seine wanted to know. He hadn't seen the AB in two watches.

"Got thrown outa the rack onto his head," said Cliff, flicking an ash and blowing smoke directly into Seine's face. "He ate two helpings of my stew and went back to bed. You sure you don't want some?"

"Put the fucking cigarette out!" Seine shouted.

Cliff winced like he'd been struck. He dropped the smoke into the sink.

"The Chemist is sailing the Gulf by Braille!"

"I feel bad for him," said Cliff. "He been good to me. He requested me when nobody else would gimme the time of day."

"We need more chains on the gob rope," Seine said.

"More chains'll help, but we need rhythm, boy!"

"There *is* no rhythm in these waters," Seine said. "Wavelength is all over the place. The Chemist is hell-bent on staying with *Vigilant.*"

"*Vigilant*'s a line hauler, different animal," said Terje Narvik. "We can't stay ahead of her in this."

"What do you suggest, we kill him?"

Narvik let out a nervous laugh. "I'll get the chains."

If they could add enough of them, the hold-down might hold no matter how chaotic the seas were. Seine stepped aft down the short hallway, past the main deck head, holding to the aluminum railing as *Fearless* crested a wave and plummeted into the trough, beat hard into the next wave, and rose up again. Through a watertight door, Seine stepped to the fiddley deck, to the ungodly noise of the screaming mains.

Deperod appeared behind, looking peaked, zipping an orange float coat. Seine nodded to him and pushed out the watertight door to the afterdeck. Wind and spume hit him like a series of frozen shotgun blasts. He held his breath. Since he'd last been outside, the seas had deepened. The tow winch stood before him, a six-foot jangle of gears, the main drum holding the tow wire. As he came around the winch, Seine felt the roar and slam of the trough and walked into what amounted to Class 5 river rapids. "Oh, God," he said aloud, clamping his fist around the deckhouse rail.

He looked left and right and saw only walls of ocean. He felt sunken and small in the trough. He smelled rubber smoke. He held to the lip of the main winch drum and with his eyes traced the line of the tow wire aft to where it disappeared off the stern of the boat. But he couldn't see much of anything beyond, only gray mountains of water, couldn't hear anything but the deep orchestral moaning of the ocean, a sound interlaced with engine noise, and the rippling of his own rain gear. Wearing a flotation vest over the rain suit left him bulky and uncoordinated. Still, he hoisted himself on a ladder that led to the boat deck immediately above. Free from the rush of water, he had a better view, and could now see the hold-down. One chain had already snapped and lay rolling around in the wash of the deck.

Just as he registered this, the boat fell down the face of a wave. The remaining two hold-down chains snapped taut with a metallic *clank* and then quivered in place. Seine felt a force shoving him *upward,* as if he might fly away into the close gray sky. He hugged the ladder and then felt his stomach sink into his boots, before the force flung him straight down from the boat deck in a heap. Inexplicably, he found himself lying on the aft side of the tow winch, exposed to the sea. He grabbed the tow wire and pulled himself upright, peering back over the winch to where Narvik and Deperod stood at the fiddley door, their eyes hunted.

Hand over numbed hand, Seine made his way aft down the fat coil of the tow cable, feeling the stress on it as the hold-down came taut again with its cold, metallic *clank.* He couldn't believe it didn't break. Each jerk sent a chill up from his tailbone to the base of his skull.

The tug labored up the face of a wave. Only the short bulwark separated him from a thousand feet of dark water. He saw the wire stretching downward, disappearing into the catenary—the long bow-shaped arc of the heavy tow wire, submerged for most of its half mile, then rising to the thick chain of the tow bridle and, at last, black against the deepening gray water of dusk, the blunt bow of *Early Warning.* A remote, distant slab of responsibility. Seine cupped a hand over his eyes to block the spray, stood as if on a mountaintop.

Then the tug dropped out from beneath him, roaring down the backside of the swell. Seine's stomach lifted into his throat. He held the bulwark and crouched low as the tug hit the trough and seemed to stop dead against a wall of water, the entire vessel shuddering as twin chutes of ice water thundered straight at him down the side decks. Blue smoke surrounded his face, curling off the rubber chafing gear as the tow wire slid back and forth. He choked on rubber smoke—needed a breath before the waves hit him. He felt the sudden rise from his stomach, and before he knew it he had thrown up all over the deck.

He gulped noxious air and jumped and clung to the tow wire, hugging it like an arboreal ape, using arms and legs to hold himself two and a half feet off the deck. If he'd had a tail he'd have held with that too. Beneath him, white water flushed the deck clean, his puke sliding overboard in a glassy rush.

When the tug lifted on the next swell, Seine dropped to the deck, breathed, held tightly to the hold-down chain, and checked its entire length for marks of wear. Midway up he found several stressed links, including two that showed tiny splits.

As the tug lifted, climbed, and reached the peak, Terje Narvik appeared from around the winch, with Joe Deperod hanging out behind him with a look of stark fear. "Here ya go there, boy!" Narvik yelled, shoving a milk crate full of chain toward him. "Two more wraps at least!" The crate caught a sheet of glassy water and slid along the deck. Seine saw the wall of dark water rise over the tug like a horrible monster and felt a chill coursing up his spine and spreading out over his scalp as he let go of the railing to move for the chain.

The milk crate slid fast. He reached down to catch it but like an incompetent infielder felt it slip past his reaching hands, catch him at his feet and trip him. As he went down, feet scrambling, Seine reached and caught a hand on the edge of the metal crate. White water swallowed the house, knocked Narvik off his feet, and the engineer washed toward Seine like a flailing kayaker, his eyes wide, his mouth screaming. Deperod clutched the winch-room railing with two fists. Then all was gone. Five tons of ocean water swept Seine aft and slammed him hard into the base of the bulwark. As the impact tore through him, the Gulf loomed past the bulwark, a foot away. He groaned and just wished it would end, one way or the other. *I don't care take me take me I don't care,* he thought, but the torrent pressed him against the bulwark, pounded his arms and legs, thundered a frozen blast into his face. He held his breath against foaming cold that rushed away from his mouth and allowed him to gulp air as the tug labored again toward the peak of the next wave. Narvik lay ten feet away against the starboard bitt, his chest heaving.

Seine pulled himself up, felt his face throbbing like a raw nerve. He grabbed two lengths of chain from the crate and crawled for the hold-down, hooking his arms around the tow wire so he could work with two hands. With his left he held the shackle and with his right he threaded the chain, then awkwardly, with fingers he could not feel, he unscrewed the pin on a new shackle and anchored the new chain to the deck padeye. He breathed once, then again heard the searing thunder of the trough, felt a chill bolt through his body, and looked forward to see a wall of green water rising over the deckhouse, with Terje Narvik running full out for the winch room, and then twin chutes of white water came flushing straight at him.

Seine knew he couldn't make the winch room. The white water was on him. He hooked both elbows around the tow wire and felt the water tear his legs out from under him. He hugged the steel cable tight in the crooks of his elbows while his legs flailed on sea foam, the vague shouts of the engineer fluttering overhead. He felt himself going, felt his arms slipping down the twisting cable toward the aft railing. He caught a finger on the hold-down shackle and clung like a sloth to a tree branch.

When the wave finally released him, he dropped to the fantail, took two deep breaths, and pulled himself to his feet. He sucked air as he ran forward, the boat driving deep into a wall of water and shuddering to a standstill, the force launching Seine into a garbled apparatus of gears and sharp steel outcroppings. He felt the impact of cold steel on his cheek, felt the flesh laid open and the warm blood flow down over his cheek and into his mouth.

A torrent of white water swept around each side deck and eddied at his knees, biting at his feet. Clinging to the giant tow winch, he heard the rifle crack of the gob rope, not unlike the previous ones. He felt the pull in the vessel, and then the lean. As the night water rushed in sheets away to drain the afterdeck, he grasped for whatever he could hang on to, but before he could gain a grip, he was flung forward as the vessel skidded down the backside and threw him like a doll against the engine-room door. In the roar of wind and spume and grinding main engines, he did not hear the hold-down go, but when he looked aft he saw the tow wire lift out of the water and swing hard to starboard.

He shouted even before he moved. "Hold-down! Hold-down's gone!"

From his knees he pushed open the fiddley door and fell inward to the grated deck, gelid salt water draining off his rain gear. "Hold-down, hold-down," he said, drowned by the scream of the main engines. He crawled inside, breathed the odor of engine oil and heat, and pushed himself to a standing position.

He ran to the deckhouse door, jerked on the dog, and pulled the door open, timing the pitch of the vessel to move inside the galley passage, where Joe Deperod sat against the bulkhead coughing and holding his head while bobbing back and forth. Each time he bobbed, his head thunked against the bulkhead as if he were beating it there on purpose. Seine tasted blood as Terje Narvik stared up at him, disoriented.

"Hold-down is gone," Seine said, running past for the internal stairway as the force of yet another wave hurled him forward, and he ran out of control down a steep slope until he fell crashing into the galley bench. The coffeemaker leapt off the counter and threw steaming coffee and hot grounds all over the galley.

He pried himself free of the galley bench. Coffee grounds clung to the blood that ran down his face and seeped down his neck. He looked down. Deperod and Narvik both had been thrown forward and now lay sprawled out on the deck beneath the mess table.

Even from here, inside the galley, he could feel the barge swinging on them, pulling the wire hard over. The boat heeled in response, leaning hard left. Seine put his feet up against the bulkhead and tried to clarify his thoughts. What to do? Options ran through his head. Radio for help. Cut the tow line and let the barge drift. Change course. He could feel the barge pulling sideways on the vessel. He saw Deperod roll over, push himself to his hands and knees, and disgorge two helpings of beef stew all over the deck.

"We gotta get the Chemist to cut tow," Seine said.

His arms and legs moved outside his conscious control as he took the seventy-eight spiral steps up through the tower, with Narvik behind him.

"You seen Cliff?" Narvik asked, about halfway up.

"No," Seine said, his voice hollow. "He was cooking before; now I don't see him."

"Shit, boy, I got a bad feeling here."

And they hauled themselves topside, stepped up into the cone of the chart-table lamp. All around, the wheelhouse windows showed black and those that could be opened whistled at their edges.

The Chemist sat in his stool, strapped in place by a yard of wrapped and rewrapped bungee cord, his face illuminated by the glowing green of the console meters showing engine rpms and rudder angle. The window heaters blasted full out. It felt like an oven up there, and the Chemist wore no shirt. When he turned, Seine saw that he had indeed pierced his nipples, both of them, and wore rings in each, connected by a swinging gold chain.

"We have no hold-down."

"Good work, Seine. When this piece of shit goes down, we'll have your incompetence to thank."

"You gotta be sensible there boy!" said Narvik. "We gotta turn north at the very least."

They both advanced now. "If not then we should cut tow."

"Cut tow?" the Chemist said. His entire body heaved and he seemed to shrink a foot. He waved them off. "I don't care what the fuck you do." He shook his head as if the very notion of cutting tow made him ill.

They leaned hard to port, a top-heavy boat being pulled over. The radio chirped, *"Fearless, Vigilant. . . ."*

The woman's voice. His *love.*

Seine held to the chart table. "Why are we here, Bill? Tell me that."

The Chemist turned away. Seine advanced on him. "Why are we here, Bill? Because of your girlfriend? We're out here because of your *girlfriend?"*

"This ain't the time for this one way or the other, now!" said Narvik. "If you don't turn north then I'm cutting tow, boy."

"Fearless, Vigilant. . . ."

Her voice again. Seine pulled himself around the left side of the chart table. Over the console shone the digitized red of the sideband, the distress channel there, open, offering itself like a lifeline. He didn't know whether to answer *Vigilant* or call the Coast Guard, but as he pushed off the edge of the chart table and reached his arm for any radio he could, the wheelhouse turned sideways.

In the back of his mind Seine knew it was a knockdown though he had no direct experience, only stories, imagined sensations compared

with present truth. In the horrific slow motion of radical action, Seine
watched the Chemist launch and fly before him, tackling him, wrap-
ping his arms around him as the two of them hit with a grunt of es-
caping air. And then the falling, forever falling, the entire wheelhouse
going over. The chart light went black, behind a crashing tumble that
chased them: books and papers and pens and clipboards and nautical
charts and parallels and an ashtray of ashes and a can of Copenhagen
and a Styrofoam cup filled with chew spit and a Bic lighter flying and
falling and splattering all around them. He smelled the Chemist's tobacco breath, heard a crack and a groan from somewhere in blackness.
Terje Narvik, he thought with a long low groan. Where he was Seine
didn't know anymore, the stuffy confines of a seagoing coffin, maybe.
A great weight lay on him. His numbed hand traced a line across the
smooth surface of something beneath him and, emerging through
that something, bubbles. Bubbles behind a black surface. And then he
realized that he lay facedown on the portside wheelhouse glass, looking downward into a churning swirl of night water, at the sprawling
limbs of Terje Narvik. He thought they'd continue over, turn turtle
and go down. He felt his father's mouth to his ear, knew the voice saying *going down down come on down with me,* turning—

Real-time motion returned. The wheelhouse flung back upright.
That the vessel managed to right itself was a miracle of randomness.
And though it saved them from plummeting right then to the Gulf
bottom, the righting was no picnic. A steel box flew ahead of Seine just
as the Chemist launched off his back, and he followed behind, flailing.
An instant later Seine landed on the wheelhouse settee. The steel box
slammed the glass window just above his head and shattered it. Gale
winds burst into the wheelhouse, shards of glass rained down on
Seine's head, and the steel box landed in his lap. He held his shoulder
and felt the stinger of nerve pain burn down his arm to the base of his

hand. Then it all turned numb, his entire right side. He turned stiffly toward the broken window and felt the wind tear at his face, saw nothing but night wave after night wave.

The Chemist scrambled to his feet—"Free radical, free radical"— and took up the radio—"Uh, yeah, *Vigilant,* we took a knockdown—"

Seine remembered the Switlik, the covered life raft that he figured was their only hope for survival now, but it was two decks down and outside and impossible to reach, it seemed. Terje Narvik lay sprawled on the wheelhouse deck, unconscious. A line of blood ran from his ear and fanned outward on the wet deck. The Chemist reached for the wheel and swung hard to starboard in an effort to take the next wave bow-to. "We can still make it," he said. "Hold tight."

Hold tight. Feeling returned to Seine's right arm with a burn. The radio crackled, and he heard the woman's voice again. "We have you at a relative bearing of zero-two-one at eleven miles—"

Vigilant had dropped farther back. They were moving slow ahead, the woman said, the voice, the soft calm of her voice. "We're moving ahead on one engine, *Fearless,* we have a blown turbo in our port main, over—"

Calm, Seine thought, a voice calm like seas he could only pray for. Julia, this would be Julia, he thought.

The Chemist turned to him. "Knockdown. . . ."

His lips parted. His face held a horror, a realization, a shock as if at the magnitude of his own failure. Seine thought of the engineer's torch. He'd have to make the engine room to get to it, string leads, and blow through a five-inch-diameter steel cable. He didn't think there was time; still, he pulled himself to his feet and fought his way toward the external door.

The Chemist barked at him. "Seine!"

Seine turned to look just as the Chemist stumbled over some debris on the wheelhouse deck, tripping and shoving a white pack at him: a stiff vinyl bag that held a Bayley suit, a survival suit that was the only thing between a single man overboard and a cold deep death. "I'm cutting tow," Seine said. "You call the CG."

The Chemist's eyes refocused on Seine, or tried in their blindness to find him. The hollow cheeks and drawn blinded eyes, hopeless eyes searching outward and finding nothing. Seine couldn't tell if he was saving Seine's life or asking him to witness a suicide.

Seine did not run down to cut tow, thinking now: where was that torch? Calculating: could he get there? Wondering: would he die trying? Should he try the external ladder? Would he be flung overboard? He needed the Bayley suit. His brain fragmented then, watching himself as he opened the zipper on the Bayley suit bag, simultaneously thinking opposing thoughts—*you can cut tow in a Bayley suit* and *there isn't time for Bayley suits*—while pulling the suit out of its bag in a long orange trail. "Save yourself," the Chemist muttered, seemingly resigned to his own failure.

Getting into a survival suit was no easy task on flat water. Now it seemed impossible. Seine put a leg in and lost his balance, falling backward against the chart table. He looked up and the Chemist held a hand, reached for a leg. "Here," he said, and helped Seine's leg into the wide boot. Then he laughed, a mirthless release out of some primal source. He squinted through lids like some kind of amphibian. He pulled Seine to his feet and yanked the rubber suit, pulling it over Seine's hips, letting out a little laugh, reaching and pulling the tight hood over Seine's head. Seine zipped the long front zipper to seal himself into it.

Narvik was still lying on the deck, his unconscious body rolling port to starboard with each wave, the wind howling through the window. "That was one wicked free radical!" the Chemist shouted, nodding in twisted appreciation.

The Chemist reached up and brushed Seine's face. He wiped away

the blood and with that simple gesture Seine felt himself floating in a
sea of acquiescence, a languid warmth pervading his muscles, sooth-
ing his mind, carrying him off—he knew the feeling, from deep somewhere far off he knew and embraced this moment as an old friend,
a moment of recognition and clarity and self-service. The Chemist
seemed to be aware of it too, and for a moment Seine thought the
Chemist was really a walking Deadman, a living ghost there to haunt
him with the corrupt choice, as if to say, *I know you I know you, you let
your father die.*

In the survival suit, Seine looked like an orange Gumby with nothing but his white face showing. Inside, his scalp itched. Narvik rolled
against his legs, stared up blank-faced, blood-wet, shards of glass
clinging to his hair, his neck twisted at an impossible angle. Outside
the broken window the Gulf roared and hissed, soaring in pitch until
somewhere amid all that chaotic sound Seine thought he heard a pattern emerge, a rhythm that blended with highs and lows to become
music.

He opened the aft door in slow motion and stepped outside to the
wing deck, which sat perched like a penthouse terrace with a view of
the abyss. The Chemist was right, he *was* out of time; he lived *out of
time,* a gone, half-dead, half-made ghost of a human being, wallowing
in self-loathing, realizing he had no chance to cut tow, as *Fearless* took
her second knockdown and he flew, ejected by force with a curious
feeling through wind and ocean air. He screamed and clawed at the
wind, reaching for something—anything—solid.

Then he was overboard and tumbling down the face of a wave.
Underwater an instant. Then up—gasping, half air, half water, disoriented, the burning through his chest of salt-water lungs. He felt the
tug falling over on top of him; oh, God, it would land on him, crush
him, force him down and hold him under. He hit the trough skidding,

butt first, the suit buoying his head as he backed up the next wave and saw clearly the tow wire hooked on the quarter bitt just thirty feet from him. The wire lifted up and away from him. The boat let out a metallic creaking sound. The wire chewed the paint from the quarter bitt, bit into the steel, and lifted, and just like that—fast—flipped *Fearless* on her back. The tall wheelhouse knifed into the wave and disappeared.

The hull bellied up as if exposing herself to the storm, the nakedness striking him even as it sank in a groaning swirl. Seine felt himself cry out, or maybe not; no sound came that he could hear, only the rush of salt water into his body to choke him out and blind him. *I'm a free radical now, spinning out of control, flailing through space.*

He thought he might die right there, his heart stop dead rather than go forward, but then he was past that moment almost without knowing it. For some reason he thought about Irons and how his frostbitten nose must have looked before some surgeon carved off the black part. It made Seine cover his face with his Gumby hands to keep from freezing his own nose off.

But the crest made covering his face impossible. Despite the impressive buoyancy of the suit—maybe because of it—the violence of the windblown crest tossed him. He flailed his arms to stay righted. Wind and spume tore into his face like a scattershot of pea gravel, and he tumbled.

The wind tossed his legs and he spun on his butt, head down, feet hauling over his head as the wave fell out from under him. He hit the trough with eyes open, belly down, water burning into his eyeballs as if somebody had opened up a pressure nozzle into his face. The spray burned through his skull. He choked on salt water like a balled sock stuffed down his throat. He coughed an explosion. Felt himself foaming at the ears, and with that came deafness and the sound of his own blood. He managed half a breath. He fought panic with an image of a woman, the photograph on the glass, doing duty. Julia—her name was Julia.

The wave crests were physically precarious, but the wave troughs plunged him into the psychological pit. In his mind, that's what he called it. "Here comes the pit," he would say to himself, and cover his face and descend, swallowed by a swollen sea. He climbed and dropped and sensed a thousand feet of black ocean eating him from below, and the adrenaline surged.

He closed his eyes and drew inward to combat the torment, to meditate. But closed eyes accentuated the sinking feeling. The pit seemed ten miles deep, twenty miles, stretching down and down, his body falling until he realized his falling was actually rising, a sensation of flying too fast as his inner ear struggled to keep up with the reality of his body's movement. He had to see. He had to look or he would die, he thought. He opened his eyes and faced downwind, the spray and scattershot of spume blowing away from him and then an instant of hovering. He saw a reach of sky, a distant light gray, a flare of moonlight. He wished for running lights, prayed for warm deck lights making toward him. But he saw nothing but the veined distant shimmer of ocean surrounded by nothing but close clouds and blackness.

And then he was down again. In the pit he heard her voice, the storm sea shouting in Heather's voice, embittered and lonely, deriding him for his stupidity. He pushed her away and let his mind fall to this woman called Julia. Her picture came to him. A literal black-and-white snapshot now flapping in black current a mile down. The woman in the photo would be working now. He saw her in the glossy two-dimensionality of the snapshot. A walking photograph, flat, unreal. She would move to the sideband, spin the tuner to 2182 kHz, and depress the mike button. "Ship down," she would report. "Ship down."

She soothed him and carried him outside himself. He imagined her motions and tried transmitting them as if by some cosmic radio. The survival suit floated him butt down, legs up, so that he fell into a surfing rhythm of cascading and turning and backing and turning and cascading. He counted troughs and descended and rose and said, inside himself, "Three thousand one hundred and ten" before he saw a blast of light on top of him. At first he thought he'd been found by a UFO until he heard the loudhailer and saw the Coast Guardsmen in float suits lining the cutter deck, and even then he wasn't sure if he had made it alive, even as they hauled him on board, voices telling him he was the lucky one, that he had *Vigilant* to thank, the cook-deckhand off *Vigilant.*

The Salvage Job

When he finally saw the woman, Seine was in the process of dragging himself aboard the *Vigilant*, feeling like he'd absorbed the physical maladies of Cliff the Cook. Thanks to the knockdown, his entire right side burned like a tweaked funny bone from ankle to ear, and the skin of his cheek bore the tightness of thirty-two stitches put in by a Coast Guard medic.

The *Vigilant* crew greeted him like a school chum who went off to some foreign war and was long-thought dead, only to turn up now a survivor. They nodded with grave appreciation and closed-mouth smiles and shook his hand like Terje Narvik, ignorant of the electrical burn that rolled down his right leg as they pumped his hand. "Thanks for your help," Seine said, wincing.

He knew the mate from a Seattle–Honolulu run four years back, a taciturn thin man named Lager. Even Lager managed a terse smile. He said, "Don't thank us, thank Julia Lew."

"Julia *Lew.*"

"That's right. You know her?"

"I've heard of her," he said.

He'd heard quite a lot, actually. Heard things he would never repeat. Suddenly the insane actions of the Chemist snapped into a clearer relief.

"Where can I find her?" Seine asked.

"Galley," they said. "Working."

She was running cook-deckhand to earn the sea time to sit for her mate's license. She'd been working eighteens every day for three months.

"She works her ass off," said Lager.

"And a fine ass it is," said the ordinary.

When Seine found Julia Lew she was whipping a wooden spoon through cake batter, striated muscles fluttering up her forearm as she stirred. In Seine's mind all that time surfing the open sea he'd imagined a two-dimensional girl, a flat-edged worker bee, flitting from chart table to radio and back again. Seeing her now a fully formed woman took his breath away. Her hair hung down her back in a blue-black sheen that ran to a long ponytail, and where she'd pulled it back behind her ears he could see the luminous line of her neck like beige pearl. When she looked up, her eyes had a deadness about them, as if she harbored some ancient malice toward him. Then she seemed to realize who he really was and her eyes instantly acquired depth and sent a smile down into her lips.

Seine thought if he said a word he might start crying absurd tears that nobody would understand, least of all her. "I don't know what to say," he finally managed. "Thank you seems lame."

She wiped her hands on her white apron and held out her hand to shake, a girl's hand. "That's the best part," she said. "You don't have to say anything."

He could barely shake, his right arm so feeble that her tight small hand seemed capable of crushing him. She looked him straight in the eye.

"I heard you're joining us for the salvage operation," she said.

"That's right," Seine said. "Macky said it was cool."

"You're sure you're up to that?" Julia said, nodding toward his right side. "Your hand is fucked up, looks like."

Seine massaged his right arm with his left, trying to knead some feeling into it. "First knockdown threw me across the wheelhouse," he said.

And Julia eyed him then, the entire crew staring and nodding silently as if his words made the knockdown a momentary reality.

"So how is it you made it out and nobody else did?" Julia asked.

Her eyes had that dead quality again.

Seine didn't know how he made it out. Or he couldn't say, or form a rational explanation. The truth ran through the Chemist, took all the turns of his whacked personality, and contorted Seine's understanding of his own survival until he had no idea how to define it. "I was thrown clear trying to cut tow," he said, sounding and feeling like a liar.

Shipboard tales and rumors filtering from boat to boat had featured Julia Lew for as long as Seine had worked for Biller Ocean Transport, far longer than he had understood her to be the Chemist's Julia. One moment his mind rose to the clear crest of truth, understanding how these stories weren't to be trusted, knowing they were little more than the lurid fantasies of demented personalities. Yet the next moment he fell into a personal trough and, in the darkness of his own torment, accepted all rumors as indisputable fact.

So he anchored himself off a different reality, that of her act in saving his life. He began thinking of her as his savior. *My savior,* he would say inside, as if to ward off evil, *the saver of my soul.* Nothing else mattered. She had been on radar watch that night. She had sat in the pounding wheelhouse of *Vigilant* with her face submerged in a green radar world, not once rising to see the light of day shrinking out of sight around her. The scale of the radar screen showed eleven miles to the fat rectangular shadow of the barge called *Early Warning*, twelve miles to the dewdrop shade of *Fearless*. She listened to the Chemist and his voice of need. She heard her captain focus on *Vigilant's* own engine-room problems, their own difficulty keeping headway into the bite of a gale.

In the wheelhouse she heard it all. She heard the knockdown, she heard the tumble and crash, she heard the Chemist's last words: "Mate's abandoned ship . . . we're going over—" and then an empty channel.

Mate's abandoned ship. They all heard it, but only she saw the radar image, the green radar outline of *Fearless* fading like an electron ghost. She looked up for the first time in an hour as the bow of *Vigilant* took green water over the house. She caught a glimpse of a bleak reach of dark sky and ridge after ridge of ocean swell. "They're down," said Julia with eerie calm, "*Fearless* is down," and she moved to the chart table to calculate a set and drift line. She figured two possibilities: one for a raft, another for a man overboard. Their difference was minor, but she radioed both to the 17th Coast Guard District at Juneau.

This was his only truth, the truth according to Seine. Now, in the dying light, lying at anchor at Cape Spencer Light, Alaska, he watched her every move.

They put Seine into her cabin to make room for the salvage crew, a group flying in by float plane from Anchorage that night, and Seine thought Macky somehow liked the idea of them bunking together, was kind of tossing them together to see what would happen. He saw the crew wink, felt them nudge, heard them whisper.

Seine lay half numb in his bunk listening to boat sounds filter through the door. Engine work replacing a bum turbo, the dull monotonous rattle of a Lister generator motor. *Mate's abandoned ship* kept playing over and over in his head, *mate's abandoned ship.* He lay there wide awake for hours, though he was exhausted himself, turning the last moments over, seeing the face of the Chemist rise before him and with a paternal calm swiping blood off Seine's cheek. When Julia finally came to bed at midnight, he turned to the wall while she undressed and slipped into the lower bunk, and only then did he turn back and say out loud, "Just for the record, I didn't abandon ship. I told the Coast Guard investigator all about it, the best I could. I may not have done everything right, but I didn't abandon ship."

At first he heard nothing from below. Then a simple, "Okay. If you say so."

"Do you believe me?"

"I have no reason not to. Auric wasn't the most reliable source I ever knew, Seine."

Seine closed his eyes and thought how the Kuskokwim story and Auric's heartsick paranoia gave him a triangulated bearing, something Seine thought he could rely on even though he didn't want to. He didn't want to imagine her in that role, the role of cook aboard the *Laurie A.,* who in the bunkhouse accommodations during a New Year's party, did things with every man on board, one after the other, while the others watched.

He hated himself for listening to such stories, for believing, for caring, for being disgusted, for being aroused. It took him four hours to fall asleep. By then Julia Lew was up cooking breakfast.

The salvage crew came by float plane to surf-land into the cove behind Cape Spencer, and when he saw the faces in the Plexiglas, motoring toward them, Seine smiled from the foredeck of the *Vigilant,* waving his left arm because he couldn't lift his right hand over his head. He called out, "Didn't know a float plane could carry so much dead weight!" and heard Irons's voice growl across the water.

"The Buff gets fatter and fatter every year!"

Minutes later Irons climbed aboard, half nose and all, followed by Buff Errol and the Big Man, and close in their wake ran a chill. On the afterdeck Seine shifted from foot to foot, shaking his head back and forth in disbelief: this was his crew, his real crew; despite piss cups and shit piles he had never been happier to see three people in his life. He felt somehow like his family had come to rescue him. His face flushed, and he thought the cut on his cheek had begun to bleed again.

"Ahoy, survivor," the Wolf growled out of a sidelong smile. And in his handshake Seine felt that all had been forgiven, that he had attained a new standing with the Wolf simply by making his way through the shit and coming out the other side still breathing.

The Wolf loved survivors. He himself was one. He'd survived Inchon in Korea, survived '75 in Prudhoe and '82 off in the polar pack, and he stepped up to Seine with that broken face and nodded to the thirty-two stitches on his cheek, and shook his hand like he might break it, then pulled him toward him in a back-slapping bear hug. "Good for you, son, goddamned good for you."

"Mr. Seine," said the Big Man. "Good to see you."

"Damn, Seine, better make sure you never go to sea with me," said the Buff.

"He is definitely lightning rod," said the Big Man, with a big smile. "If there was doubt prior, no longer."

"Bullshit!" Irons bellowed. "He's my first mate! Forever, goddammit! Can sail with me anytime, I don't give a shit you got no license!"

And he dared anybody to contradict, and he howled at the steep mountain of trees that jutted skyward behind them.

"Look at there!" he bellowed. "Goddamn! Trees! You ever seen anything like that? Trees?" He even laughed when ten minutes later a
williwaw hit them hard and cold from over the top. Winds reached
eighty knots for about two minutes and then subsided. But for that
two minutes they were bounced all over hell, while Irons laughed and
yelled out, "I love this godforsaken state! Let's go find us a frickin'
towboat!"

When the *Fearless* fell out of sight, she sank trailing a half mile of
eight-inch tow cable, settling to the bottom like the world's costliest
anchor. The barge called *Early Warning* drifted on the wind and lay at
anchor off the downed tugboat, while two days later, *Vigilant* came
charging out to salvage both.

Seine had trouble walking, felt his right side drag in pain as he
climbed the ladder out of the winch room so he could hold to the railing of the Texas deck as the boat knifed through a lazy sea swell. The
skies were open and blue and calm now, the only seas a leftover from
a distant gale. He wondered where Julia Lew was, wondered if she'd
find him so they could talk their way through his gratitude.

On the horizon, lifting on the languid blue of the fall seas, the *Early
Warning* emerged, still at first, then slowly gaining motion as if ani-
mated, sitting high on deep seas. Eight Ford Ranger pickups stood
lashed to her center deck in a line, with three tons of retrograde cargo
piled aft.

Off the bow, the thick chain of the tow bridle hung down at a 45,
merging at the pigtail, where the steel cable of the tow wire angled
tight into the ocean swell. At the other end of that wire lay the tug
Fearless, settled in the crags of the Gulf bottom. Seine forced himself
across the Texas deck to the rear of the deckhouse, climbed a short
ladder to the wheelhouse wing, and pushed through the door. Julia
stood wheel watch, turning at the wind behind her, tendrils of hair

blowing around her face, and smiling at him as if in victory, as if only she could understand what Seine saw in that double-decker cargo barge, anchored off a sepulchre.

They tried reeling her in like a giant steel fish, and Seine worked alongside his crew, scaling rung ladders up the side of the barge, hauling cable and hoisting the foot-long links of the chain-tow bridle, and hanging them from the forward cleats like a five-ton steel garland. Gradually he worked his way through the pain and stiffness of his right side until he felt the muscles loosen and elongate, and for the first time since *Fearless* he felt he could actually stand upright.

Using the barge's giant Skagitt winch, they fed the long tow wire onto the oversized drum and reeled in. Powered by a CAT 333 diesel, the winch rotated slowly; by then Seine and Julia were watching from the afterdeck of *Vigilant,* directly adjacent to the spot where *Fearless* would rise, thirty feet from where the wire passed through the fairlead of the Skagitt winch and made biting sounds as it wound its way onto the winch drum. Pulling through tension, the wire ran from the water steadily and slowly, Seine's eyes fixed on the blue-green surface, waiting for the appearance of *Fearless.*

"There's no chance it's the tug, you realize," said Julia. "I've seen this twice. It'll be the tow winch."

"Oh, I know that," Seine said.

"Then why do you look like you're about to see a ghost?" She smiled and reached up to touch his cheek. He took her hand and clutched it—awkwardly, too tightly. But she let him hold it, and before long the shadow of a rounded fantail came into relief, and then an image of the wheelhouse railing emerging upward through the dark seas. "Holy shit," Julia said.

The tow winch lay intact, holding strong amidships. Seine turned to Julia, checking for reality, and her look said everything.

From their position on the afterdeck they had a clear view. The buoyant seawater lifted *Fearless* from below while the winch hauled her out from above. She tipped forward, the fantail and tall wheelhouse rising out of the green sea.

Big Man gave a yell from above, on the deck of *Early Warning*. Buff stood next to him, watching expectantly as the wheelhouse drew into full relief, angular, painted white, its radio antennae piercing the surface first, then the full wheelhouse breaking the surface in a rush of raining water, shaking off like a downed boxer coming up sweaty off the canvas.

Standing next to him, Julia drew a breath inward, and then Seine felt her tight muscular hand on his arm, and if not for the presence of a waterborne tomb before him he would have turned to her and held her. But the sight of rising water held him instead, eyes straight overboard, staring into the glass aquarium of the *Fearless* wheelhouse. An aquarium with two dead men in it instead of fish, the floating faces of drowned sailors. One was the Chemist, eyes like black glass marbles, the other Terje Narvik, his hair a shock of Nordic blond waving in seawater like some kind of museum exhibit: DROWNED HUMANS, CIRCA 1990, IN UNNATURAL HABITAT.

As the tug broke from the surface tension, the wheelhouse swung toward Seine, water rushing out of the broken glass, the bodies dropping and draining away into the internal passage.

Then the tow winch broke free of the deck. It tore loose with a metallic explosion, and the tug fell. The wheelhouse slammed the bulwark along *Vigilant*'s stern quarter, crunching the railing and pitching sideways before dropping down in a rush. Seine and Julia grabbed each other to keep from falling over, eyes welded to the sight of *Fearless* going down for a second time. They held each other a moment. Julia said, "Jesus, I been at sea since I was fourteen and I never saw anything like that."

She clutched his hand tight in her strong fingers. Something like hot water bathed over Seine, as if his head had torn free from his body, watching the dangling bolts of the *Fearless* tow winch hanging by the tow wire, clanking against the bow of the *Early Warning*. He floated in midair just like it, bones exposed, blood draining from his face, hanging alongside this woman. The heat came in waves, like a force barreling up over the back of his head, submerging all the crew, his father, himself, the Chemist, the cold.

SEVEN

Inside Passage

Juneau looked like a city clinging to the side of a mountain, inches from falling into the sea. Buildings and trees both grew straight up off the waterfront, where Seine sat on a dockside bollard looking at snow-dusted mountaintops, contemplating an offer by Macky to run AB for their southern leg to Seattle.

Coniferous green rose off the water, colored the water, brought living smells to Seine's nostrils for the first time in how long he didn't know. As he tallied time, he kept remembering the black bubble of Cross Island in winter, the white bubble of North Dock in May, the stark gray of the western coast, the grim rocky Aleutians as they ran False Pass heeling, and after that the sea-gray nightmare of the Gulf. Seine realized it had been almost a year since he'd seen a tree.

In front of him, the salvage team stepped to the fantail to pile their seabags there. "Did you call a cab?" said the Buff.

"That is the third time you have asked me," said the Big Man. "And now I refuse to answer again. Of course I called a cab."

"Thanks for refusing to answer," said the Buff, and laughed toward Seine.

The pile of seabags made Seine remember what he'd lost aboard *Fearless:* seabag, boots, clothes. He traveled light now. He had his float suit, the clothes he'd been wearing when he went overboard, his locking seaman's knife, his wallet, and a neck pouch that contained his passport, Merchant Mariner's Document, and two hundred dollars in cash. The Buff nodded in Seine's direction. "We oughta call him the Big Ass, whattaya say, Seine?"

The Big Man shouted out, "Mr. Seine! Do you not think we should call him Buffalina? Yoo-hoo, Buffalina!"

Seine thought his heart might burst open right then, though from joy or loss he couldn't have said which. He stretched his leg out; the stiffness and the shooting pain of the stinger had returned.

"So what are you gonna do?" Irons asked as he swung his seabag onto the wooden dock.

"He's gonna fuck the broad that saved his life," said the Buff. "I know him and I know her."

"Errol," said Irons. "Shut the frick up. So what is it, Seine? Stay or go?"

"I'm thinking the best thing to do is get back on the horse," Seine said. "If I don't stay on now, I'm not sure I'll ever work on the water again."

"Could be right," Irons said. And he didn't say so, but Seine knew he approved.

A taxi pulled up then, the Big Man booming, "There, a taxi cab for Buffalina—as I told you!"

Even the Buff laughed. Seine hated them and loved them at the same time. They shook hands in a circle, and Seine watched them load into the cab and slide away with lifting chins of acknowledgment and a short stubby Buff arm rising out the window to wave, Buddha tattoos and all. Seine sat there a long time until he heard someone behind him.

"So you're gonna sail south," she said.

"Yeah," he said, glancing at her, then turning back toward the fan-

tail and stuffing both hands in his jacket pockets. He shivered off the
October chill and felt a raindrop smack his nose, then the *tap-tap* of
rain on his canvas jacket. The buzzing pain still extended from his
right shoulder to his hip, but he knew he could work now. He felt the
Dear John letter against one hand, two fat joints against the other.
Dry as a bone—the letters and the pot had both gone through the
whole damned thing unscathed.

"Going into town to have a drink. Wanna join me?"

But with that, Heather spiked her way in, appeared on the afterdeck at her gentlest best, mouthing *I love you.* He turned to look at
Julia, to see if there was some truth in her eyes, to see what she really
wanted from him and maybe in their reflection to know what he
wanted from her. He thought maybe she could just lift him with both
hands by his jacket lapels and shove him . . . *that* way . . . and say, "Go!"
Or else curl a diminutive finger around him and tuck him to her
breast and say, "Come. With me."

He wanted some shared experience that would shred the stories
and judgment of sailors. He stared at her and thought she might be
the most beautiful woman he had ever seen, yet in her eyes was a dark
inhuman beauty that somehow paralyzed him. Half his body couldn't
move, half his mouth drooped. He felt like a stroke victim. He wanted
to cry but knew he couldn't. If not for her he would be dead.

"You think about him? The Chemist?"

"Auric? Of course I do," she said. "But you know, he was lost long
before the *Fearless.*"

"Was he? I don't know. I never knew him, not well at least. Not the
way you did."

"I didn't know him *that* well."

"He said you were lovers. He said you left him."

She laughed and shook her head. "You're one of those guys who believes everything you hear, aren't you? I sailed with him once, Seine. *Sailed.*"

And the dark look came again, as if someone had pulled shutters down, and no light emitted from her face at all.

"Auric was a bully. Not to speak ill of the dead, but he never got over being rejected by some girl in seventh grade, and he took it out on everybody he ever met afterward. I don't usually go for guys like that. I like men who are more secure with themselves."

A creepy cold feeling came over him. He recognized the chill in her face. Cook or deckhand or whatever, underneath she was an outside sailor, suffered from what old Arne Olleson had called DWD—Deep Water Disorder. They were aberrations, strange clouded human beings who understood the faces of waves better than the faces of people.

"Let's go buy alcohol," Julia said, and stared at his mouth as she said it, and in that one look he knew just what she wanted from him. But he still didn't know what he wanted from her, wondered if he hadn't already gotten all he needed, or all he could possibly ask.

Before he knew it she was walking away. Hands in pockets, tight blue jeans moving up the sidewalk for downtown Juneau. He wanted to grab her, even stood up and tried to follow because he wanted her, because he didn't want her to leave him with the image of her cold self, but wanted to see her change again. He was only hours removed from the Gulf itself, and now his right leg was asleep and burning and again he could barely lift his arm. He sat back down and felt himself flood with tears. "You're alive," he said to himself. "You're not dead, you're alive." And it was almost true.

When she returned she had rum, a bottle tucked into her sweatshirt. She found him in the stateroom staring out the porthole. She pulled the bottle free and peeled the sweatshirt over her head, her tee shirt beneath riding high up to reveal the smooth skin of her belly. She turned and cranked the wall heater. "Let's take all our clothes off and pretend it's summer!" she said, laughing. And then proceeded to take off her jeans, revealing a man's boxer shorts.

"You feeling better?" she asked.

"I guess." He couldn't stop looking at her. At the skin of her legs. He hadn't seen the skin of a woman's legs since before he'd last seen a tree. "I guess I don't know what I feel. Glad I'm alive, wishing I weren't. Heather. The Chemist. You."

"Me? What the hell did I do?"

"You saved me."

He wondered then if his feelings for her were nothing more or less than an extension of gratitude. He knew he wanted her, but that was easy, that was physical. What he felt inside was more complicated. Watching her face, like a wave ride in the Gulf, an up-and-down face, appearing and disappearing, her eyes brightening at the foamy crest and deadening in the depths of the pit, he wasn't sure if she was crazy, or if he was, or maybe both.

"Maybe going slow down the Inside is what you need. A milk run to purge the bad thoughts."

"Maybe it is," he said.

Besides, if he got home too fast he'd find someone he might have to kill, or someone who might kill him, or, worse yet somehow, no one at all.

She turned, looking more sensual in the simplicity of tee shirt and boxers than any woman he'd ever imagined. She poured rum into paper cups. They drank a toast to survival, a toast to ghosts, a toast to dead people he had never really known, overlooking the black water at gray-green sunset on the Inside Passage. The *Vigilant* motored south, towing doubles.

She stared at his mouth again, her eyes like glowing embers, her mouth melting. He wondered what experiences drove her, what made her so comfortable in a world of men. He wanted to ask but he didn't want to ruin it, didn't want to insult her, didn't want to reveal himself. She said, "I'm off watch until four A.M., when I cook breakfast. So let's party. You have a lot to celebrate."

Seine no longer had much of an inner compass. He saw the rain out the porthole, then opened it to hear the patter on calm water. He smelled land. It intoxicated him more than the rum, and made him think still more about the Chemist, how he claimed he could smell land. "I've never been unfaithful," he said. "We've been together ten years."

She smiled. "You've wanted me all along."

"What are you talking about?"

She grinned, as if she'd caught him. "I know about you." She talked like she was scooping out his insides with her finger. One thing she knew, she knew men. Better than they knew themselves. Better than he did anyway. "Are you always so goddamned uptight, Seine?"

"I don't know. My head hurts."

"You're so serious." She reached down, let her fingers splay through his hair, fingertips dancing lightly on his scalp, draining it of tension.

"I'm thirty-two. My wife left me for another man, I've been offshore for a year, and I feel like I might start drooling out the side of my mouth any minute."

She stood before him, paused, Dixie cup in hand, and then laughed. "Wait a minute there, you're right—" She reached down, wiped rum-saliva from the corner of his mouth, then slid her finger into her own mouth and stared as if she'd been hunting him and now that she had caught him would suckle the shreds of his flesh.

Her eyes locked down on his mouth as if this would be the first place she'd attack. "You wanna touch me?"

He could barely breathe but managed, "Yes."

"Good," she said. The way she said *good* made it sound like a fifteen-syllable word. She moved one of her legs between his, so that she hovered there, straddling his knee. She reached down with both hands. She traced the ragged bristly line of the suture on his cheek. He thought for a second she was going to pull on it, thought if she did it might unravel him completely. But she didn't pull. Her fingers moved to his mouth instead, sliding her middle finger between his rum-moistened lips. They looked like little-girl hands but felt calloused and rough from boat work. He sucked on her finger, looking at her eyes as she sat down on his leg and rocked back and forth, sliding, and then he thought he was unraveling anyway.

"I want you to make love to me," she said, with a voice all innocence, a girl-voice that belied completely the meaning of what she said next: "I want you to fuck me," she whispered.

He said nothing in reply, only gazed back at her.

"You're thinking about your wife, I know," she said, and she was right. "So, is your wife going to be waiting at the dock when we arrive?"

"Yes," he said, unsure why he lied. Giving himself an out. He was in need of a bright red hatch in the deck that said ESCAPE in bold stenciled letters.

"So when we get there, I won't be on deck. I'll occupy myself. She'll never know I was aboard. She'll have no need to be suspicious."

"It's not that," he said.

"So then I guess you think badly of me."

"No, it's not that either." But it was. Partly. Also the unspoken debt, like she'd reached out with a simple vector line and hauled him to safety. They would always have that between them—unless. He felt her move against his leg. Ohhhhh, he said inside. *Unless.*

"I want you, Henry," she said.

She raised up off his leg and swung over his lap, lowered herself again, and pressed herself onto him. She took both his hands, held them up and surveyed them, and placed them around her waist; pulling her own hands around his head, she clutched his face to her breast. Her skin felt at once tight and soft. He kissed her skin, licked her skin, tasted her skin.

"And I want you to tell me you love me," she whispered in his ear. "I know it's not true. Don't worry. I just like to hear it. So tell me."

He looked up at her in a panic, her face hovering inches higher than his. He searched her coal-black eyes, the brown skin of her face, the shining black luster of her hair. He wondered where she was from. With Julia you could pin down no defined ethnicity—she might have been part African, certainly Asian, maybe East Indian, a world of genetic information all mixed and wrapped in a five-foot two-inch muscle-body.

He felt for Julia's lips with his own and didn't for an instant imagine kissing Heather. Felt Julia's hips move on his lap, felt Julia's warmth, felt Julia's skin. "Please," she said. "Please, Henry. Oh, God"— she moved, breathless—"I love you I love I love you—"

"Oh, Julia, don't," he said. "Don't say that, please. I can't say that."

"I know you don't really," she whispered, "I know you don't, it's okay; please just say it, please. I need to hear it. I like to hear it. I can't come unless you say it."

And she pushed him backward to the bed, striking the back of his head on the wall; and as she stripped him of his jeans and herself of her boxers and sat on him, holding tight to his body, his mouth went to her ear, his lips pressing, whispering, "I love you, Julia, I do. I love you. I do. Oh, God, please. I love you."

And he felt warmth flood through him, filling him with a kind of fluid sunlight, and oddly enough, at that moment, he felt certain it was true.

Seattle

"You're my savior," he said, as they stood side by side on deck while the *Vigilant* approached Terminal 116 in Elliott Bay, swinging her barges in for off-loading.

"Savior's a pretty strong word," she said.

"You are. Without you I'm down."

"Well, be careful of it. You say I'm your savior, next thing you know you realize you owe me. Then you realize there's no way to pay me back unless you save *me*. And if you can't save me you start to hate me cause you resent that you owe me. And that really sucks. Since I don't need saving, you're bound to hate me, Seine."

She had that cold look again, but she gave him a friendly check with her hip as she pushed into the galley. Twenty minutes later, the tug *Vigilant* had dropped both her barges at the terminal and ran light those last miles to Pier 19.

Pier 19 was home port, and Seine knew it well. He had never harbored any illusions about Heather really being there to greet him, but now as he saw the familiar pier offices and the parking area beyond he wanted to see Julia.

Julia wasn't anywhere to be found, though, not in their stateroom, not in the engine room, not in the galley, not anywhere. In the wheelhouse, Macky was filling out his final salvage report. "The company investigators will want to debrief you, Seine," he said. "Make sure they have an up-to-date phone number."

Seine gave him the number he'd last called, the new number for the Bainbridge house. "I'll be there eventually," he said. "You seen Julia? I didn't get a chance to say good-bye."

"Oh, she got off at Terminal 116."

"She did? You know where I can find her?"

"I think she lives in Everett, but I heard she's trying to buy a house, so I'm not sure."

"A house in Everett?"

"Queen Ann Hill, I think."

"Well, if you see her, tell her I said good-bye. Tell her I said thanks. Again. Thanks for everything."

"No problem. If I see her. I probably won't, though. I'm shoreside for three months, and I heard she's going outside in a few days. She's working hard for her license. She's tough."

"Yeah. You have a local phone number for her?"

He moved over to a book, flipped it open—a crewing sheet—and shook his head. "Nope. They'll have it in the Port Captain's office, if you want to stop off."

Seine went outside, carrying his bag over his shoulder, and stepped over the bulwark dockside. He felt a kind of wonder at his own survival. A split came, a feeling of simultaneous relief and horror at his survival and the deaths of others.

For an instant as he stepped to the wooden dock, he felt it wobble and ripple underfoot. For some reason, he didn't want to move too quickly, didn't want to leave behind the tug *Vigilant* or the water or the temporary nature of that moment. He felt a kind of warped strength in it. Survival did that to him. It felt like an injection of importance. Made every moment and every image strike him as the most critical, the most aching, the most sublime he had ever known. He wished Julia were there, but even her absence left him with a sense of relief. He would not have to face the truth about his feelings—whatever that truth turned out to be—and with that he bypassed the Port Captain's office, leaving behind her phone number and her image both.

Less than a half hour later, he sat on the bed of the Harbor Light Motel, a simple two-story strip motel two blocks from the main harbor, with a view of the waterfront and the smell of the sea. He sat out front on the first level and watched a hooker walk back and forth on the street out front. He was about to go talk to her when a fifty-something businessman driving a rented Ford Explorer came along and picked her up, so Seine went to a corner market and bought a pack of Philip Morris Commanders and a twelve-pack of Rainier, and sat on the front porch of the Harbor Light and smoked and drank beer until it started to rain. The rain came like a mist, pattering from the afternoon air, and warm as it was, he rubbed his arms and wondered where he would go next.

He couldn't quit thinking about the Chemist and about Julia, first separately and then together, like twin apparitions. In a dream that night, they held hands, kissed, laughed at him. Waved him on. *Come on*, Julia said in a dream that night, *come save me, save me hard, oh God, oh God—save me.*

Next day he considered going straight to the union hall and hopping a tanker headed out for foreign ports, leaving Seattle behind forever, but he knew he'd just be trading one aberration for another. He'd end up like Julia and the Chemist and all the outside sailors he knew, carving his life from the pit of a sea swell.

Seattle never felt more foreign. He felt like an outsider in his own town and, with the rain still drizzling, he sat outside the Harbor Light for another day and watched clouds of cigarette smoke rise up through the noon mist, and by the time he finished his first smoke, the hooker appeared again. She wore plain gray slacks and a black sweater and she had no raincoat. When she looked his way, he waved her over.

He carried a chair outside and they smoked and drank two beers each until she finally asked if he wanted a date, and he said, "I thought we just had one," and handed her twenty bucks.

Her mouth smiled as her eyes frowned, and only then, in a moment of innocent surprise at his gesture, did he realize how young she was. She couldn't have been more than sixteen, and he had an idea she was even younger. She wore a sweater to cover her arms, and tattoos at her ankles to cover the bruises where she'd sought battered veins with needles.

"Not into sex? Or do you just like boys?"

"Naw, it's not that. I just can't do it."

"Can't do it? I've been with grizzled old dudes who lost their virginity in World War Two, and they could do it. You can't be more than what, forty?"

Seine shook his head. "I'm thirty-two."

"Don't get huffy. I *said* you couldn't be more than forty. Anyway, I like older guys."

"I guess I don't mean I *can't*, I just can't "

She frowned at him. Then took a long drag from a smoke and stared with eyes dulled by drugs and grizzled old men who'd lost their virginity in World War II. "You seem so lonely," she said.

"Don't pity me, thanks."

"Just saying what's obvious. Don't you have anybody in the area?"

"Yes, there are people in the area. I just—I guess I can't go see them right now."

"For another twenty bucks I'll sit here an hour longer with you—if you give me another beer and a smoke."

"Twenty an hour? Your pimp wouldn't like it."

"He don't care. I'm already ahead for the week."

Seine thought, fuck it, why not? and held the smoke dangling from his lips, squinting like the Chemist and practically gagging on smoke while he dug into his wallet and pulled out another twenty. She brightened. "Thanks. Cool. I could give you head if you want."

"No thanks," he said. "Just tell me you love me."

"Oh, I love you."

"Thanks. Once more with feeling."

"Don't fuck with me." Her eyes deadened. "I'll give the twenty back if you fuck with me."

"It's okay, forget it. I'm sorry."

She shrugged and helped herself to another smoke and a beer. "Strong smokes," she said.

"A guy I knew smoked them. He's dead now."

He tried to tell her about the Chemist and *Fearless* and the Wolf and that feeling he got riding the *Vigilant* out to the salvage job, how the shipmate feeling ran between them, how it was the only love he knew anymore.

But she just frowned at him, smoking. He thought of asking her about all the things she'd done, when it all started, how old was she, and how bad had she really been. He wanted a nasty story. Had she ever been in a gang bang with five towboaters while pushing a barge up the Kuskokwim River?

"You *sure* you don't wanna fuck me?" she asked.

"I'm sure," Seine said. He had never been more sure of anything. "No offense. It's not you."

He watched her go, walking through the rain, down toward Pike Street, and he was glad she'd gone. She made him think too much, made him wonder why he couldn't bring himself to go home, made him face the fear of what he'd find. So he smoked another cigarette and drank another beer and wondered if Julia was at that moment steaming out the Strait for open sea. That night he slept with the window open, so that in the middle of the night he woke up to the surface numbness coupled with the inevitable stabbing pain deep inside his palms. He soaked his hands in hot water, and groaned out his relief, and then lay back listening to the sound of the rain and to the tires slashing through rain-soaked streets. He stretched his right side and felt the pain sear through his shoulder. He shivered, cold, but somehow couldn't bring himself to close the window. He wrapped a blanket around his shoulders, put on an old warbly tape of Bob Marley and sat by the open window, smoking his way through "No Woman No Cry."

PART TWO

Ocean of Ghosts

Braindamage Island

From the middle deck of the Washington State ferryboat, Bainbridge Island loomed before him like a bright green garden of lies. He liked being a passenger now, leaning on the second-deck railing with the floating parking lot of cars beneath him. Partly he still hoped he'd find Heather there in the house, sleeping in their bed in the vast space of her dream bedroom.

But the house was vacant save for a few pieces of furniture that had been his before they'd met: a cold leather sofa, an ancient wooden desk etched by years of use, and the bed they had once shared. He just stared at it and couldn't bring himself to lie on it or sleep in it. She'd left it made, and he wondered if the sheets were clean. Only the garage was full, not with cars, but with the worthless details of vanished youth. The old Triumph Trident he had bought from his cousin in 1976, boxes of schoolbooks, newspaper clippings from high school basketball. And Heather: letters, pictures, dead memories killed and buried by her own handwritten admissions.

He climbed on the Triumph and stood on the starter stiff-legged, a pain shooting up from his heel to his ear as he turned it over, and felt mild surprise that it started at all. He rode out over the floating bridges to Port Townsend, cruised into the offices of North Sound

Realty, and waited while Heather's assistant, a post-punk slickster with narrow black-rimmed glasses, two earrings, and sideburns, threw sidelong glances at him.

Seine didn't know why, but it took him five minutes of sitting and waiting before he noticed the guy's nameplate: LARRY DEHAN. Seine's cheeks flushed. He watched Larry work, fielding phone calls with his headset well placed, his hair spiked black, and somehow the just-correct blend of conservative practicality and edgy rebellion. So acute was his rising bitterness that Seine could only think how much he hated men who spent more time contemplating their hair than what happened under it.

As Larry concluded his phone call he made eye contact, and Seine saw right off that Larry knew he'd been recognized. His eyes grew sleepy, and a smile crept into his mouth with the merest hint of smug superiority, as if daring him to say, So, you're fucking my wife? But Seine said nothing, merely stared at him until Larry's smugness gave way to the implicit threat of psychosis in Seine's face.

"You can go in now, she's ready for you," said Larry.

As he went in, Seine wondered if this was one of those times people went berserk and killed five in an office and then turned the gun on themselves. He had no gun, of course, but that didn't stop him from thinking about it.

Heather looked cool, her hair tight, business suit crisp, the skirt hemmed just above her knee, at a line that defined precisely the boundary between sexy and professional. She was elegant and smart and beautiful, and Seine wanted her even as he hated her. He finally said, "Is that him?"

"What difference does it make?" She laced her fingers together on her lap.

"I don't know."

"How unusual. You *never* know, Henry."

He wanted to tell her about the *Fearless*, about all that he'd been through, but then again didn't feel up to offering it. Maybe he wanted her to divine it by the look on his face, or just care enough to ask.

"I was working to make money for the house, Heather," he said, an edge of defense bolting involuntarily into his voice. He watched her face. "It *is* him," he said. "You left me for *him*."

"You are so full of shit. *You* left *me* a year ago. I haven't seen you in a *year*, Henry. And you sent about five letters the whole time." She sat behind her desk, leaning back, legs crossed. "So full of shit."

His mind stumbled and he felt himself sinking into his chair; he patted his pocket, feeling for the long letter he'd never sent. But it wasn't there now. He didn't know where it was. He wanted her to understand what had happened to him, and he thought maybe the letter could explain it.

"Did you even think about me at all?" she asked.

For so long he hadn't—couldn't. Now he couldn't explain why. The frustration and the anger it caused. "I had to be in the moment," he said.

She laughed. "Must have been one hell of a moment."

Maybe he didn't love her. Maybe he only wanted her. "He answered the phone when I called, did he tell you that? *Larry?* What kind of stupid fucking name is Larry?"

She smiled then—*look at yourself*—a smile that for an instant came as warm humor. Then a deep, disdainful laugh replaced it, rising from somewhere in her belly. "I'm just so sure you've been Mr. Pristine."

He wanted to say yes. Until a week ago, he could have. But not now, and something inside him wouldn't allow the lie, no matter how recent and justified he had felt.

"So, what now? Sell the house? Split our money?"

"I don't care about the money."

"Neither do I." Then he laughed. After everything he didn't care about the money. "You can have whatever you need or want. I don't care. I have a good job."

She laughed again, in a way that seemed like she was about to spit on him. "You have a shit-for-brains job, Henry. Look at you. Your job is beating the hell out of you. You look forty. You look like hell."

He knew he looked like hell. He certainly felt like hell, and it didn't help to hear it out loud.

"Why do you even do it? You're smart, you could do a thousand things. You claim you were going off to make money for us, but I really think you were just going off."

She might have been right. He thought now that she probably was, but that knowledge made the moment no less painful. His mind went blank and he felt tears press at his eyes. He frowned toward her then, like he might say something, might beg, or plead, or simply break down. But nothing came out.

The ride out beyond Port Angeles dizzied him, so he pulled to the side and sat overlooking the blowing overcast of the Strait of Juan de Fuca, watched the steamers beating their way out to sea, and a tanker tracked by escort tugs. From here he could stare at the spots where both his father and his marriage had drowned.

The feeling that he was bad news for others came back, displacing the good sense that he might be able to save somebody someday, cure them of sorrow, snatch them from the clutches of cold.

He was no lightning rod, he knew that. A lightning rod *drew* fire, offered itself up as a conduit for a violent nature, kept people safe at its own expense. He was more like a latter-day Charon of Greek myth, running the ferry across the River Styx to the Underworld, charging a fee, picking coins from the mouths of the deceased. A ferryman of the dead.

*   *   *

At home, in the bathroom, he stared at his face in the mirror, an ugly face of stitches and scraggly beard. He cut the beard with scissors and shaved his face with a blade gone dull on Heather's legs. He laid himself bare, pale, civilized. Then, using scissors and tweezers, he clipped and tugged each stitch of the Coast Guard suture, pulling out each of the bristly black pieces and setting them on the cold porcelain sink. The scar left behind was pink and a little ragged, and still surprisingly tender.

Then, driven by images of Julia Lew and Heather both, he rode his motorcycle into town with the vague intent of finding the Pike Street prostitute in the gray slacks. He wanted something from her, or maybe just wanted her. Maybe he could find the woman underneath the layers of imagined acts, and in this way prove to himself in some contorted whisper of logic that Julia Lew didn't deserve the rumors of shipboard life, and that his wife didn't deserve his hatred.

But the hooker wasn't there, so he went to a downtown bar called the Chase Lounge, which looked like any Formica-countered waterfront bar except it was split in half, dance club on the left side, hardcore drinkers' lounge on the right. Seine sat on the right side and watched through the wide passage between the two as the metal heads and gutter punks milled around. He'd always harbored a secret desire to come here with the Buff and the Big Man—walk off the barge and into the Lounge. Lug-soled firejumpers in exchange for Doc Martens. He kept thinking about the Chemist while he listened to the punk riffs and little-girl voices of a girl band called Edible Electra.

The scene annoyed him, but he loved the way the lead singer's voice turned and contorted around the lyrics, liked her snarling fuck-me attitude, liked the suggestion of her body beneath her black tights. He watched her, semi-dazzled, and afterward tried to buy her a drink, but she said she didn't do that.

Seine had no idea what *that* was.

He sat alone at the short leg of the L-shaped bar and drank eight beers by himself and afterward staggered down along the waterfront and watched the lights of the autumn night sparkle on the Sound. He saw couples walking along in overcoats, heard music drifting on the night, and suddenly he wished he'd never left the freeze of the north. More than ever he felt convinced he had no business among normal people anymore.

When he was south, he missed things he couldn't account for: the smell of the barge, with its mix of oil and grease and fuel, and its outdoor wind filled with diesel exhaust, and the smell of smoke from steak and steak fries for supper. The patterned ground of the tundra plains flying in, like a geometric field reaching to forever. The incongruity of a land that was at once desert and frozen marsh, the smell of the sea when it finally thawed, the sound of a lone seal, the distant horn of a buoy tender or the gentle moan of the buoys themselves. The breaching release of spouting humpbacks migrating through ice fields, lumbering giants that somehow made you feel as small as the sky did. All measurement came back to sky, whether the white bubble of May or the steel gray of June or the ten-hour sunsets of August—when the sun drove north dipping toward the horizon and then rose up and turned miraculously into a sunrise without ever touching ground—or the descending dark of September, when you lost twenty minutes of light a day, and clear weather brought an aurora borealis that took up half the night sky.

He missed all of it. He missed the Wolf. He missed the Big Man. He missed the Buff. He missed his mind.

Mostly he stayed alone and lonely on Braindamage, but when he was about to explode from self-imposed isolation, he'd pay the ferryman and ride east. One day in late fall the sun shone like spring, so he climbed on the Triumph and rode to the Seattle Fish House for drinks and dinner, feeling the air in his lungs, posing as normal. In the restaurant, people gathered after work on a Friday evening and Seine sat among them, drinking in the midst of a crowd, completely alone. Sipping a pint of draft ale, he looked out and saw a face moving up the sidewalk, a lanky face from the north, one he hadn't seen in six years. He ran outside without hesitation, saying, "Marco! Marco Barn!"

But Marco walked right by him. Seine stopped and watched him pass, said, "Marco, it's me, Henry Seine," but the face didn't register anything, not so much as a fluttering eyelid or a nanosecond of eye contact. He was either brain-dead or harboring such a grudge that he'd blocked Seine out of existence. Seine wouldn't have been surprised to find that either was the case.

Marco Barn had been Seine's roommate his first year in the arctic, a welder and a stoner by trade who along with Buffy Errol once smuggled four pounds of high grade bud into camp using two large Tupperware containers wrapped in mint leaves and aluminum foil. The buds lay inside the plastic containers, lined up like stuffed zucchinis, and over that summer they smoked every ounce of it.

Everybody had a theory about what happened to Marco Barn, but in the end he became the poster boy for why not to smoke three bowls of high-grade Afghani *indica* before breakfast. Not only was Marco Barn stoned all day long, he also refused to wear a hard hat, even though he was a welder and every rule ever written about marine welding made hard hats standard issue. But Marco hated them, as he hated all things restrictive and protective, and he refused to wear one despite Irons's insisting.

Seine even chimed in to no avail: "It's just common sense, Marco," he said one night as they lay in their bunk beds. "Why risk getting your head split open?"

"Hey man, it's too bulky," said Marco in his stoned voice. "I like being free. I hit my head twice as much when I got it on as when I don't. Anyway, it's my head," and then, as if to prove it, he sucked down yet another bong load and passed the silver tube Seine's way. "Besides, dude, nobody mentions arc burns."

"No one said getting hit on the head is your only occupational hazard. You're so stubborn about it. It's *obvious*—"

"I'll tell you what's obvious, man. Arc burns are obvious. I gotta smoke the whack just to ease my pain. I'm self-medicating, man. You don't know about arc burns, dude."

But Seine did know. He'd worked a season as Marco's helper, though evidently Marco had forgotten all about it. Seine had spent twelve hours a day handing him welding rod and stringing welding leads, and in the process caught countless inadvertent glimpses of the supernovalike welding arc. The accumulated effect felt like beach sand shoved into his eyeballs.

Next day, Marco was just stepping out the string when Irons pushed his rag face into his. "You're playing games," Irons barked. "I told you once I told you a thousand times, get your noggin into a hard hat or you're gonna regret it."

"Yeah?" said Marco. "Well what about arc burns, man?"

"What about 'em?"

"I got arc burns, you don't care about that!"

"What are you doing, staring at the arc for fun? Huh? I bet you are."

"You think I'm stupid?"

"Of course I think you're stupid! Now get a goddamned hard hat!"

In his pot-induced haze, Marco Barn looked at Wolf Irons and imagined him like a wire sculpture, a thousand lengths of baling wire folded and twisted together and spot-welded. Marco Barn had flirted with sculpture for a while. He liked using his welding talents to produce wild beady steel things he called art but that everybody else called junk. The problem was he couldn't sustain an idea. He couldn't even sustain any lasting anger toward the Wolf for calling him stupid. While stoned he found the world was a drifty place, where no one was his enemy and nothing bad could happen.

So Marco went to work inside a barge tank, vaguely noticing a pallet of half-inch steel padeyes stacked by the entrance hole. He recognized them because he had cut them himself, six-inch squares of thick steel with holes in the middle. Eventually they'd be welded to the steel decks of barges and used for lashing down cargo. But Marco Barn didn't quite understand how or why they'd made their way to this manhole. Down in the tank he welded all morning, repairing a break in the bulkhead between tanks. At lunch he started up the ladder. He was about six rungs up when he heard a stick of dynamite explode on top of his head, the noise so loud it deafened both his ears and made the top of his head feel as if it were shoved down into his chest.

When he woke up he was lying on his back on the bottom of the barge tank looking straight up. Seine knew because Seine was right there next to him, kneeling on the tank bottom, the first person to get to him. The world encased Marco Barn in black, as in a grave. His ears didn't work, except for a kind of pressing deafness, and when that lifted, he could hear nothing but an intense ringing. As for sight, he could see only the rising black walls of nothingness, just space and infinity, a sweeping dark without depth or distance or definition. And up top was a single round hole that seemed nine hundred miles off, a vague pinprick at first, swelling to a circle of streaming light, growing until there within the bright came the face of Wolf Irons, wrinkled from arctic winds, his nose half frozen off by the Bite, his lips moving first, and then his voice saying, "IS HE DEAD?"

At the time, Marco got the idea that the voice hoped he was dead. Then he figured it was true, he was in fact dead, and now had to face the cold and unavoidable reality that God looked just like Wolf Irons.

Seine said, "Just stay there, don't move, don't move."

"Seine . . . Seine . . . ," Marco groaned. "What the fuck, man?"

Seine saw the realization in Marco's eyes that he had never left the barge tank, saw the steel padeye next to his head with blood and a tuft of his hair sticking to it. Somehow it had fallen into the hole and landed flat on Marco Barn's skull, which was lucky; if it had landed on end it would have buried itself somewhere south of his pituitary gland. Then Marco's eyes rolled up and showed white, his voice still moaning, "Seine, Seine, ohhhhhhhhh—"

Marco Barn slept for seventeen hours, and after that he couldn't seem to get his socks straight. He seemed to puzzle over sorting pairs, and then finally gave up entirely and went to work barefoot, until someone pointed out that it was just 15 degrees above zero and that maybe a pair of boots was in order.

Everybody who knew him before the accident said Marco was never the same again. When he finally went south, he climbed into the crew cab with his jeans on backward, steadfast in his belief that Wolf Irons or Mr. Hanson or his roommate, Henry Seine, had tossed the padeye onto his head as some kind of twisted lesson in safety first.

The night he saw Marco Barn outside the Seattle Fish House, Seine rode back to Braindamage Island, swinging the bike up the gravel drive. Headlights flashed across his dark house and he felt a surge in his throat as out front stood Terje Narvik, broken glass clinging to his bloody scalp. He came and went in the flash of a headlight.

Inside the house, he tried pushing the incident with Marco out of his mind, finally pulling Hang Mann's blunts from his pocket, and to make them last he broke them apart and smoked them in small bits from a pipe fashioned from a dented beer can. A wave of happiness washed through him, filled him until he thought his chest might burst. He stumbled out to the garage and pulled the boxes into the driveway and looked off into the black woods and felt the darkness close over him. Somehow the trees and the beauty dropped him as far as it had lifted him, and having smoked Hang Mann's pot he was somehow not surprised to see the Chemist standing there at the doorway when he went inside. He mouthed the word *feckless*. Or maybe it was *fuckless*. Seine couldn't tell.

That night he curled on the floor on a bedroll next to the bed and stared out the large frame window to the woods until he drifted off. But just as suddenly he found himself awake, and aware somehow that he wasn't alone in the house. He heard a door creak, and then a voice in the living room: "Seine!"

Work aboard tugboats had trained him to shake off sleep, and he did that now, quickly, trying to place the voice as he stood and stepped carefully down the hallway. Here not even a glimmer of moon showed him the way. He turned on the overheads, the open great room flooding with pools of light. But there was no one there.

The next night, he heard the voice again, calling a single sharp *"Seine!"* When he awakened this time, he wasn't so sure he'd heard it or dreamed it. Again Seine went out and turned on the overhead lights, and this time, outside past his own reflection in the glass he saw a man pass by the window and then away from the house, disappearing into the woods.

Seine's breathing quickened. He ran for the rear door, snatching a heavy Maglite and carrying it outside on his shoulder like a cop, ready to bring the steel barrel of the flashlight down hard on someone's head. But he found no one. He flicked on the floods to snap the forest into brightness. He looked for footprints. He called out "Hello!" and finally went back inside and turned out all the lights and sat there, awake on his bedroll on the floor, listening to every creak, every scrape of every branch on the cedar-shake roof.

By the next night, he knew there was no one there at all. At first he thought Deadman, his father again appearing as he had on *Fearless,* or the Chemist—but this one was distinct, faceless, a shade—a shade with a voice he could only pretend he didn't recognize: Marco Barn.

He called it his autumn of sloth. He wandered the halls and high ceilings of the wooded house, through nights and gray days, his mind swallowed by divorce, his body digested by rain. He did little more than walk around the house in boxer shorts—stoned—and carry on conversations with dead men. By February he felt like a ghost himself and wasn't entirely convinced he'd survived *Fearless* after all. The Shade appeared sporadically, often not a vision but a feeling, like somebody crawling inside him.

Sometimes in midafternoon if the sun hinted its way through the trees to tempt him with a vision of spring, he would lie on the floor of the great room and drift in a painless cloud of near-sleep where he would dream controlled dreams. He sometimes imagined Heather then, and in the null zone between waking and sleeping he could make her respond as his conscious mind chose. He could make her beg for forgiveness, or beg for his touch, or simply beg. In real dreams she never wanted him, but in the half-sleep of winter afternoons she released her hair in a tumble and hiked her skirt to her waist and lowered herself onto him.

When he dreamed of Julia Lew it was always the opposite. She came to him through a haze of false I love yous, emerging from a crowd of merchantmen, and even in controlled dreams she could never be his.

Heather appeared at the door one dreary day in early spring, wearing a business suit, looking ravishing and slightly appalled at the condition of the house. "Hello, Henry," she said.

He didn't say anything, just stepped aside and let her in. She lin-

gered on him a moment as she passed, frowning. "Have you stopped
showering?"

"I take walks in the rain," he said.

"You smell bad." She glanced at the floor as if studying it for de-
fects. "Let me guess. You have a pile of money and you're going to
blow it all during the off season and then be forced to go north again."

"That's the plan."

"How original," she said, and then retreated into business, where
her mind operated with the cushioned security of the quantifiable. He
understood it; after all, it was the only way he'd survived the gravel
haul. "I have a plan too," she said. "I've been doing a lot of thinking,
and a lot of figuring, and it comes down to this: we need to do something about the house. We have three options: you buy me out, I buy
you out, or we sell to a third party."

The thought of Heather buying him out and living in the house
with someone like *Larry* made Seine's skull throb. He imagined *Larry*
walking down halls and touring the great room as if the house were
his, wearing Seine's boxer shorts and making love to Seine's wife.

"Do you really want to live here?" he asked.

She pondered that, pivoted on the Berber weave and surveyed the
open beams. "It's a beautiful home," she said, sounding like a real estate agent now, "but I can't really afford it by myself. You?"

He frowned, succeeded in not looking at her body. He stared her
in the eye and said, "The truth is, I feel like it's ours—" He caught
himself, choked on saliva, and paused to swallow. "If we can't live in it
together, then I don't think either of us should live in it."

Almost imperceptibly, she flinched and regarded him with a puz-
zled expression, as if she hadn't expected that. "I guess I understand
what you mean," she said softly.

She stood there then, watching him as if something might come along and shove them both off the track they were on and they'd fall into each other's arms and laugh and make love and it would be like waking from a bad dream of imagined selves.

But no such thing came along, and she finally said, "Okay, I'll list it."

"Do I have to move out in the meantime?"

"We can time the close of escrow with your going north if you want, but if you're going to stay until then, you'll have to make the mortgage payments. I've got rent on this condo where I'm staying. I can't afford both. It would go into your share of the equity, of course." She pulled out a date book and jotted a note. "And you should probably get an attorney to handle the sale once you're gone."

She clicked her pen and smiled briefly.

"I don't need an attorney," he said. "I trust you to handle it. In fact, I'll pay you a fee to handle it. I'd rather you have the money than some attorney."

Her lips parted slightly; she appeared completely incapable of understanding him. She muttered, "Thank you, Henry."

The last act of cooperation in their marriage was to clean the house together to prepare it to be shown. She arrived on a rainy Saturday wearing work jeans and a gray sweatshirt. He answered the door freshly shaved and showered. She had bunned her straw-colored hair tightly back, and she walked past with a mop bucket, not seeming to notice him at all. Together they labored through the morning, listening to rain patter on the roof. Without wind the rainfall made straight lines in the forest air.

He enjoyed the work. He enjoyed watching Heather's bun fall out as she vacuumed and he knocked down webs from the tall ceiling and dusted blinds in the bedroom. He enjoyed listening to reggae as they had in old times, dreaming of the tropics to break up the wet monotony of a Seattle winter.

When they'd first moved in together, into a beat-down house in the U district in 1982, they had this ritual they called the Cleaning Blitz. Once a week they'd make a party out of housework, drinking semi-copious amounts of blended margaritas while dancing to The Cure and cleaning toilets. It was the best two years of his life. What he did now bore more resemblance to running ordinary on the gravel haul, except that Heather was there to torment him in person. The further her hair fell, the more she aroused him, and the more he wondered where in the house she'd actually done it with Larry, and before long the images crowded him.

He ducked into the garage and lit off a quick bowl for the sake of perspective and put on The Cure, a kind of musical narration for the last act of their marriage.

"This room is disgusting," she called from the bedroom. "You've been sleeping on the floor?"

Seine walked into the room. She was standing there with an eight-foot feather duster, looking at his bedroll.

"Well, yeah," he said. "Most of the time."

"That's weird, Henry. Why are you doing that?"

"I just couldn't sleep in the bed. It felt—"

She turned to him and tilted her head, half in disgust, half in pity. "Felt what?"

"It's not my bed anymore."

She eyed him until she figured out what he meant. Abruptly she pulled out her clip and her hair fell down completely, past her shoulders. Then she curled it back up and started pinning it into a bun again. She didn't once look at him for a facial response—distancing herself, he thought. She doesn't want to know what I mean.

"All right," she said when they had finished. "You'll need to make arrangements for your stuff when you leave. Can you make sure you do that? I don't want to have to deal with it."

"I'll do it," he said, and sank a little further into the deep. He pulled himself out long enough to move some boxes out to the garage. The Chemist sat on Seine's old desk with skinny legs crossed, thumbing a Bic lighter. *Ever heard the sound of one Bic flicking?* he said with a buoyant smile.

"Get out of my way," Seine said, then went inside and turned the music off.

"Good, then," she said. "Try to keep the house picked up, and I'll give you as much notice as possible before I show it. Deal?"

"Deal," he said, and they shook hands.

They both seemed like such reasonable people.

Outside he stood on the huge wraparound front porch and watched her step into her Volvo wagon and drive off down the long gravel drive. When he turned around to step inside, there the Chemist stood with a nerdy menace, a tobacco mouth, wearing a timing chain off a '57 Mercedes for a belt to hold his pants up, and wraps of electrical tape on both wrists. He spat Copenhagen on the porch and cleared his throat. *You saved yourself and then you fucked my love and this is what you get.*

"Fuck off," Seine said, and brushed past.

In the bedroom Seine stared at the bed and saw Heather lying back with Larry between her legs, their cries bounding inside his head like a migraine. Holographic porn flicks played in every corner of the house.

When he couldn't take it anymore, he went to the bedroom, where he dragged and hauled and lifted and pushed the king-sized Beauty-rest by Simmons to the front yard. And out of the garage under pale yellow lights he came up with a five-gallon can of gasoline. And he doused the mattress of her adultery, and he burned it. The flames *whooshed* into a gathering pull, reached high into the night air, where Seine stood and breathed and watched flames lick the stars. He imagined the flames igniting the house, leaving nothing of his former life but ashes and smoke. He heard the cries of shipmates and the moans of the steel tug *Fearless* sinking. Seine wondered if he'd ever see Julia Lew again. He tried to remember her voice on the radio. He wondered if he'd ever taste the succulent warmth of her mouth or hear her say *I love you I love you I love you* in a voice that made men wild.

Sitting back in a lawn chair, he smoked the last of Hang Mann's crumbled joint and watched the bed flame up like some kind of marital incinerator, heard voices swirling around him, saw Marco Barn standing on the other side of the flames, smoking cigarettes and laughing.

"Go away," he said quietly.

The Shade of Marco Barn sat laughing.

Seine knew then that he would return north. He would fly on turbojets into the black dash of the outland airstrip, flee in every way one could flee except possibly from the law, though a goading whisper said this too was possible. He had a lurking suspicion he'd done something heinous in his life, something he couldn't quite admit himself, and for that the ghosts would surely gather and come for him. For now he tried to ignore them, even as they moved around the fire to close in. He shut his eyes and felt the blaze of flames burn them all away.

False Horizon

W hen he opened his eyes he didn't know where he was at first, only that he felt the rattle and rumble of main engines beneath him, felt the pitch of a flat-bottom push boat through sea swell, and heard Buffy Errol telling him all about how he was going to fuck Julia Lew.

He heard Julia too, or thought he did, distant and kind, saying, "Hey, Seine, I didn't think I'd ever see you again."

He couldn't quite pull himself out of the fog.

This was how it went. His life leapfrogging from moment to moment, with nothing but blank spots in between. Migration was the main cycle of his existence, a flinging back and forth between mutually exclusive extremes. He awakened fully to realize he was indeed north, offshore, in what looked to be the Chukchi Sea. He had been in the arctic all season, he realized, remembered months passing to bring him to this place, steering a course north toward a false horizon. The Buff was saying, "She's north, Seine, she's north and we're north, and I'm sliding in. You got nothing to say about it."

Seine didn't figure he had anything to say about anything. He stood up and rubbed his eyes. In the distance the line of the polar pack stretched by refraction into a sheer wall a hundred feet high. Arctic mirage closed in.

"Did I hear Julia or was I dreaming?"

"You heard her, but you're dreaming if you think I ain't taking over."

"Where is she?"

"They just rounded Barrow aboard *Terror.*"

Through a fatigued brain, he could barely make sense of the *concept* of *Terror,* much less the reality that Julia was sailing on her. He hadn't seen the boat since that day, now a year gone, when he'd boarded her sister ship and met the Chemist. *Fearless* and *Terror,* the best example of dualistic nomenclature. He wondered what twisted soul in the company hierarchy had thought up that pair of names.

His entire face hummed, his ears hissed white noise. He'd been subsisting on catnaps for a week, working twenty-hour days preparing North Dock for its fate: shipment south. He wasn't sure of the date anymore, and frankly he didn't care. He'd even lost track of the money. In his mind he replayed the image of *Fearless* in that last instant before she heeled over and sank.

Buff fished into his pocket for a tobacco tin he kept filled with fresh nutmeg. This season (since the advent of dogs) he'd taken to grinding and chewing the stuff for a jailhouse high. He packed his lip full of the sweet-smelling powder. "I feel like someone removed half my brain," Seine said. "I need real sleep."

"So go below and get some. I'll talk to Lew for you, set things up for her and me once we get back to North Dock. She'll be there in two days." The Buff cackled, sending wet flecks of nutmeg spattering across the wheelhouse console.

"Am I gonna have to hear that kinda shit forever?"

"Nope. Just as soon as I fuck her, you won't hear a peep outa me."

"You're such a dick, Buff."

"No, I *have* a dick, not like you, Seine. Putz."

"Putz? Where'd you get that word? You don't even know what it means."

"What the fuck I care what it means? I know what it *sounds* like. It sounds like a weak-dick who passes up the hottest piece of tail in four oceans because he's still technically married to a cold-ass bitch who fucks some real estate agent called Larry! A putz! That's you."

Seine shook his head. "Who's skippering *Terror*?"

"Korso."

"Jesus Christ." Seine pressed his palms against his eyeballs and felt the pressure. An ocean of perverts. "If it ain't you, it's Korso," Seine said.

"You're just jealous," the Buff said. "You can't stand thinking Lew and me got a *relationship*."

This was true. Anything close to a relationship between Julia and the Buff made Seine question the boundaries of reality, so he wrote the suggestion off to the Buff's testosterone-laced fantasies and buried the image under a sea of gravel.

Seine checked his radarscope, where Muktuk Island appeared as a perfect circle on the green screen. The Buff pointed off. "Out there, man, you know what's out there?"

"Let me take a wild guess: ice."

"You're a regular comedian, Seine. I mean outside the ice. Way out. I'm serious now. Skeemos talk about it: Rottingmule. Can't see it with your eyes. It's where old Skeemos walk off to die, where everybody sails in the end. Bet you never even heard of it."

He hadn't, but that meant little. The Buff had a lot to say about old Eskimos, even though his father had taken him south at the age of four and moved him to Wyoming. Since then, the only Eskimos the Buff had contact with were those he used as sources for polar bear hides and native artifacts he sold down in Anchorage.

"*Muktuk* is Eskimo for 'whale blubber,' " the Buff said. "We're sailing to Whale Blubber Island."

Seine didn't know what to believe of the Buff's talk, so he decided not to believe any of it. He could barely believe how quickly time had passed, much less some mythology concocted by a Wyoming Eskimo. He focused his eyes downward and saw the ship's log: September 6, 1990. Seine took back the wheel and motored north with a set of images all his own, one of which was a feeling Columbus must have had at least a few times: that despite his best estimate, he was sailing off the edge of a flat earth.

As he approached Muktuk, Seine steered east to survey the island's perimeter, circling the north side against a steady northwesterly wind. The blunt bow of *Whale* thumped against short chop. A flat low disk, the island rose four feet above sea level, protected by a bulwark of sandbags that terraced the island's edges. He turned south along the island's windward side and looked for a good place to push ashore.

To the north, the polar pack refracted into a split image now, the wall of white ice actually hovering two or three degrees above the horizon, as if floating in midair. They called it ice blink: an insane, inverted image which to Seine was worldly proof that perception was a joke—true in matters of geography as well as relationships.

So what did it matter what the Buff or anybody else thought of Julia? She had saved him, and that was no illusion. They would always have that. At times it seemed the only certain thing. So he didn't understand why the other men bothered him so. He kept repeating to himself that she would soon make camp, climb the catwalk of the camp barge at North Dock, and stand outside his door, waiting. The image thrilled him, even if it was a dream.

He maneuvered the bow against the island, easing forward into a notch between sandbags, pressing ahead dead slow on both engines. With the vessel holding itself in place, Seine left the wheelhouse and climbed backward down the external ladder to the narrow side deck. At forty-five feet in length, the *Whale* looked like a flattened World War II landing craft. The two-story deckhouse rose off the stern of a rectangular hull, leaving a long foredeck where the hydraulic crane angled upward like a giant steel arm. A grated steel landing ramp jutted upright off the flat bow.

Seine didn't much like the idea of taking a boat the size of *Whale* this far offshore this time of year. She had little power and even less rudder. The bilges leaked perpetually. She spent most of her time on routine daily runs around camp, deploying oil spill booms for environmental containment and transferring fifty-five-gallon drums of slop with her deck crane. But most of the slop came from her own bilges, and Seine never saw a single oil spill that *Whale* ever contained, only about a half dozen that she herself caused.

In the tiny galley, he found the Big Man seated at the table with his chair atop the engine-room deck hatch. The entire area, bunk beds included, was the size of a big walk-in closet. The engines vibrated the bottoms of Seine's boots until his feet tickled. "What's for dinner?" he asked.

The Big Man's voice boomed. "Ohhh, man. The Buff is insane. Do you know what he brought aboard? He brought aboard nothing more than dill pickles, mayonnaise, Wonder Bread, a ten-pound sack of onions, and a case of Spam! It is your fault, Seine, for asking the engineer to load the stores."

Seine let out a little laugh. Ever since *Fearless* he and the Big Man had an understanding, a mutual respect that bordered on friendship, and since Seine had no real friends, he had to take all the borders-on-friendship he could get. "I don't think I've ever had Spam," Seine said.

"Whatever else that you do," the Big Man said. "Do not watch Buffy Errol eat it. You will never eat meat by-products again."

Seine thought that was probably a good thing. Then he set about making himself a Spam, pickle, and onion sandwich. After seven hours on the wheel it tasted like well-seasoned dog food.

The Big Man rattled a recent copy of the *Anchorage Times* and announced there were two hundred narwhals trapped in a freezing fjord off Melville Island. "They are launching international effort to break ice to free them," he said.

"Maybe we should get in on it," Seine said. "Do something useful for once."

He stepped out the back door to the tiny afterdeck, took a breath of cold westerly wind, and caught sight of the Buff just as he ran a garden hose out the rear railing and began pumping bilge slop overboard. Bilge fluid was mostly a mixture of diesel fuel, motor oil, and seawater from the leaking hull. The Buff had mixed it with fresh water and Westlode—a nonfoaming industrial detergent—creating a mixture that looked something like a licorice milk shake. When it pulsed into the gentle wheelwash, it mixed with virgin seawater and sank out of sight. "What are you doing?" Seine asked.

"What's it look like I'm doing?"

"It looks like you're polluting the Arctic Ocean."

"You're a goddamned genius, ya know that? Why don't you just get the fuck outa here. Go hug a goddamned tree, if you can find one."

Seine shook his head, a pointless argument, so he stepped around to the foredeck, the Big Man moving up behind him. They stared across the empty island. "Ah, Mr. Seine," the Big Man said. "This is an odd kind of tragedy. Exxon spends twenty million dollars to build Muktuk and move a rig to it and I spend three winter months of my life here and we get dry hole. It makes one's heart break."

"My heart always surges when Exxon loses money," Seine said.

"Jah, jah, make joke if you want. But before long I will have to move to some hellhole like Kazakhstan, where ex-KGB run oilfields."

Joke or not, the Big Man was right. Muktuk did seem a personal failure. The island would die in infancy and his work there would have meant only a paycheck, a way to stay alive. It produced nothing usable in the long run, nothing memorable but his divorce papers.

"Do you know what tonight is?" the Big Man said, as the two of them stepped to the bow to survey the job. "First Dark. The first night of black sky of this year. I love it because it marks time for me. Do you think the camp will be there when we return to North Dock?"

"Maybe not," Seine said. "There isn't much time to get everything packed up and shipped south before freeze-up."

"It is hard to believe, you know?" said the Big Man. "I always thought the Wolf would convince them to keep going."

"They're corporate guys," Seine said, as if that explained everything.

Tearing down Muktuk Island felt like the most futile act Seine had ever committed, if only because a short year ago he and a hundred other men had worked like Egyptian slaves to build it. He accomplished this small contribution to universal entropy by running Buffy and the Big Man around the island on the boat. They took turns operating the hydraulic deck crane, extending the boom to its full length, hooking the sandbags, and tearing them loose. The Buff worked the shore during the first twelve hours, using his fat Special Forces blade to knife open the bottom of each bag. He sliced cleanly as if gutting an animal, and let the sand drain out to the island shore, then nodded to Seine, who craned the limp, empty bags onto the foredeck of *Whale*. Seine couldn't help but think of the Chemist, couldn't help but notice the inner boom was no longer the color of a dog prick.

With his seaman's knife he even scraped a line of paint away, several layers down showing the ancient coat of pink. He imagined all the boats that way. He had painted them all so many times over eleven years, their deckhouses would bear layers of paint like rings on a redwood.

Tearing down was a misnomer, he thought. The force of arctic ice meant the island required no tearing down, only a leaving alone. They pulled the sandbags to keep them from floating away and fouling the wheels of work boats, and even as they worked they felt the ice move in, ice shear with the force of the entire polar pack behind it, setting down on this spot to scrape the island out of existence.

After twelve hours draining sandbags, Seine lay back on the wheelhouse settee and absently monitored the sideband. The Big Man snored down below, his nasal tone rising and falling over the idling rumble of the main engines, while way down in the basement the Buff worked on.

Maybe because of his image of Julia Lew listening to *Fearless* and in the process saving Seine, the long-distance low-frequency sideband made Seine feel a kind of connection to the world, and now he tracked a Canadian rig tender running in light ice off Tuktoyaktuk in the Canadian arctic. Amid fuzz and fade and interference, he caught some cross talk—merging channels of separate conversations coming in via sideband, and then a voice falling like a faint echo from somewhere out there in the circumpolar twilight. At first he thought it was speaking Russian; then it seemed to morph into a garbled English.

Radio waves did odd things over the polar dusk, bounced off the ionosphere, blacked out, faded, skipped like erratic children in a playground. Distorted by atmospheric clutter, the faint voice now twisted into a ghostly chirp like a cartoon chipmunk: "... *research station Flaw Island, research station Flaw Island* ..." It wasn't just the eerie pitch of the

voice that disturbed Seine but something in the repetition, a professional calm that belied a lurking urgency.

So Seine twisted the clarifier and the voice slowed into a Quaalude
low, saying, "... *naaame is Doc-tor Looouis Moneeey-maaaker,*" and then
faded completely.

Seine fine-tuned but couldn't pick up the frequency. The voice
bugged him and he kept after it, thinking, Moneymaker, an odd
name, or else a nickname for the greediest son of a bitch ever to make
his way north. And there were plenty to compare against. One was
below Seine at this very moment, pumping bilge muck overboard
while turbo-drying a polar bear hide he'd traded for 110 gallons of
embezzled gasoline.

Seine rotated the fine-tuner dial and wondered where Moneymaker
was anyway and why he kept repeating his message the way he did
unless he was in some kind of trouble. Then, all at once like a pop he
hit on the voice again: "... *satellite navigation system is out, and the fact is
we may have drifted another two hundred miles since then, and there is little
doubt about the ice—the island is rotting out from under us—over.*" Seine didn't
hear the response, a radio fluctuation that frustrated him, if only because he couldn't find out who the hell Moneymaker was talking to. He
waited a minute or more for Moneymaker to return, but he never did.

Seine tried to contact him over SSB but heard only the warped hiss
of the ionosphere in return. So he gave it up and did his job, focused
not on ghosts or memories or possibilities but on the truth of work.
He was a boat operator. He lay idling against a manmade island a hundred miles offshore, on a day boat operating five days away from
camp. Ice was settling all around them. After that first shift, all three
of them started looking over their shoulders, as if the polar pack were
coming after them.

Seine kept thinking about Moneymaker. He looked around and
imagined how it would feel being out there, adrift. At night he again

tried contacting him, but Moneymaker was barely there and didn't seem to hear anything at all, but just talked through his own random world. Seine turned the *Whale*'s radio direction finder until he gained a bearing; he pulled a chart and plotted it. He kept staring at the line, angling east into the Canadian arctic. He wanted to file a report with the Coast Guard but couldn't raise anybody over the normal CG emergency channel—too far out, too weak a transmitter. He'd have to wait until they returned to camp, where he could make a report by ship-to-shore.

He wondered how the hell you could lose an island. He curled into a fetal ball and dreamed of Julia Lew. Together they floated in the Great Salt Lake. They were naked, and the warm saline water floated them as if sitting in recliners, the same way a survival suit floated you in open ocean. They sat there grinning at each other, eyes opening and closing like pond frogs, mouths kissing water.

The next day, as they worked hooking sandbags, Seine taped open the loudhailer mike and listened to Moneymaker's errant conversations blaring out over the deck. He talked about Chaos Theory and the swirling movement of the polar pack, about fractal geometry and self-similarity. Finally the Buff yelled, "What the fuck's wrong with that guy? He running for some kinda office? He gives speeches that don't end!"

"I think he's lost," Seine said. "What do you want him to do?"

"I don't know, shut up about it."

By the second day, the Buff couldn't take it anymore. He threatened to go homicidal if they didn't at least play some music or something, but Seine refused. Truth was, he liked Moneymaker's voice. It held a strange familiarity, a deep smoothness, even with its underlying urgency, and it made Seine imagine that something in the world really mattered.

By the third day the Buff was throwing rocks at the loudhailer speaker and soon hitting it regularly, until he bent something inside and made Moneymaker sound like a frozen peep a million miles off in space.

Sandbags emptied like hourglasses. When all the bags had been craned limp from Muktuk to a fifteen-foot mound on the long foredeck of *Whale,* Seine walked one last time onto the flat gravel pad and stood dead center in a summer snowstorm. He turned a circle to view the flat sweep to the horizon on all sides, spinning circles until he was dizzy, the last man standing on an island that a season of ice would scrape out of existence.

Out across the twilighted north, the polar pack loomed. And there in its midst was an orange drill ship, the rig derrick rising out of its middle like an orange-shrouded Eiffel Tower. The illusory horizon showed the ship cruising through midair, a good 3 degrees above the line of ice. Below the wall of pack ice, superimposed on the gray seas, the ship's image appeared upside down, tracking its mirror image like a ghost ship.

Seine stood still with the realization that he was not only the first person but now in all likelihood the last to walk on Muktuk Island. Standing there dead center, he heard voices on the wind. Ice floes littered the offing like flotsam. Voices fell from the sky like jetsam. He looked around but saw no trace of the old man, or Terje Narvik, or Cliff the Cook, or the Chemist—or Marco Barn either.

Maybe the good mood was a hallucination like all the rest, but Seine felt elevated. The thought of Julia Lew being at North Dock somehow stabilized him. He stamped his foot on the hard surface of Muktuk and thought how much harder it was this time than the year before, how no way now could it swallow him up.

ELEVEN

Nautical Twilight

Since the season's start, Irons had made it clear to the crew that he had lost his battle with corporate forces and that this was the last year for a full operation in the arctic. Steaming back into North Dock with a deckful of nylon sandbags, Seine rounded the point to see that, in their absence, camp had been packed up for shipment south. The string barges lay in an orderly line down the causeway, piled high with equipment. Along the flat steel dockface lay the bullet-shaped icebreaker barge called *Arctic Odyssey*, a line of eighteen-wheelers groaning past in a wide circle, pausing just long enough for a swarm of forklifts and front-end loaders to pick them clean and transfer their contents to the flat open deck of the icebreaker barge. Rig cargo of every sort, bound for a late-season job to supply an offshore drill ship—the one Seine had seen from Muktuk, he guessed. Drill collar, drilling mud, and tall mud tanks had been staged on the edge of the dock and were being loaded by crane.

With *Whale* made fast alongside the camp barge, Seine disembarked with his log sheets, making his way topside and realizing along the way the extent of the invasion. Anchorage longshoremen had descended on camp, a motley and scary crew of union men: ILWU guys who took over the poker room and kept to themselves, ignoring the merchant seamen who were the erstwhile full-time inhabitants of camp. The merchantmen had built the place, at the orders of Wolf Irons, but the longshoremen didn't care. All they knew was they'd been hired to load the contents of camp onto the backs of barges and lash it all down for a permanent trip south.

Seine went topside in search of information, to find out how much time they had and if maybe somebody in Canada knew something about Moneymaker. But he found Irons holed up in his room, in a funk over the final reality of liquidation and forced retirement. He was refusing all visitors. When Seine knocked on the door, all he got in response was an outburst of fists pounding on mobile-home walls and low guttural screaming—"Fuck off!"—that shook the entire upper portion of camp.

Seine wondered if the Wolf hadn't found some booze left over from the old days, but he knew that Irons had quit drinking and smoking sometime during the offshore fiasco of 1982. So Seine went below and found old Al George in the tool van, etching his name into a set of combination wrenches. "I figure they owe me," he said as an explanation.

Al said Irons had agreed to sign off on as much overtime as the crew wanted. He had a list of jobs that needed doing, so the Big Man went on burn duty, gathering up every shred of scrap wood in camp so they could torch it rather than ship it. Seine agreed to inventory deck equipment and survey barge tanks for an insurance report. Meanwhile, Al George kept scratching his name into the necks of wrenches that until now had belonged to the company.

"How much longer till we're out of here?" Seine asked.

"Day, maybe two," said Al. "Soon as *Odyssey*'s loaded. *Terror*'s taking her north, 737's taking us south."

Working alone into the heart of a wintry-cold September, Seine toured camp with his clipboard, counting equipment. As he wrote the numbers down for the company controllers and the Lloyd's surveyors, he felt a hollow place grow inside his belly. The job felt like an inventory of his own past. Each tugboat dry-docked on the deck of a barge, each shipping container, each pump, and each generator forced a memory of a job, a shipmate, a moment in life now irretrievable.

His melancholy grew when he ran into Al George in the Pinup Van. Al stood just inside the door, staring at a frozen picture of Miss August 1974, lying belly-down by a campfire. "Ain't that a beautiful ass?" Al said.

"The campfire looks pretty good too," Seine said.

"She's a TV weatherman now; you know that?"

"Weatherman, huh? Didn't know that," Seine said.

"Yep. Least I think she is. I mean, I'm sure she *was*. Been fifteen years ago now." Al spoke with a nostalgic ring in his voice, as if remembering some grand time curled up in front of her weather broadcast.

"How come you never come to my room, Seine, and have a drink like Olden Days?"

"Mostly because there's nothing to drink like Olden Days," Seine said.

It had been a boomtown party back then, the days of cost-plus contracts, unlimited overtime, unlimited alcohol, the bipolar grind of hard work and hard play. Back then, Al George and Arne Olleson were Seine's mentors, Marco Barn his roommate. As camp foreman, Al George had been gentle and funny and friendly to all Newmen. When Seine was a Newman, Al George used to invite him and the Big Man over for drinks, to share in his stash of two cases of Black Velvet half gallons kept in a locker in his room. They'd drink Black Velvet and 7 UP until Al couldn't stand up. They hadn't done it in years, primarily because Black Velvet hadn't been tolerated in years. The constant threat of room searches and drug-sniffing dogs had eradicated such problems, even though the closest thing anybody had seen to a dog out at North Dock was a three-legged arctic fox that roamed around the dockface in August and turned white in September.

"Don't matter about dogs," Al George said, and winked. "Dogs ain't trained for what I got."

Seine didn't guess they were, since rumor had it Al had recently taken to drinking aftershave, a regimen that gave entirely new meaning to the term Aqua Velva Man.

Seine imagined the old guy there all alone in his room swigging Ice Blue, an image that made Seine twitch with pity until he agreed to come by for a visit. "I'll do it before we're out of here, I promise," Seine said.

"Better hurry," said Al George.

After dinner Seine took the long way around, touring the bow-end living units, past the watermaker, up the wooden staircase that he and Arne Olleson had built eight years before, and up to the open sky. From there he could see offshore, where he saw the outline of the deepwater line-haulers, powerful ocean tugs that had recently arrived to perform the backhaul. And there, amid them, lay the stretched wheelhouse of *Terror*, evoking in Seine the image of her sunken twin. Somewhere aboard *Terror*, Julia Lew slept, or worked, or lay reading. Why Korso was hanging out in the stream with the deepwater guys was anybody's guess.

Seine ducked into the movie van, to the familiarity of flickering darkness. A voice he didn't recognize asked if he was a crewman off *Terror*. "That Lew broad come ashore yet?" the voice asked.

"I don't know," Seine said, failing completely to conceal his irritation.

He squinted, trying to see who it was—some scraggly faced long-shoreman, he guessed—there were about a half dozen of them in there, along with the Big Man and a few others, all watching a movie called *The Red Tent*, which was about the 1928 attempt by Umberto Nobile to reach the North Pole by dirigible. It struck Seine as oddly appropriate to his overall view of life that the camp was in its last week of existence and whatever crew not working were all sitting around watching a whacked-out Italian trying to ride a helium balloon to the North Pole.

Seine had already seen the movie. Everybody in *The Red Tent* died except one. In movies about polar exploration everybody always died except one, but in reality history books were full of expeditions that went out and never came back. In fact, they were full of expeditions that went out to save other expeditions and *neither* of them came back. Seine called this the Lemming Effect. In this case, Nobile saved himself, leaving his crew to die. Sean Connery was dead for the entire movie. He played the ghost of Roald Amundsen, discoverer of the South Pole, who ended up being little more than a hump of frozen meat while attempting to save Nobile. Amundsen died a lemming, Seine thought, as he backed out.

He saw the long gooseneck silhouette of *Terror* hanging out there among the line-haul tugs, and like the voice in the movie room he wished Julia Lew would come into camp, even if he would have to fend off a half dozen Anchorage longshoremen just to talk with her.

His sense of short time drove Seine to visit Al George. In his Carhartts and stocking cap, Al George looked like Santa Claus, but after work, in his tee shirt and tattoos, he looked like the drunken pervert he really was. Al was an outside sailor to the core, a guy who spent eight months a year staring at open ocean and pictures of naked women, a combination that contorted his perceptions into jam knots of sexual obsession.

The rumors were wrong about Al George; he wasn't drinking Aqua Velva at all, he was drinking Listerine. In fact, he had a case of plastic half-gallon jugs of it stuffed into his locker. Seine had nothing in the way of booze, but he wasn't about to drink any Listerine. He did bum a Lucky Strike and drink root beer while they talked.

Al George had a habit of sucking on a quarter whenever he drank. The coin clicked inside his mouth and made Seine's fillings ache. Al liked the metallic taste, he said; then he poured a chug of mouthwash into a Styrofoam cup and hoisted it. "Speaking of taste! Cause it tastes so bad, you know it works so good!" And he laughed until he coughed. His eyes pooled up and tears streamed in rivulets down and around his high, fat cheeks.

Al was the barge engineer, a man of respect and seniority and position in camp, so he didn't have to share a room. They listened to the Ink Spots on an old monophonic tape recorder: *"I don't want to set the world on fire, I just want to start . . . a flame in your heart. . . ."* After Al finished coughing he cried out, "This is just like Olden Days, Seine!" and then started coughing again until the quarter flew out of his mouth and landed on the bed.

"That's what I'm thinking," Seine said.

Only it wasn't like Olden Days. That's what Seine was really thinking.

Al George could smoke an entire pack of Lucky Strikes and use only one match doing it. He lit each one off his last and told stories about his new wife, whom he'd acquired since the old days. That was the word he used, *acquired.*

"How long you been married now?"

"Two years. And you know what, Seine? I never had it so good. I like her. We got an understanding."

"What's that?"

"I tell her what to do, and she does it."

"What happened to your last wife?"

"Oh, she run off. Last outside trip I took I come back and she'd cleared the house out. Anyway, no big loss, cause she was a whore. And ugly. I mean *ugly*. And a whore. Did I say that?"

He shot back another cup of Listerine and reached over to grab the quarter off the bed. He dusted some wool fibers off it and popped it back into his mouth.

"Yeah, you said that."

"I mean it too, she really was a whore. Back in San Pedro she walked the docks when she still had a body."

He downed yet another shot of the Listerine. "They get better after you've had a few."

Seine wasn't sure if he was talking about the Listerine or the whores on the docks at San Pedro.

"Shit's forty proof!" he said.

All at once Seine thought *oh why not* and reached out a fresh Styrofoam cup and held a shot of Listerine, heard Al George say "Here's how!" and slammed it back. The mouthwash exploded down his throat and rose up through both ears and skyward through his nose. "*Jeeez-us,* like—like—" Like an aborted shot of Everclear he'd once attempted in college, he wanted to say. But he couldn't speak just then. Of course the Everclear hadn't made it much past his lips. The Listerine was somehow worse if only because he'd managed to swallow it.

Al George giggled and rose unsteadily from his chair and stood there, his jeans sagging down around his ass and his tee shirt pulled up short to reveal his potbellied tattoos. He turned the quarter over in his mouth and made it click against his teeth. Seine could hear it echo inside his head.

"You stay here, now, don't go nowhere," he said.

Al George stumbled out his door and stepped down the open hallway to the head. The wind beat its way in through the door. While he waited, Seine looked around and saw an old windup alarm clock that had two bells on top, no numbers on the face, and no second hand.

But even over the drone of the generator he could hear it *ticking*. By the time he started wondering if the thing might explode, he decided it was time to go to bed.

He remembered fueling operations with Al George at the end of his first season, a late-September job to Challenge Island, hanging out in ice fog for two days, smoking cigs and watching daylight die. Once, to demonstrate the effect of ambient temperature on the flash point of fuel, Al threw a lit cigarette down into a diesel tank and laughed when Seine took off running.

Seine stepped out of Al George's room to feel the norther snapping down the passage to the head, where he leaned inside and called out, "Hey, Al! I'm hitting the rack!" But he got no answer. So he stepped inside. The head was warm, a wall heater glowing red to his left. The showers were empty, the fluorescent light glowing its harsh white light. "Al!" And he stepped around the line of stalls, and saw the gray tuft of hair down on the linoleum deck. Seine moved fast and knelt down to check him, saying silently *airway—breathing—circulation*. He found none of the above. Al George's tee shirt was hiked to his chest, where a tattoo of a clothesline streamed blue-ink laundry with women's names on each garment. Al's briefs were bound with his jeans in a bundle around his ankles. The stench of Listerine vomit rose off him like a toxic cloud. Seine felt his entire face flush, his mouth drain hot water from saliva ducts, and for a fleeting instant he thought he might puke.

About the time Seine became certain Al George was dead, the Big Man stepped in behind him. "Ah, my God," the Big Man snarled. "What in the fuck did he do to himself?"

"He died."

"Ah, fuck, as if all the rest of this is not bad enough." The Big Man looked inside the stall. Then he stepped up with his size 19-EEE boot and pressed the handle to flush the toilet. "I suppose we should be grateful that he managed to crap into the toilet."

"I suppose," Seine said. Then he noticed, lying on the linoleum floor by Al's head, the shining circle of a newly minted quarter. Seine picked it up and rinsed it in the sink, and without knowing why he slid it into the front pocket of his jeans.

Together he and the Big Man hoisted Al George's small, fat, half-naked body out of the head and back to his room. The Big Man took him under the arms. "There is something under here," he said. "There is something under his arms."

Inside the room, they laid him out on his bunk and the Big Man checked his pulse out of some hopeless duty, and found nothing. Seine felt his hand. "He's already cold."

"Do you feel that? What is that?" the Big Man asked, prodding up under Al's armpits. "Tumors. He is riddled with tumors. Feel."

Seine probed gingerly with his fingertips, still numb from carpal tunnel, feeling in a remote way the cold round lumps like big marbles in the pits of the old man's arms.

The Onset

S eine didn't know if it was lack of sleep or the death of Al George or the gruesome discovery that the tug *Terror* had run over a walrus, but the next day the Shade of Marco Barn returned. At that point, he realized he had barely noticed its absence, the way you forget a headache until the pain returns.

The Shade came while Seine was working tank survey with an androgynous Newman named Stuart Wanless, who had long golden hair that most women would die for, and who spotted for Seine topside while Seine squeezed down into the dark tanks with a miner's light, an O_2 sensor, and his clipboard. On the way down the string, passing from loaded barge to loaded barge, the kid talked nonstop. He was a design major at UW and had made something called a tunic and won a design contest sponsored by a magazine. He had some long-lost brother who used to work up here and tell stories about it, right up until he wandered off to sea and disappeared forever. The Newman suspected his father was making a last-ditch effort to make a man out of him by sending him north for the last week of camp.

"Be careful, dude," the Newman said, as they came to a barge tank and Seine prepared to go down. The Newman hunched his shoulders and turned his back to the wind. His hair blew in a curl around his face. "Cause they, like, told me you were a lightning rod."

Seine sat down with his legs dangling into the tank hole. "Gee, I wonder who told you that."

"That big guy. He said *you* never get it, but everybody around you does."

Seine laughed without mirth, without even actually laughing out loud. He had spent so much time alone on barges fifty miles offshore that he didn't know anymore when he talked out loud and when he just thought things really intensely. Besides, he was still reeling from the self-induced death of Al George and still wondering if he wasn't somehow to blame for that too. He reached down and patted the spot where the quarter lay in his pocket.

"Big Man's just trying to scare you."

"Yeah, okay." The kid was jumping up and down. "Dude, it is fucking *cold* here! Nobody warned me."

"You think it's cold now, come back in February."

"No *way*. I'm, like, in Mazatlán in Feb."

Seine flicked his miner's helmet light on and then raised his arms over his head and slipped down into the tank, thinking it was a good thing this Newman would get only one week of work before camp disintegrated into nothing, because anybody as innocent as Stuart Wanless would either be killed, driven mad, or fired within two.

Seine climbed hand-over-hand down the steel ladder into the dark depths of the rusted-out barge tank, thinking about his own reputation for being bad luck for others, and in the echo chamber of the tank he swore he could hear his own heartbeat.

The arctic norther quieted to a whisper as he hit bottom. A faint dusting of snow filtered down in a glittering frozen mist. He looked up to where Stuart Wanless stood, looking down as he had been asked, trying to keep an eye on Henry Seine. He looked familiar to Seine now, the eyes of someone he knew. Biller was a family company, so there had always been legacies through the years, little brothers or cousins who appeared and disappeared during Seine's time.

As Seine climbed down into the tank, his eyes adjusted to the dark. He thought he smelled arc smoke from a welder, then looked up and saw, in the dim light of his helmet lamp, the Buff hanging upside down in the manway like a fat bat clinging to the roof of a cave. "Seine! We got *Terror* coming into camp with something in her starboard wheel. Need a crew."

Seine started up, realizing all at once that this was Marco Barn's barge, the rusty reality of the C-240.

Topside he found the Newman bouncing up and down, still trying to keep warm. The Buff on the other hand stood there wearing thin coveralls unbuttoned halfway down to his belly. Not only did it expose his bare chest but also the scar, looking like a shining dome of hard pink flesh about as big around as a quarter. The Buff glared at the Newman, fingering the scar.

"Why me?" Seine asked. "I'm doing things."

"Cause unless you count longshoremen, which I don't, or this faggot, which I also don't, then everybody's gone but you me and the Big Man. So we're it. You hang here, Newman."

"My name's not Newman, it's Wanless."

"Oneless?"

"Wanless."

"Whatever."

Wanless looked at Seine. "You want me to just stand here?"

"Just monitor the pump over there on the 320-4. Move it around if it gets clogged. I'll be back soon."

Wanless nodded and then looked back at the Buff, who didn't seem to intimidate him much at all, even though he'd called him a faggot and refused to use his real name. Wanless just smiled, flipped his hair from his face, and said, "Cool!"

The Buff looked like he was about to put the shake to him: snap his neck and leave him in a blond-haired heap. "Jesus Christ," was all he said, and marched off.

Terror lay backed into the causeway just past the camp barge but short of the dockface where the longshore crews continued loading the *Arctic Odyssey*. The crane operator had walked a tread crane the size of a small house as far down the beach as he could get and had the tug's stern end hoisted out of the water to reveal her underbelly. In the process he'd dragged half the vessel up the shore, the wheelhouse tipped forward like a giant steel bird doing a header. As the three approached, Seine caught a glimpse of Julia standing on the stern with a radio around her neck and her cook's apron trailing out from beneath a heavy jacket. The thought of seeing her again now—*right now*—made his chest tighten. His strides lengthened through the soft gravel, but a moment later he heard the indistinct crackle of the tug's loudhailer and watched as she swung through the galley door and disappeared. "Awww, too bad, Seine," said the Buff. "Don't get to see my lover yet."

"She's running cook," Seine said. "Korso's got his foot to her neck."

The Buff laughed and shook his head. "Putz."

As they approached, the vessel loomed overhead, the crane stout and stiff with an upright boom and crane treads sinking into the wet gravel. Seine kept an eye for Julia, but she didn't come out now, so they gathered on the gravel beach beneath the raised stern to survey the six-foot stainless-steel propellers, both of which were encased in cylindrical Kort nozzles, steel shrouds for added power. The starboard wheel glistened and dripped seawater, but in the port wheel, a gnarled black form lay knotted within the Kort, obscuring the steel screw.

The three stood there for five minutes with heads cocked to one side, arguing whether it was an inner tube or a seal.

"It ain't an inner tube," said the Buff. "That there is an eye."

Seine stepped up and looked into the folds of dark brown hide, and sure enough there was a glassy black globe. "Looks like an eye to me."

"Now watch this," said the Buff, and he reached in with his Special Forces knife and started sawing, and a minute later pulled out an ivory tusk clutched in a bloody fist. "It ain't a seal either, it's a walrus," he said, and shoved the tusk into his coat pocket.

Seine knew the Buff's game. He'd add the tusk to his seasonal haul, get an additional grand for it in the black market of northern artifacts. While everybody else worked double-time, the Buff had been running baleen, antlers, tusks, and bear hides, making fivefold what any of the others did.

Once they'd finished arguing about what it was, they argued how to get it out. The Big Man suggested cutting it out with knives, the Buff suggested burning it out with an oxygen-acetylene torch, and Henry Seine finally marched to the tool van and brought back a chain saw. He started it with a quick pull of the rope and shoved the running saw straight into the hide. Within five minutes he was shoving blocks of blubber and hide and bone out of the wheel.

After ten minutes they all looked like they'd pulled a shift in a slaughterhouse. When the walrus was nothing but a pile of hacked-up flesh on the beach, Seine spied down the thick steel shaft to see if it had been bent. "It's got a turn in it, right there," Seine said, indicating a place about two feet from where the shaft entered the hull, a point of subtle change of direction.

"I do not even want to hear it," said the Big Man. "My back is killing me."

The Big Man's ability to dead-lift 450-pound tugboat shafts notoriously evaporated when there were no bosses around to witness it, never mind that this shaft weighed closer to 2,000 pounds.

"The season is over," said the Big Man. "There is one job left for this vessel and then time to go home. Every boat in our fleet has bent shaft by this time of year. I have changed out my share of this particular shaft, and I can tell you right now that we do not want to do it if it is possible to avoid."

The Buff checked the shaft and nodded. "He's right, Seine, we don't wanna change this fucker, not just the three of us with a forklift and come-alongs. We need a week of work out of this tub and that's it."

Seine imagined the shaft job. Trying to keep a forklift from sinking into the beach gravel while dangling a one-ton shaft of solid case steel. They'd have to bear at least part of the weight on their shoulders to guide the shaft through the shaft tube and connect it to the main engine fly wheel. Seine ran his eye up the rudder struts. "What's that?" He pointed to a weld line.

"Who are you, Mr. Surveyor now?" said the Buff. "Wolf's got you looking for every little problem, huh?"

The Big Man chimed in. "Mr. Seine is quite good at finding *little* problems. The problem is he cannot do anything about the big ones."

Despite protests, they peered up to where the rudder strut connected to the underside of the hull and both of them groaned. "All right, looks like a split," said the Buff. "We'll get Mr. Hanson on it, it'll be stronger than ever."

Seine tapped finger to thumb and felt the numbness. He stood there on the hard gravel beach and looked out to where the line-haul tugs lay at anchor in the stream, their black silhouettes like half-submerged ax blades.

While Mr. Hanson welded the split underneath *Terror,* Seine heard via the crane's cab radio that once the tug was repaired she would come alongside the camp barge for stores. So he made his way up the main gangway and picked through the passageways, moving back toward the stern end of the camp barge. A minute later he heard *Terror* roaring off the beach, grinding gravel in her wheels. The loud-hailer boomed with the voice of Dale Korso. "Where's that fucking cunt?"

Seine shook his head and tried hard to throw a dirty look, but Korso was still a hundred yards off and oblivious to anybody not him-self. Julia, wearing a jacket over a white cook's apron and a radio slung diagonally across her chest, came bursting out the galley door.

"Get them lines flaked or I'm gonna run you off the water!" yelled Korso.

"Get a new pair of glasses!" Julia called back, and pointed to where she'd already flaked two deck lines in precise patterns up the side deck.

Seine stood there, caught eye contact with Julia, and she lifted her arms in a prolonged shrug, then broke into a smile. "The Arctic Dick-head!" she shouted. "Where the hell you been, sailor?"

"Belowdecks!" he called back.

"Time to move topside!"

Meantime, Korso was topside with his head sticking out the wheel-house window, yelling down. "This is my boat, goddammit. I ain't gonna put up with jack shit from you, Julia!"

As the Buff came up behind him, Seine turned. "That fucking perv. I hate that guy. He sounds like the goddamned Chemist with all his *my boat* bullshit."

"Korso kick your ass, man," the Buff said.

"So what? What does that prove?"

"Proves he can be a perv and a tyrant and you ain't got nothing to say about it."

Dale Korso was best known in Alaskan waters as Captain Fuck, a moniker that came primarily from his fondness for the word in all its forms and secondarily from his fondness for the act in all its forms. The first time Seine met Korso, he told a story about picking up underage native girls while running the Yukon River. "I ain't shittin you, Henry, fuckin A, that Al George is such a goddamned fuckin perv. We pick up this homely fuckin Skeemo chick, fourteen years old, no fuckin teeth, and we take her back to the boatswain's locker and old Al's fuckin her in the ass while she's swabbin my knob. Al George! What a fuckin perv!"

Seine figured the story told you everything you needed to know about Captain Fuck and probably a good sampling of what you needed to know about Al George, too.

When *Terror* powered past, white water flushed from her stern. Seine could see she was a powerful boat, a point he often overlooked when he remembered *Fearless*. He kept his eye on Julia there on the side deck, lifting her chin to him, looking straight and dour now, as if she hadn't just seen Henry Seine for the first time in a year, as if it took all her energy just to deal with Captain Fuck.

By the time Seine thought about the Newman again, it was quitting time and the kid was still down there on the end of the string, standing alone in the cold on the precise spot Seine had left him. "Stuart!" he called. "Quitting time."

Wanless nodded briskly and bounced over to him, shivering like a man on the verge of heat death. "It feels like the temperature's dropped twenty degrees!"

"It has," Seine said.

Wanless let out a frozen-lipped laugh. He had rusty-water stain all over his coveralls. He'd gotten dirtier watching a pump than anybody Seine had ever seen. "The pump plugged up so I went down to clear it. And then I got wet, and then when I came out my coveralls froze."

He looked as if his entire face had frozen.

When the Buff heard that Wanless had not moved an inch in four hours except to move the pump and get wet and dirty and frozen, he decided the kid deserved an initiation into the wonders of nutmeg, so he invited him over to Room 5 for an after-dinner cocktail.

It turned out the Buff had been holding out. He'd smuggled up four shampoo bottles filled with Irish whiskey and hadn't told a soul, not even his roommate. It was under the influence of a double Irish over snowballs that the Buff managed to talk Seine into taking a taste of nutmeg, but Wanless needed no encouragement. He knew all about the psychoactive nature of nutmeg, primarily from his time working in the restaurant business in Seattle. When he and the other busboys had to pull double shifts they often ate nutmeg when they couldn't get ahold of any crystal meth.

" 'Meg's got MDA in it, did you know that?" Wanless said. "Naturally occurring. And MDA's the mother compound to E, and you know how good that is!"

"E?" Seine asked.

"Ecstasy! MDMA! You haven't tried Ecstasy? Dude, you're missing God."

It came as no surprise to Seine that he was missing God. He knew he was missing something.

When the Buff found out the Newman was not only already initiated into the medicinal powers of nutmeg but actually appreciated the difference between canned and fresh, he practically peed himself with joy and promptly broke out the last golden shampoo bottle. Then he ground up the fresh whole nutmegs using his Waring coffee mill. The resulting powder might have gagged Seine completely had he not chased it down with the whiskey.

Seine checked his watch, realizing he'd been on the clock for forty-eight hours, but worse yet was the fact that he hadn't even had a catnap for thirty-six. His brain function was about the level of oatmeal mush, and he was curious how a little raw MDA might affect him. He planned to spend that night on the job, in the Com Shack, talking to Julia if at all possible. "You ain't sleeping enough," the Buff said. "Now me, I'm sleeping like a baby. They got nothing on me."

The Buff didn't care for overtime—for one thing, it involved twice the work at only twice the pay. If he had to work twice as long he figured the effort was worth at least four times the pay. The only way to make that kinda bread, he claimed, was in the Trade, which he contributed to by stuffing the walrus tusk in with five polar-bear hides and a narwhal tusk he kept stored inside his locker.

Seine was no fan of the Trade, but he enjoyed the Buff's illicit drug combination. The nutmeg sent him soaring over the whiskey and the whiskey eased the rush of the nutmeg.

The Buff bent his head over a tobacco tin and shoved his tongue into a mound of dark brown nutmeg. "Numbs your tongue, notice that?"

Seine laughed, nodding vaguely as the nutmeg started gaining altitude, bringing with it a rush of unbridled happiness, in which everybody—the Big Man, the Buff, Irons, all the crew of the ill-fated *Fearless*, even Heather—took on a beatific glow. Julia Lew was a goddess waiting for him out there in the stream. They could be together again soon, he thought; he might again feel her embrace. No restrictions this time. No marriage. No moral judgment. Only *joy*.

Seine suppressed the sudden urge to give Buffy Errol a hug, thinking he might get his ass killed, so he decided instead to get topside to stand his radio watch. "Some of us have to work for a living," he said, hoping he wasn't slurring his words.

"Why the hell you beating yourself into the ground? For an extra two grand?" the Buff said. "I told you you could go into business with me."

"That's all right," Seine said. "I told you I don't do furs and shit. Animal artifacts. Ugly business. No thanks."

"You're such a goddamned moralist, Seine. He's an environmentalist whack-nut," he said to Wanless.

Wanless looked up from a photograph he was holding.

"Why do *you* do it?" Seine asked. "You probably have enough to retire, Buff. Admit it."

The Buff smiled. "Yeah, well. Maybe. But you can never have too much, I say. You never know what's gonna happen, Seine Man. The markets collapse, currency goes to shit. Ya gotta take care of business while you can. Now, me? I'm diversified. I got my mutual funds and my equity investments, and my muni bonds, and I got some gold, and I got my guns, of course, and I got my house . . . and just for safe-keeping I got a hundred K buried in coffee cans in the back lawn!" And he burst out with a laugh that made everybody jump.

Seine couldn't quite process the concept of a hundred thousand dollars buried in a backyard, particularly not with three whiskeys and two tablespoons of nutmeg under his belt. "Why in the hell are you *here*?" he wanted to know.

"No shit, dude," said Wanless. "If I had a hundred K I'd be like *so* far south right now."

Still he was holding the photo.

The Buff peered at Seine past his cup of whiskey. "I'm here same reason you're here, Seine."

"Well, *I'm* here because I got shit since my divorce."

"That's such bullshit. That ain't why at all and you know it. Or maybe you don't; fuck it, I don't care. Just for once quit blaming it on that bitch. She was *worthless*. She fucked that real estate fag, right? And him, you ever thought about giving him what *he* deserves? I mean, that's fucked *up*. I maybe done some bad things in my life, but I ain't never fucked another man's woman."

"Now you sound like Marco. He used to say that exact thing—*I ain't never fucked no other man's woman, man*—like that was the worst thing you could do in life."

"Look what it got him."

"I been thinking about Marco," Seine said. "How's he doing? I saw him in the off season."

"What the fuck you talking about?"

"I saw him. At the Seattle Fish House. We didn't talk or anything, though."

"No, I bet not!"

"What's that mean, like he's still pissed at me?"

"Pissed? He's fucking *dead.*"

Seine's brain started spinning in tight little circles like some kind of psychotic ice-skater. "I just saw him."

"Well, you saw him and then he died." And the Buff started laughing "Or maybe he's one of them ghosts. *Whoo-oo.*"

"How the hell he die?"

"How do you think?" the Buff said. "Blew a gasket topside. Started bleeding out his ears."

"Oh, man." Seine held his head in his hands.

The Buff had his eye on Seine. "Whole time he's saying, *That fucking Seine did it to me, that fucking Seine killed my brain.* Hey, that rhymes!"

"I have to hear that old line again?" Seine asked.

The Buff looked at Wanless, like talking to a witness. "Seine here is—whatta they call it?—*deluded.* He sees dead people."

Wanless looked back and forth like watching a Ping-Pong match; he had no idea what they were talking about, he just looked like his eyelids were pinned to his forehead.

"Marco needed somebody to blame," Seine said. "Either me or the Wolf or Mr. Hanson, he couldn't decide which. I was the first one to get to him, so he decided me."

When Seine blinked, there sat Marco on top of the lockers, legs dangling. Camp was a small town. Truth was ruled by gossip, rumors were mongered by liars, and if you were the subject of either you were always the last to know.

Marco Barn sat grinning. Then he sat next to Seine, right up on him, and Seine could smell his hot Marlboro breath against his cheek. Seine thought he might not be able to breathe then, or if he did it might come out like a scream.

"All I know is that padeye didn't jump up and *fly* down that hole on its own," the Buff said, then finally took the photograph from Wanless. He looked at the picture, narrowing his eyes. "Who's this?"

"My brother," Wanless said. "Taken a long time ago."

"Your brother?" The Buff let another one of his hand-grenade laughs. "This is great. What a fucking great day."

Wanless flinched. "He's missing in action, so to speak. We haven't heard from him in ten years. It's why I was curious about coming up here. See if people knew him."

The Buff said, "I don't know—Seine, you know him?" He handed the photo over to Seine, who took the picture and felt the speed of the nutmeg snap it into sharp and immediate focus. It was a graduation picture, taken about 1975 from the look of it, and at first it didn't make any sense to him. But then the mouth curled into position, tight and round and small as he remembered it. And the glasses, horn-rimmed Buddy Holly glasses. He was young, but there was no mistaking the face of the Chemist.

Wanless took up the shampoo bottle and poured himself an Irish over snowballs and drank, his girl-face wrinkling. "Zachary P. Wanless the Fourth. Skoal!" And he downed his whiskey in a burst. He shivered and went *"Bluhhh!"*

"The Fourth? Mean there was three more before him?" the Buff said.

"Family tradition," Wanless said. He looked at Seine. "He hated the name. Used to call it a family curse. You recognize him? It's an old photo."

Seine handed the picture back but couldn't look Wanless in the eye. "Never seen him before," he said.

"Are you sure? He's like in his thirties now. I was nine when he left home. He and my old man—they *hated* each other."

The Chemist sat on the top of the lockers then too, side by side with Marco Barn, cackling silently, both of them mute with cigarette smoke furling around their faces. Seine could smell the smoke even if nobody else could.

The Buff watched Seine for some clue what to do and then made an executive decision and turned to Wanless. "Look, Newman, I got something to tell you. And I ain't good at pulling punches so I'm just gonna say it. Your brother? Look, I do know him. He used to work up here. And he's—well, he's . . ."

The Buff paused, gave Seine a sidelong look, and then gazed downward into his empty cup of snowballs.

"What?" Wanless asked.

· The Buff took a breath. "He—he don't work for the company no more," he said, and looked at Seine like he'd been caught in some lewd act. Then he started fingering his scar.

"Oh," said Wanless. "I know *that*. We would have known if he was working for the company, dude. You think we didn't check that out? *Sheesh.*"

Wanless laughed while Seine downed his Irish and reached for the shampoo bottle to pour another. He didn't even ask. And the Buff didn't say a word in protest, just held out his cup for a refill of his own.

THIRTEEN

Radio Daze

The snow eased off, and a break to the northwest brought a shaft of evening sunlight onto the barge. In the Com Shack, Seine stood before the bank of radios and endured the hovering presence of Marco Barn, standing inches from his face and doing nothing besides breathe all over him. He turned his head away instinctively, but the Shade followed. Seine grimaced and rubbed his face, listened to radio chatter and watched the Big Man.

The Big Man ran a Cat 966 front-end loader up and down the causeway, diesel exhaust billowing off downwind, balloon tires singing down the frozen gravel, hauling chunks of scrap wood large and small to the dockface. There the burn pile rose like the rubble of a fallen home. It would be a sight to see it burn, Seine thought, a way to mark the end, like a funeral pyre for the camp itself. Maybe the Wolf would die of a heart attack or refuse to leave and take a fire ax to his own head, and they could stuff him into the midst of it like some old-time Norse king and send him on to the afterlife.

Seine had never been a believer in a plan, had never seen God's orderly face in any action among the tormented dreams that constituted his memory, but as the evening of work settled down around

him, as the line-haul tugs left and the wheelhouse of *Terror* rose up off
the water, at anchor in the stream, he wondered.

The camp had disintegrated in two short days of work, and Seine
felt on one level like the reign of entropy was gaining power. But ob-
servable action wasn't the only reality, he thought, because everything
that evaporated condensed and everything that condensed rained out
like a great hydrologic cycle of truth. Standing in the midst of it,
watching camp go south, he felt a strange and exhilarating sense that
his entire life was congealing in patterns he couldn't resist. Maybe it
was fate. Maybe a choice lay before him. Maybe this was all you could
expect in the way of order.

He thought of Julia going to sleep on the middle deck of *Terror,* her
door locked against the undoubted persistence of Captain Fuck. He
listened to the radios. Just listening made him feel connected, even if
to an outside sailor's world peopled by sea creatures, accustomed to
the ocean's rhythms, accustomed to night watch. The Com Shack
housed an array of radios, several VHFs, two marine sidebands, and a
radio direction finder. He caught sporadic transmissions: fishermen
and whalers speaking foreign tongues, towboats slamming their way
home across the Gulf.

Seine stood fiddling with the sideband, trying to find something
diverting. Sailors always complained of radio boredom, particularly
on night watch, moaned of sleepy-eyed tedium watching their own
red reflection in a night-lighted wheelhouse. But night watch made
Seine imagine Julia Lew aboard *Vigilant,* saving him. In his mind she
focused intently, remained calm, and simply did her job.

Seine turned out all the lights in the Com Shack and imagined how
Fearless must have seemed from her perspective. He wondered why she
did it, concluding finally that it was nothing more or less than an expression of character. And with this his respect for her began to swell.

Not like the overwhelming ecstatic gratitude of their first meeting, clouded by reputation and rumor, but something deeper and quieter and somehow sadder, if only because he was starting to realize how completely he had missed her the first time around. He had labeled her, put her in a hole in the ground dug out by the stories of others, and covered her over with dirt.

So with that he couldn't help watching the silhouette of *Terror*, couldn't help calling over VHF. He repeated the call ten times before he finally got the groggy voice of Dale Korso. "If it ain't Henry In-sane. How's the madness coming along there, Henry? I hear you cracked up last winter. Went to some asylum or something."

"Where'd you hear that?"

"I think it was . . . damn, can't remember who told me that. Some driller who worked with the Big Man, I think."

"I was on Bainbridge, in my house, Dale. Listen, your mate around?"

"Lew? By God, she is. And you know what, she *is* my mate. Heh-heh! Seine, I can't say over the radio how this trip has been without breaking about fifteen FCC regulations! Hah-hah!"

"You're a funny guy, Dale."

"I am, by God. One of my underappreciated talents, don't ya know."

"Can I talk to her, Dale?"

"Not right now, we been sailing shorthanded, just the two of us, so we're getting shut-eye. Call back."

"You hear about Al George?"

"Naw, what happened?"

"He died yesterday. Right here on the barge."

"I'll be damned. The old perv lasted longer than I'da figured, smoking the way he did."

"I'm the one found him."

"That right? Still finding dead people everywhere, are you? Look, I gotta hit the rack. *Terror* out."

Seine remembered the Chemist trying to talk to her all the way across the Bering, and how Macky had stopped him. What was it made people think it was their job to erect barriers around Julia Lew? Was it just male possessiveness, the ancient chieftain inside a skipper?

He wanted to talk to her and for some reason an urgency hung over him. He wanted to board *Terror* and rid himself of the ghost of her sister ship once and for all. More than anything he wanted to remove Korso. He closed his eyes against the breath of Marco Barn.

A radio call came through then, the drill ship *Alpha Dog* making its way north from Barrow, where it planned to drive east through ice into the northern Beaufort Sea. Seine gave them an update of progress at North Dock. Any day now *Terror* would cruise north, pushing the loaded icebreaker barge called *Odyssey,* to deliver supplies in what everybody was calling the Last Job.

Seine would fly south.

The thought of him and Julia going in opposite directions made him pace the Com Shack, desperate. Until he heard the pale voice of Moneymaker. The bounce was good this time, the SSB signal clear, Moneymaker's voice coming like a chant: *"This is research station Flaw Island, our position is unknown, repeat position unknown. . . . Island is breaking apart, repeat breaking apart, my colleagues and I have been separated. . . ."*

Seine felt a confused surge of electricity. He didn't know what it meant that an island was breaking apart, unless it was a manmade island like Muktuk, succumbing to ice shear. He turned to the radio direction finder mounted along the bank of radios and punched SCAN, then watched it peg on Moneymaker's voice and show a precise gyrocompass heading of 351 from North Dock. "Three-five-one?" Seine wondered.

He ran below, rattled the catwalk and returned with his chart from the *Whale*, laying it flat to trace his previous line. From Muktuk, two hundred miles northwest, the line stretched east. He superimposed the two, and they crossed almost due north of him, about two hundred miles. Seine was stunned. He looked north at the darkness. He imagined being out there floating, spinning helpless.

Seine picked up the mike and tried to reach Moneymaker, but in return the voice grew weaker. Moneymaker faded, fizzled, popped. Then he was gone.

Seine telephoned the Coast Guard District headquarters in Juneau to file a report. "This guy's in trouble, sounds like. I first heard him a couple of days ago from my position at Muktuk Island."

The dispatcher wanted to know the make and model of his RDF unit, his precise positions, the hour of contact.

"This last signal was strong. The earlier one from Muktuk was weaker, I admit, but still—"

"We've heard nothing from anyone else, sir."

"He's been inconsistent. I've been wondering. How do you lose an island?"

"It's probably an ice island. Scientists use them sometimes as floating research stations. In any case, we'll investigate. Thank you for the report, sir."

After he hung up, Seine couldn't get Moneymaker out of his mind, kept thinking he was just right there, north by west of his current position by two hundred miles. With the icebreaker barge *Odyssey* and a line-haul tug they could break their way out to him in a day.

Seine moved over to the chart and figured his statistical margin for error; then with a mechanical compass he drew a circle of uncertainty around the point where the two RDF lines intersected. He tapped the pencil on the chart, pondering the circle, tracing its outline with his fingertip.

Only three barges remained in camp. The causeway stretched

empty and gray toward the flow stations and burn stacks of the oilfields. Seine traced the circle, tuned to Moneymaker, and heard nothing for a long time. Finally he picked up the phone and called the
Coast Guard again. "We found a listing out of Russia," the dispatcher
said. "Ice island NP-32. They're really the only ones still using ice islands for research. It's been out there since last spring to take meteo-
rological data."

"But this guy's American or Canadian."

"Well, this Russian island is affiliated with the Polar Science Center
at the University of Washington. Could be him."

"So NP-32 and Flaw Island are the same thing?"

"Could be. Sometimes they do that, name their station. But we've
been unable to establish any contact ourselves; it's a difficult radio
zone. Skip zones and fade are the main problem. In any case, the
Canadian CG has a fairly recent direction fix in the Greenland gyre.
That's east of the Canadian archipelago."

Seine shook his head. Smelled the breath of Marco Barn. "No, not
east. I've got him at three-five-one from my position at Prudhoe.
That's north by west. That's not Greenland gyre. That's the Beaufort
gyre."

"North by west of *Prudhoe*? That's not consistent with the Canadian efforts. But listen, they aren't regarding this as an emergency
anyway. Let me give you their number. I think direct contact is the
best idea."

So Seine called the Canadian Coast Guard out of Tuk and passed
on all his information, including his plotted circle, then sat back and
listened to the dispatcher shred it. "Your error calculations are way
off. At this time of year, with your equipment, eh, I'd put your circle at
more like a thousand miles."

"A thousand?"

"That's right. We'll just have to monitor. He doesn't seem to be broadcasting over twenty-one eighty-two kilohertz, which is the standard low-frequency distress channel."

"I'm aware of what it is. Maybe he's got equipment damage."

"Maybe. Or maybe he's got his situation under control."

"He doesn't know where he is! That's not under control, that's lost."

"Then why is there no Mayday? If the island is breaking up underneath him and he doesn't know where he is, then why isn't he transmitting a distress call?"

"I don't know. Maybe we're just not hearing it. Do you have any satellite imaging of ice islands?"

"Yes, but we've been unable to locate NP-32 for some time now."

"That's because it's broken up!" Seine said.

"Listen, we have limited resources, right? You understand that. But we also monitor emergency channels, and we'll be on the lookout for any word. Keep in mind that we get a number of false alerts, and they strain our ability to cover everything."

Seine had to suck a breath down just to feel like he got any air at all. He bristled, felt a knot of frustration turn in his abdomen, and hung up the phone. The newspaper headline lay face up on the counter next to him, and he saw the updated report on the narwhals trapped and freezing in a fjord. Pictures showed a smiling crew of Coast Guardsmen aboard an icebreaker, leading the white whales southwest out of danger.

That night Seine remained in the Com Shack as ice settled around North Dock in floaters called growlers and sections of grease ice like slicks running down-current. Seawater froze at 28.6 degrees F, so Seine figured the water a half degree above that. The *Arctic Odyssey* remained along the dockface, three hundred feet of inert steel, her icebreaking bow raked like a shark's nose, her deck piled high with rig cargo, lashing lines angling down to the deck to hold everything in place.

"That's damned near it, then."

Seine spun to the voice, the Wolf standing like a gnarled length of tow wire. Right off, Seine noticed he was wearing a prosthetic nose and was dressed up as if for a meeting, so Seine knew he'd been out at the BP offices, or over at Exxon trying to drum up work, and didn't want to look like the Elephant Man while doing it.

He wore a look of defeat, his cheeks gaunt, his eyes watering, his thin gray hair sticking straight up. The fake nose made him look like something out of a bad horror movie, a prosthesis that was probably brand-new in about 1918. Made of heavy metal, it hung awkwardly and whistled when he talked. When he sniffed it sounded like an echo in an empty room. Seine wasn't sure which was worse, the fake nose or no nose at all.

"Looks like we lost the Endicott rig move to Crowley," Irons said, then took a deep breath and let it out in a burst.

"Hard to believe this place is out of oil," Seine said.

"Outa oil! It ain't outa oil. They got more oil up here than you can shake a stick at. Just wait. Soon as all them Yuppie cocksuckers run outa gas for their BMWs they'll be slapping oil rigs up so fast you'll think the arctic sprouted trees."

Seine laughed. "So what's next for here?" he said.

Irons turned on him. "For *here*? There ain't no here. We're eight hours from sending the camp barge south by line-haul. It's time to pack. We're going home."

Irons drew silent then, and looked off toward the silhouette of *Terror*. The sun dipped north and set in a bleeding streak along the ice horizon. The length of sunsets astounded Seine even now.

"Beautiful, ain't it?" Irons said.

"Yeah, almost makes up for October," Seine said, thinking about Julia again, smelling the Shade of Marco.

"We been through the snot up here, ain't we? But we always got ourselves out. Company don't understand what we did here, maybe two or three of them suits in Seattle. But otherwise, they don't know, they don't care."

Seine realized by watching him just how addicted Irons was to the edge, how he lived for the fundamental necessities and the clarity of a decisive moment. Seine understood its allure. Everything southside was a jumble by comparison. He enjoyed just standing there with the Wolf. He kept thinking about all the dead ones. They all floated around him in waves. "I heard you told Korso you wanted to skipper the last job," Seine said.

"Goddamned sentimental of me, huh? Anyway, he ain't going for it. Won't come into camp or talk to me on the radio until I get a crew up from Seattle to replace the three people who *quit* on him. Won't even let you guys on board as his crew."

"Korso's an ass." Seine spied *Terror* again through the Com Shack window. Darkness was falling. He turned to the Wolf. "What do you say we light off *Whale,* slip out there in the dark and tie up alongside Korso and have a talk with him. Make him see reason."

"Ya think? That'd be a frickin' first."

"Well, maybe he won't, but I've been thinking about all this. This camp disintegrating and everything, and this radio signal bugging the shit out of me."

"Radio signal? What the hell you talking about?"

"Some guy. Lost. Name of Moneymaker. Some researcher from Canada or Russia or something."

"A Rooskie called Moneymaker!" Irons got a good belly laugh out of that. "That's a good one."

"He's not Russian. Canadian CG says this station's a joint thing between the Russians and UW."

Seine showed Irons the RDF line. "I got him drifting somewhere in
this circle," he said. "The Canadians say his last known position is
here—" and he stabbed a spot a thousand miles east of his own estimate. "Needless to say, I think they're wrong. So what do you think
about . . . ?" he paused, knowing how it would sound. "We have to ren-
dezvous with this drill ship fifty miles due north, right? Well, it looks
to me to be about another fifty miles north into the heart of the circle.
I think we should bust up there and find this guy."

"Seine. I got enough to worry about."

Seine reached over and tuned the radio, hoping Moneymaker
would fade in for once. Nothing. "I have a triangulation on him. No
one else does. I got him from Muktuk, and I got him from here. He's
not where they think he is. He's not east, he's north."

The Wolf eyed Seine. "Coast Guard's job, Seine."

"Well, yeah, but we're closer than they are. Besides, they got this
whale problem."

Moneymaker came in crisp and clean then, that eerie monotony to
his voice, and Seine could see the Wolf react. He turned. Frowned.
"That him?"

"That's him."

"Jesus, what a voice. Sounds fucking lost, don't he?"

"They don't know where he is. They think my numbers are wrong.
Say we have outdated equipment."

"We do have outdated equipment."

"He's out there. He's lost." Seine pointed again at the chart, to the
circle of uncertainty inscribed there in pencil. "We can find him."

The Wolf frowned, like he still didn't trust the notion, but Seine
could tell it was working on him. "You up for that? You think Buff,
Big Man—think they'd want to do that?"

"What the hell else they have to do?" Seine said.

"Retire," Irons said, and let out a guffaw. He unhooked the prosthetic nose and took a grip as if to crush it. Then he threw it hard against the glass, and to both their surprise it flew through the window like a baseball, making a neat round hole as it went out, rolling across the roof of the adjacent van.

"So whatta you say?" Seine said.

"It's the craziest goddamned idea I ever heard," Irons said. "I love it!"

FOURTEEN

Pirate Nights

Dale Korso had once made the taxi squad for the Dallas Cowboys, but his professional football career had less to do with any particular skill as a player and more to do with the strength in his arms and his willingness to endure massive amounts of punishment. He played two seasons for the LA Express of the defunct USFL before blowing out both knees, then retired from his lackluster professional football career to begin a lackluster towboating career, running push boats up the long rivers of western Alaska.

That evening the Big Man torched the burn pile while Seine boarded the *Whale* with Wolf Irons, motoring off the camp barge to chase down *Terror*. Irons pushed *Whale* full ahead on both engines and still only made about six knots. A tugboat hull wasn't designed to hydroplane atop waves like a speedboat but to plow through the water like a seagoing tractor. The faster they went the deeper they dug. As she approached *Terror*, *Whale* looked like a giant bathtub on the verge of burying herself in the waves. A hundred yards off, Korso pulled anchor and powered away, circling back and coming over the radio to tell Irons to back off and get him a crew.

"*We're* your crew!" Irons growled.

"Like shit you are," Korso said.

"This is my operation!" Irons snapped back. "Until it's finished I'm still GM of Arctic Ops, and your boat is under loan to Arctic Ops."

"There ain't no more Arctic Ops," Korso said. "Just look at your goddamned camp! There ain't one!"

Irons slammed both fists hard down onto the wheelhouse console and boomed out, *"You fuckhead!!!"* and then jammed both engines full ahead until it seemed to Seine the whole boat would rattle apart. When Irons tried to approach the bigger tug, Korso backed up, circled around the Wolf's starboard side, and turned to face him. With the underpowered *Whale*, there was little Irons could do. One time, he came within fifteen feet and kept yelling at Seine over the loudhailer, "JUMP! BOARD HIM! JUMP!" but all Seine saw was two hundred tons of tugboat coming right at him.

He jumped all right, but in the opposite direction, just as Korso rammed their starboard quarter. By then, Seine was hiding around the stern of the deckhouse, peering out to see Julia Lew burst onto the side deck of *Terror* and scream, "What the hell is going on?"

Seine stepped out and shrugged. "He's crazy."

"Which one?" Julia wanted to know.

"Both!"

An ice fog started to settle over things as Irons finally limped the dented *Whale* back to camp, where they made her fast and sat there to reconsider their plan. Out on the dockface the flames of the burn pile reached upward, burning a hole in the fog, a column of clear hot air going straight up like a giant's campfire.

Back on the barge, Seine went to Room 5, where he found the Buff packing to move aboard *Terror*, thinking Last Job was a done deal. As he packed, he drank the last of his Herbal Essence whiskey, straight from the plastic bottle.

Before Seine could say a word, the Buff held out a letter to him. "Here, I found this."

"What is it?"

"Some old letter." He scanned the room. "We're never coming back here, Seine. We'll never sleep in this room again. You believe it? Too fucking weird. I ain't one to mourn places, but we sure as shit have spent a chunk of our lives on this barge, ain't we?"

Seine recognized the letter. It was from Arne Olleson, his roommate after Marco Barn. Seine had carried it for five years at one point, and finally stuffed it into his desk drawer. Now he stuffed it into his pocket.

"It's a good thing you ain't stuck on Lew no more," the Buff said, "Cause I'm going for it."

"For *it*? What's that supposed to mean? She's not an *it*, she's a *she*. Besides, who ever said I wasn't stuck on her?"

"You had your chance and fucked the dog. Now it's my turn."

"Why don't you just leave her alone?"

"Why the fuck should I? Nobody else ever has."

"Maybe that's why you should."

"Fuck that. Don't be trying to introduce some kinda moral thing here. This ain't about morals. It's about sex. And Julia's *all* sex."

"You know, that's just fucked-up shipboard rumor. I'm sick of hearing it. It's twisted up, man."

"You're such a fucking pussy, Seine. I got a new idea why you wouldn't fuck her. It's cause you knew about her rep. Not cause of your wife, cause of *Lew*. Cause you're such a fucking *prude*. But Lew ain't ashamed, man. She ain't done nothing wrong. She's just done what she wants to do. And you can't fucking handle it."

"I don't believe all those rumors. I never did."

"It ain't *rumor*. It's *fact*. She had a fucking gang bang with the whole crew of the *Laurie A*. going up the Kuskokwim outa Bethel! She pulled a fucking train. Deal with it."

"Shut the fuck up. She did not."

"Get off your horse, man. She *told* me. That's why you didn't want her. Just cause you got some prude thing, don't mean she has to."

By this time, Seine had had about enough of the Buff. But before he left he told him the Wolf wanted the crew to assemble in the Com Shack, then added, "Listen, you want a fact, I'll give you a fact. Julia and I spent three weeks together, coming south down the Inside Passage, after the *Fearless*."

The Buff stopped everything and slapped the desktop with an open palm. "Hah! So you fucked her too! Hypocrite."

"I made love to her."

"Oh Jesus Christ spare me." He waved Seine off and kept stuffing his seabag, his big arms shoving socks and underwear deep inside. The outline of his bulging arm against the fabric of the bag made Seine vaguely sick.

"Anyway, don't matter," the Buff said. "Fuck it."

But Seine could see that it did matter.

In the Com Shack the four of them stood around in a square with arms crossed and Irons offered up what he wanted: a way to do this last job together. The Buff stood wide and chewed on his lower lip. Seine looked out to where *Terror* floated, and Stuart Wanless sat by the burn pile like a Boy Scout on an overnight.

The Big Man shook his head. "You must ask yourself if there is anything to be done here. Clearly it is corporate decision."

"I'm just saying I want this job. It's still my operation until I step on that flight south, goddamnit!"

The Big Man kept watching Seine, and with eyes wide he pleaded for some reasonable talk here. "Say something, Mr. Seine."

"I'm on his side."

"Jesus Christ, you people have all lost your minds."

"I know what to do," said the Buff.

All eyes shifted to Errol.

"What?" snapped Irons. "Tell me."

"SEAL operation if I ever seen one. Give me one guy to run a Zodiac out there, and I'll have the *Terror* back here in an hour."

The Big Man clucked his tongue. "I have no doubt as to your prowess at such things, Mr. Errol. But honestly. Captain Fuck has always struck me as dangerous man."

"He's an ex-jock with no knees," the Buff said.

"And twenty-inch biceps," said the Big Man.

"Harder they fall, man," said the Buff.

"You can't kill him," Seine said. "That's not part of the deal."

"Who said anything about killing anybody, Seine? You think I'm *crazy* or something?"

"Well, yeah. As a matter of fact."

"No killing. I just incapacitate him. Choke him out. Big Man can help me carry him ashore, and then we're gone."

Seine had his doubts, but his perverse side wanted to see Captain Fuck take it in the chin. When he thought about Julia it was an easy choice. If they went to sea together, even for a short run to the floe edge, a ship job, not to mention Moneymaker—

"I gotta tell ya, Buff," said Irons with a gleam, "I'd pay to see you kick Captain Fuck's ass."

The Buff nodded, his eyes narrowing. He smiled a twisted grin and looked off toward the silhouette of *Terror*, lying quietly in the stream. Then he turned to the Wolf. "How much would you pay? Exactly?"

And the Wolf howled at the moon, even though there wasn't one.

That night *Terror* was lit up like a Christmas tree as the two Zodiacs motored slowly past the dockface, where the burn pile raged, and swung wide to the east. Seine ran the outboard on the first Zodiac, with the Buff sitting still in the bow seat, while fifty feet behind, Irons ran the second outboard with the Big Man on the bow. When Seine looked back, he saw the trailing Zodiac running way down by bow. He could hear Irons barking, "Move back, you're gonna sink us!" as he slowed to avoid losing control.

"Check it out," Seine said, chuckling and nudging the Buff's back, but the Buff swatted his hand away and grunted. "Be ready," he said. "See if we can catch Korso snoozing."

Seine throttled ahead to about two hundred feet off *Terror*'s port quarter, where Buff gave him the cut signal and he shut down his engine completely and they coasted in.

Only Korso wasn't snoozing. At fifty feet the boat's spotlight swung right onto them like a prison break. And then the whining roar of the tug's main engines erupted, belching smoke out the twin stacks, and then the rush of wheel wash blasting off the stern end.

The Buff signalled, and Seine restarted the twenty-five-horse outboard and opened her up. The Buff ducked forward, keeping low and chanting, "Hoo-wah, hoo-wah, hoo-wah!"

The tug went full out, taking water over the bow when Seine powered up alongside in the faster skiff. The Buff leaped forward and clung to a tire fender on the tug's stern end, legs dragging and flailing in the rushing water before he hauled himself up and out. He vaulted the bulwark to the afterdeck, spry as a lion.

The bow of the Zodiac lifted off. Seine let off on the throttle and leaned as far forward as he could to keep the bow down. He peered past ice-cold salt spray to see the Buff disappear into the aft door.

The bow leapt upward again, slammed against the tug, and when

Seine looked up he saw Julia Lew standing there, leaning over the bulwark. An instant of eye contact showed eyes a deep black, that dead look again. She reached out and snagged the Zodiac's bow line, giving it a quick yank and putting four fast snapping wraps onto the aft quarter bitt.

The Zodiac skimmed and hopped alongside the tug then, and Julia reached a hand to help Seine aboard. "I'm always saving your ass, aren't I?" she said.

Seine climbed aboard.

"What's going on, Henry? What's the Buff up to?"

"It's not the Buff, it's the Wolf. His orders."

She gave him a suspicious, sidelong stare. Then she turned and moved toward the deckhouse, disappearing into the winch room. Seine followed. He turned the corner of the stack housing and found her sitting on a top-opening freezer set against the wall. Her head was down. She'd cut her hair since he last saw her, and wore it pulled straight back in a short ponytail.

"Julia," he said. "It's good to see you."

She looked up. Her eyes were black as pools of ink. "Are you going to tell me what this is all about?"

But then the main engines of the *Terror* backed off to neutral, and the tugboat slogged to a standstill in the open water.

"What's he up to?" Julia said, nodding her head toward the wheelhouse.

Seine lifted onto his tiptoes and peered over the boat deck and up the ladder to the wheelhouse, where the windows were dark now.

"What *are* you people, pirates?"

"Not exactly. But nobody had to convince the Buff."

Just then the Buff appeared down the side deck, dragging the limp body of Captain Fuck by both arms.

"Goddamnit!" Julia said, shaking her head. "Buffy Errol, what the hell did you do?"

"Now don't get all irate," the Buff said. "I just put him to sleep for a few."

He dragged Korso out onto the afterdeck and dumped him. Then he stood up, stretched, and grinned. "Damn, that was fun! Too god-damned easy, but fun. I was hoping old Dale would be more up to the task. He tried, but his legs are *gone*, just like I figured."

Julia threw her arms up. "What the fuck are you people doing?"

"WE'RE COMMANDEERING THIS VESSEL!" the Wolf boomed.

They turned to see Irons cruising up alongside with the Big Man in the bow, looking about ready to sink the poor rubber boat. Julia shook her head. "I've never seen anything like this in my life. Do you know what this man did? I think he killed Dale! Did you? Did you kill him?"

"No, I didn't kill him," said the Buff, looking down at the humped form of Captain Fuck. "I killed plenty and I choked out plenty, I think I know the difference."

"You people are *dead*. When the Company gets wind of this, you're all gonna be fired, you know that, don't you?"

"Hell, they can't fire us. We're already fired!" Irons said, stepping aboard. "That'd be, whatta ya call it?—double jeopardy. Hey, Julia. Good to see you again. How you been?"

"How've I been? I just spent two months with *him*, how do you think I've been?"

She indicated the form of Captain Fuck, still out cold. Unless he was dead. Seine still figured there was a chance he was dead.

The Big Man loomed over her like a tree. "That is why we are here," he said. "We are here to rescue you from the evil Captain Fuck."

"I don't need rescue," she said, turning to Seine.

"Damn!" said the Buff. "You are so hard-core. We're like them knights of the Round Table guys and you're like the damsel in the tower—" and he jerked his thumb at the tall wheelhouse.

"Fuck off," she said.

The Buff's face lit up. "I love when you talk dirty to me, Lew."

Julia addressed the Wolf. "Robert Irons. I think you need to explain a few things here before I walk topside and call the goddamned Coast Guard!"

"You don't wanna do that," Irons growled. "You wanna come *with* us. We're on a mission. We need you. And that man was standing in our way."

The Big Man loomed. "It is the last mission in the life of Biller Ocean Arctic Operations," he said.

"Twenty-five years!" the Wolf said.

The unconscious Captain Fuck lay there like a dead belukha whale. His tee shirt had hiked up almost to his armpits and his big arms stuck out from the short sleeves like a bloated version of Al George. Irons knelt down and felt for a pulse. Satisfied he wasn't dead, the Wolf stood upright and looked at the Buff, then let out a terrific belly laugh that echoed over the afterdeck.

"You done him so fast I didn't get to see it!"

"Wasn't much to see," the Buff said. "He don't have much but them big arms of his. I had him in less than thirty seconds."

"Shit!" Irons bellowed. "I'd have paid to see *that* too! I always loved seeing them big football players get it, ya know?"

The Buff smiled and went for a dip of tobacco. "So when we leaving?"

"Just as soon as we load stores and fuel up and grab the *Odyssey,*" barked Irons. "Gotta pass off the camp barge, too, to a line-hauler."

"I'm the only ship's officer aboard this vessel," Julia said. "Do any of you even have a license?"

The Wolf dug into his pocket and produced his Washington State driver's license. "Got that. See, right there. Says I don't even need glasses. And it don't expire till next year."

And he laughed, yawning his cavernous face until Julia Lew was convinced he was out of his mind.

Seine avoided going inside the deckhouse. Too many echoes of *Fearless* still, even though Julia walked past the tow winch, the Big Man dwarfing her, following and talking at high speed. His Slavic accent kicked into eighteenth gear as he tried to convince Julia to go with them on their mission. "It is a desperate mission, to rescue a man caught way off past the line of the Beaufort Sea, in the Arctic Ocean."

"Don't bullshit me," she said, and they were gone inside.

Seine stayed out on the afterdeck. His face glowed from windburn and from the sight of Julia Lew, but she was preoccupied with the takeover of her boat. Maybe she'd become more responsible since gaining her license. That sense of ownership—*my* boat—began when you became a mate and just bloated until, as captain, you were a full-fledged control freak.

Being aboard the *Terror* had a way of eradicating all thoughts besides *Fearless,* and Seine just sat there at first, feeling the hovering ghosts of gone shipmates, and refused to look around for fear they'd enter him.

Then he went for the tow gear, to check, among other things, the hold-down. As he removed the deck hatch for the after lazarette, Dale Korso began to stir. His defensive end's body rose from the deck. He pushed himself to a sitting position and said, "What the fuck is going on! I said, *What the fuck is going on?*"

"Take it up with the Wolf," Seine said, pulling out lengths of chain and a steamboat ratchet. "But I think you're going home."

Korso held his head and sat against the tow winch. "That fucking Skeemo is gonna get it. I'll have him on charges!"

"You mean the Buff? He's not full-blooded Eskimo," Seine said. "He's actually half Irish."

Korso shook his head at Seine. "And that's supposed to be some kinda *good* combination? Jesus Christ."

Seine turned the steamboat ratchet and listened to it click freely. He liked that sound; it meant they could use it. No gob rope. It meant *Terror* would not go the way of *Fearless*.

"I bet the Big Man you'd take him," Seine said.

"*Take* him? How the hell can you *take* Buffy Errol? There ain't nothing to hold onto unless ya grab his dick and shove your thumb up his ass! Ah, fuck it!"

Inside *Terror*, the galley mess was vacant, the table there with its laced pad of green rubber. To Seine it looked like some museum exhibit of the tug *Fearless*—except the place was spotless. "You run a tight ship," Seine said. "Not like the Chemist."

"The Chemist?" said Korso, heaving himself to a bench at the table. "He was an asshole. A smart-ass college prick! Pour me a cup, will ya?"

Seine poured Captain Fuck a cup of coffee, then handed him a sheet of paper with departure times listed. "Wolf said there's a ticket waiting for you at the Alaska Airlines counter. These are the flight times."

"You people are in deep shit."

"Nobody's gonna care," Seine said. "We'll be back before they can do anything about it."

Walking topside, Seine remembered without effort that night a year ago October. He had climbed this very flight of stairs aboard *Fearless*, thrown from wall to wall all the way up. Now he closed his eyes in some odd attempt to re-create the moment, to feel his way toward the middle deck. When he opened them he saw the doors to the cabins all lighted by a red sleep light, in the glow of which he saw bodies wash down from the wheelhouse, like dead fish from a broken aquarium. He stepped over Terje Narvik and watched seawater run out of his nostrils.

Seine made the long climb up the internal spiral until he made the wheelhouse. There, the crew gathered without Dale Korso, while the Wolf brought *Terror* in alongside the camp barge. Julia leaned backward against the forward console, her arms crossed, looking gloomy.

"So? Whatta ya say, Lew? Ya coming with us?"

She didn't say a word, but her face lifted, her dark eyes angry and suspicious as she surveyed the mutineers, her eyes finally falling on Henry Seine. "You in on this?" she asked.

The Wolf laughed. "Is he *in* on it? It was his idea!"

"It was my idea to do Last Job. Not my idea to take this boat by force. But I'm going. Are you?"

"Depends. I'll cook, but I get double time, same as with Dale. And I'm the first mate of this vessel. I get paid as mate, and I get the respect and authority of mate, and I get the overtime or I don't go. I got bills."

"Hell, yes! I got no problem with that," Irons said.

"Then I'll go," she said. She stared at the deck, brooding, then looked up at everyone and said, "But afterward, I'm gonna say you kidnapped me."

And crazy as the whole situation was, a shipmate feeling spread among the crew, and all the shit jobs and mind fucking and dark secrets that had once stood between them lay down like dying ghosts and went to sleep.

A minute later, Korso stepped out the side door with his seabag. With considerable effort he hauled it to the bow and heaved it up to the camp barge and then climbed up onto his knees, pushing himself to his feet. As he walked toward the main gangway, Irons piped in over the loudhailer, asking him if he wanted a ride into Deadhorse. Korso wheeled around and flipped the Wolf off, yelling, "Fuck you Irons! You are going to *die* a slow *death* over this! You and that motherfucker Buffy Errol!"

But Seine thought Irons might die laughing first.

FIFTEEN

Freezer Burn

S tuart Wanless took one look at Julia Lew and fell in love. Stuart had a girlfriend back in Seattle, but the girlfriend was very young, not even eighteen yet, and had none of the experience of someone like Julia, who seemed to Stuart to embody all earthly sensuality. Seine was on his way to pack his gear when Stuart stopped him on the catwalk and, in a biting wind, told him all about his newly born affection.

"She's ten years older than you are, Stuart."

"Dude, I have always gone for older women. I just never had the chance to get to *know* one. So you think I'd have a chance with her?"

"I have no idea. You'd have to ask her that."

Stuart stood still in the wind. His coveralls were unbuttoned, and Seine could see his hairless chest. It was the first time he hadn't seen Stuart bounce up and down outside, saying, "It's cold! It's cold!" Apparently love had heated him up considerably.

"Look, Stuart, I gotta go now. You should get packed if you're going with us."

"What's that supposed to mean? Of course I'm going with you!"

Seine left him there. There was a small matter of room assignments. With four staterooms and a crew of six there was protocol to observe, a hierarchy to such things. Skipper got the first solo room, then the chief engineer, then the first mate. Fuck if Seine would leave it to protocol. He knew what the Buff had planned, so in Room 5 he packed like a madman. He stuffed clothes and letters and music tapes into his seabag until the thing was overflowing, and then he hefted it on his shoulder and ducked down the back ladder to the bow of the camp barge, then swung around the forward generator shack and dropped his gear to the foredeck of *Terror*.

Ten minutes later, he was unpacked inside Julia's room on the main deck, his seabag stowed under his locker. He was lying on the top bunk when the Buff came in with his bags and just stood there glaring. "What the fuck you think you're doing?"

"What's it look like? Trying to catch a nap."

"You sneaky bastard."

"What are you talking about?"

"You still got a thing for her. Well don't think that's gonna stop me, Seine."

"I don't own Julia."

"Damn right you don't!"

"Nobody owns Julia."

"Damn right they don't. Cause *I* do!" And the Buff slammed the door on his way out.

When Seine was satisfied that the Buff had actually moved into the middle-deck engineer's quarters, he went out on deck to help carry stores from the reefer vans to the afterdeck of *Terror*.

Seine lifted a cardboard box packed with frozen meat to a deep freeze set up on wooden skids in the winch room. It seemed a strange place for a deep freeze, especially since this time of year the outdoors itself was a deep freeze. He swung the lid open and found the freezer filled completely with layers of blankets. He had never seen blankets in a freezer, even on a tugboat, where you were liable to see anything.

So he peeled back a frozen layer to find a human face sleeping quietly in profile. A woman's face. Eskimo, he thought. Frost had formed
around her one visible eye and nose. She was curled in a fetal position
to fit into the freezer. Seine felt a hard ball grow in his throat. When he
tried to swallow the ball down, it moved about a quarter inch and just
lodged there. He shook his head. "No," he said aloud. "No way."

He replaced the blanket and slammed the lid closed. A flat smile
came to his face, as if someone had long been playing a sick joke that
he was just now getting. It was that kind of world, a place where people drove tugboats to the bottom of the ocean and put dead bodies in
freezers.

He opened the freezer again just to make sure he wasn't hallucinating. He lifted the corner of the blanket gingerly, and again—
still—there lay the old woman. Along her jawline ice sprouted like a
crystalline beard. Seine patted the blanket down and felt it press
against frozen flesh—and jerked his hand away. He closed the lid again
and left the box of frozen meat on top, then walked fast to the foredeck, where he slithered down the forepeak hatch and started hauling
out lines and deck gear he knew they'd need for pushing the icebreaker through ice.

He worked with a grim expression, not asking for help, just passing
by as the Big Man ran the winch wires out to get ready, and the two
worked side by side without saying a word. "You seen her? That old
woman?"

"What old woman are you speaking of?"

"On the afterdeck. In the freezer."

"Do not bull shit a bull shitter," said the Big Man.

Seine shook his head. "Not bullshitting," he said, and the Shade
hovered again, whispering things he couldn't hear, making accusa-
tions he had never stopped hearing in eight years. They crowded—his

old man, the Chemist, Cliff the Cook; *ya got a clear conscience there Henry Seine, do ya?*—and he wanted to say more but feared the appearance of insanity or superstition—*you spent a year in an insane asylum, didn't you, Seine?* The dead body goaded him. This boat was a bad one. A doomed one. Driven to the bottom.

It wasn't even his superstition. Some of the old-timers had this whole series of don'ts on a vessel: don't make split-pea soup or you'll simmer up a fog; don't whistle on a boat or you'll whistle up a storm; don't be mean to seagulls, they're reincarnated sailors lost at sea; and don't transport a dead body on a boat or she'll pilot you to the bottom. It was an ancient thing, someone once explained, from the old days of burial ships, pushed offshore on fire with the king inside. Ferryman of the dead.

Work work work, Seine said inside. He felt the Shade's breath again, and realized it had been gone for the whole takeover. He plowed face-first into work. They readied *Terror* for their trip out, and that meant deck lines and spare wires and a thorough check of the towing gear. He checked both the Zodiac power raft and the Switlik inflatable life raft, which hung on a rack up on the side of the Texas deck, encased in a bright orange barrel. He checked for survival suits, counted, and ran the zippers on the vinyl cases just to make sure. When the Buff appeared suddenly behind him, Seine let out a yelp and practically jumped into the air.

"The hell is the matter with you, Seine?"

Seine opened his mouth, speechless, and pointed aft toward the winch room, vaguely aware that his finger was quaking up and down, the Buff looking at it cross-eyed.

"What's with your hand? Why you doing this thing?" And he jerked his own finger up and down while making a mocking face. "You having some kinda goddamned seizure or something?"

"You—you check out that freezer in the winch room? You know what that's all about?"

"No I ain't checked out no freezer in no winch room. I got work to do. I'll be in the basement anybody needs me. God damn." And then he scampered aft and climbed below to the engine room.

Only two barges remained in camp now, the camp barge itself, which still lay inside the curving lagoon of the causeway, and the ice-breaker barge *Odyssey*, which lay fully loaded and lashed along the dockface. Wolf backed *Terror* to the seaward side of the camp barge, where Julia and Seine boarded the barge's stern end. Julia operated a handheld radio, and Seine followed her as they stepped along the side deck to release the camp barge from her mooring lines and yard her offshore.

They stepped carefully, Seine thinking this was it; the only thing they'd left behind were the dead men buried in the causeway and the dying burn pile. He flopped the hawsers off along the camp barge and then finally released the beach line and let the steel cable flop to the gravel.

The Wolf powered *Terror* full ahead, stretching the soft tow line, the camp barge resisting, so long had it been moored there, filling its own footprint, as if it had put down roots. But it finally gave way and coasted off the beach, the sound of the tug receding into a distant whine, blocked by the housing units and everything else. Seine and Julia stood side by side on the beach side of the barge deck. "First time I've seen this thing move in eleven years," he said.

Julia watched the job, held the radio to her mouth. "You're clear of the beach, half ahead on two," she said. Then she looked up at Seine and smiled. "I'm sorry, what's that?"

"Nothing."

They stood still, feeling that strange sense of silent motion.

"You moved into my room pretty fast there, Seine. Didn't even ask. That mean you finally miss me?"

"Of course I've missed you."

She laughed. "Is that right? Well, maybe we can do something about that later on. For now, why don't you stay put for the handoff to the line-hauler. I'll be back." And then she threaded her way back through the living units toward *Terror*.

After she'd gone, Seine pressed his back against a corrugated aluminum living unit and waited, flipped his collar up against the cold, stuffed his hands into his pockets.

How bleak the thought of being carried in a freezer, how bleak to be lost on the ocean floor. He preferred daydreaming of how it would feel to grab Julia by the waist and fly south. All the birds had done it, why not him? This time of year, flying south was as natural as breathing. One year, '83, he booked a flight to Seattle at first, but then on every stopover he had drinks in the airport bars and before he boarded again he'd already bought a new ticket, extending his flight, until by trip's end he was standing in the sand in Mexico drinking a margarita while the sun barreled its way into the Pacific Ocean. In ten hours that fall, he'd made a temperature trip from 30 below to 90 above.

Now the only heat he felt came from Julia and from the burn pile, which had blazed past its wild peak. Transparent blue flames rose out of the pulsating embers of the base. Even from a half mile off he could feel the heat of it throbbing against his face.

As he watched an ocean tug called *Vigorous* came into view, maneuvering to accept the camp barge, and it occurred to Seine that he *was* what people feared him to be, a lightning rod, bad news, the ferryman of the dead. He felt the air prickle his scalp, as if he could feel the energy of Bad Things hovering all around him, swirling there. His hair stood on end and started to glow green, engulfed by St. Elmo's fire. He rubbed it out, shook it off, and took a deep breath. I'm hallucinating, he thought, as he breathed the breath of Marco Barn.

Julia returned then, talking with authority into the handheld, directing Irons—"All stop!"—as the line-haul made its approach. In between she gave Seine a queer look, like she could read his mind, so he asked about the old woman. She said that Korso called her the Old Woman of Nunivak. They received the pickup order on their way through the Aleutians, and on Nunivak Island five Eskimo men brought the freezer on board and said she was their grandmother.

Terror's job was to transport the old woman to Kaktovik on Barter Island a hundred miles east of Prudhoe Bay, where her family in the north would see her properly buried.

"I wouldn't let her bother you, Henry," Julia said. "I know it's weird being on this boat, believe me. It's weird for me too. Just stay in the moment."

He nodded. "I know. Do the work. Fuck *Fearless.*"

She smiled and nudged his arm. "Boat's don't have ghosts, people do." And then she was gone, marching, doing her job the way she always had, saying, "Slow ahead on one," into the handheld radio.

Seine reached into his jacket pocket and pulled out the old letter from Arne Olleson. He tipped it toward the last bit of light, and only then did he realize that daylight was falling. He read:

Dear Henry Seine,

I am writing this letter from home. They finally let me come home because I told them I'd break out if they didn't. I recently had some trouble I thought I'd tell you about, since you're probably wondering where your roommate went. Well, two weeks after I got home last fall my eyes froze up on me. One turned out to the right and the other stuck dead ahead and neither would move at all. After two CT scans, an angiogram, something called a

PET scan, and an MRI they told me I have a tumor on the nerve that
controls my eyes. It messed me up so bad I couldn't even go hunting. But it
didn't stop there. They said the tumor in my head was a secondary one.
And their tests showed I had lots more. So I just wanted to write to tell you
that's why I'm not up there working you into the ground like I always did. I
hope you are doing well. I have been thinking of how you were always going
to come up to Index and go hunting with me, or at least get out to see a real
live bear in the woods. But I don't reckon that's going to happen now.
Anyway, you have a good summer, and I'll see you sometime somewhere,
I'm sure.

Your friend, Arne

Seine folded the letter and slipped it into his coat pocket. How was
that for living in the moment. The guy had been dead five years.

A brisk norther had blown ice into the bay all week, and now floes riddled the horizon as far as he could see. After they'd passed off the
camp barge to the tug *Vigorous,* they wired *Terror* up to the stern of the
Arctic Odyssey, pushing west while Seine made his way to the wheelhouse. Irons and Julia were there, steering and plotting their course
along a flaw lead, a break in the ice that ran coastwise past the Return
Islands. The Shade was there too, pressing his mutated face into the
glass, Marco Barn eyes staring at Seine and laughing. "Why don't we
drop the old woman off first?" Seine said.

"What's that?" Irons said.

In the stream, the low-cut ocean tug powered out ahead of them,
towing the camp barge away toward the western sky. Irons watched it
go longingly, as if watching his childhood home being carted away by
movers.

"We should get her off this boat!" Seine barked.

"Jesus Christ," Irons said. "Re-frickin-lax, Seine. Hell if I'm going two hundred miles outa my way just to bury some old lady in the permafrost. She's dead and frozen already, in no rush I can see."

Seine felt a throbbing headache come on, a chorus of voices ringing in his ears, with Marco Barn there breathing on him, inches from him like he might kiss him, or strangle him, or both, saying, "You're already dead, man."

"*Shut up!*" Seine yelled.

Julia and Irons both jumped, turning toward him.

Seine cranked the volume on the VHF, which erupted in static.

"What the hell is the matter with you?" said Irons.

"Sorry," Seine said, and reduced the volume. Irons glared at him and then moved to the chart table. Seine tuned the VHF to the Coast Guard working station. He got nothing on the short-range VHF but empty air waves, so he tuned the single sideband to 2182 kHz thinking he might run into Moneymaker, thinking he alone seemed to eradicate the Shade, thinking Marco Barn was dead dead dead.

Irons looked up from the chart table. "Do me a favor, Seine, and get the Newman on the sanitary. How about that? Just go below. Go below."

Julia steered a course and glanced over at Seine as if she was suspicious he might be losing what little mind he had left.

Seine stepped out the rear of the wheelhouse to the tiny Texas deck, thinking he'd go below that way, needing fresh air, needing open sky, wondering what Flaw Island looked like, how it felt to be some lost man out in the ice wilderness of the polar pack. It made Seine shiver as he came to realize where he was standing, how he'd stepped out of the wheelhouse of *Fearless* just like this, absently, only to be hurled overboard. Now he held to the railing and breathed deep gulping breaths of arctic air. He tried to focus on the job, to feel the purpose that penetrated the loss, but he couldn't help thinking they were all embarking on a grave error, going north to nowhere, and once again it would be his fault. The camp barge was towed away to the west, trailing the day boat *Whale* astern, and in the wake of both, nothing remained of camp but the smoldering burn pile and the naked causeway, a long umbilicus of gravel stretching south toward frozen land.

PART THREE

Circle of Uncertainty

SIXTEEN

Ice by God

Four hours later, they broke ice into a falling night, squeezing into a flaw lead of open water that angled north like a black lightning bolt. In the wheelhouse, Seine stood on tiptoes and scanned with the spotlight, just barely seeing over the top of the tightly loaded deck of *Odyssey*, where cargo quivered from ice impact.

The lead narrowed until ice and darkness seemed to close down on them all at once, surrounding them. Seine swept the spotlight in a quick three-sixty and saw nothing but unbroken ice against a black sky. Ice coverage was measured in tenths—five-tenths coverage meant half water, half ice. Seine pointed at the ice field that encircled them. "Ten-tenths coverage," he said.

Irons didn't even look at him. He shoved his meat-fists forward against the throttle controls, let out a yell that sounded like primal scream therapy, and launched into a sermon on ice and human expectations: "What the assholes don't understand, Seine, is things don't go perfect in the arctic. In fact, not anywhere, but it shows up more here. Ice by God! Ice'll burn you every time!"

Then they slammed into a pressure ridge. Like a mountain range in miniature, a mangled rubble of ice angled across their bow, and despite its size Seine barely caught a glimpse before they hit. The impact seemed remote in the tall wheelhouse, the icebreaker riding up a hillock of ice and heeling to starboard 15 degrees, a steel deck the length of a football field rising and tipping and flexing as a shock wave rolled aft through stacked cargo, toppling mud sacks, shifting the tall tanks and racks of drill pipe until Irons pulled the throttles to neutral and yelled, "All stop!"

The delayed force of impact rippled into the boat, where they felt a shuddering rise up through their feet. The starboard winch wire snapped like a rubber band. *Terror* swung off the barge, flailed sideways onto a slab of multiyear ice, and jammed to a stop. Seine found himself suddenly on his knees. He pulled himself to his feet and peered out the portside window to see the spotlight beam flash through cargo that jiggled as the barge settled amid the ice. *Terror* lay sideways along the flat stern.

"Damn!" Irons said, surveying the mess out on the icebreaker deck. The roar of the mains had settled to a dull idling drone. "I need shock cords on my wires, Seine. Then I'll need lookout on the breaker bow."

Seine had no desire to make his way through the dark and jumbled cargo of the *Odyssey,* but at the same time he knew they needed a forward set of eyes if they were to pick their way safely through the tighter ice. Another ten miles beyond they would, with luck, break free into another long angular lead where the *Alpha Dog* was drilling exploratory wells. There they could get rid of the cargo. There, with any luck, they'd be fifty miles from a drifting Moneymaker.

On the foredeck of *Terror,* Julia popped the dogs on the deck hatch and lowered herself into the forepeak, a belowdeck storage area shaped like the prow and housing an array of deck gear. Nylon lines lay in precise coils that she herself had organized. She went straight for the shock cords, six-foot lengths of thick nylon line, ten inches in circumference. An eye was spliced in one end and a steel grommet in the other. They'd shackle the grommet to the end of the steel winch wire as a kind of safety valve. Shock cords would stretch where steel wires wouldn't, and break before the wires could.

Julia hoisted two shock cords from their hooks on the aft bulkhead and heaved them toward the short ladder, where Henry Seine's arm extended down inside the hatch to grab them and haul them out one at a time.

On deck, in the eerie idle of night, sea ice encircled them. Irons worked both mains to shove ice away from the blunt stern of *Odyssey*. Ice insinuated itself down-current, shoving in between boat and barge, but Irons swung his bow hard to port, hammering and sweeping floes aside until he powered forward to press *Terror*'s push knees tightly against the flat stern of the icebreaker.

Seine heaved one shock cord toward the starboard winch, the other to port, then reached down to where Julia pressed over her head the tight steel coil of a new winch wire. An inch and a half in diameter, the wire weighed fifty pounds. Seine felt his back pinch as he lifted the coil out of the hole and rolled it across the steel deck to starboard.

Julia bounced out of the hole, stepping fast as Seine signaled Irons to run the winch out, the slow grind of the electric motor taking ten minutes before it finally spit out the last of the broken wire. Then they reversed the process. Wanless held the new wire tight, leaning backward like a water-skier to keep tension on it as the motor pulled the steel rope through his hands and drew it onto the circular winch drum. Julia used a crowbar to lever each wrap in a tight spiral and Seine a sledgehammer to beat the factory-stiff wire flush against itself, winding around and around the lumbering drum.

Without a word, Wanless dragged the first shock cord toward them, and Seine used a shackle to connect it to the winch wire. Only then did Irons run the winches out, and the deck crew walked the wires up to the barge, stretching the heavy nylon line attached to the still-heavier wire cables. They climbed to the stern deck of *Odyssey*.

They leaned backward with all their weight to keep from being dragged overboard, leaning and walking the wire out to the nearest steel cleat, where they looped the eyes over, then stood up to watch as Irons ran the winches to take up slack.

They sweated and their sweat froze. They breathed hard and their lungs ached. And when Irons had pulled the wires tight, drawing tugboat and icebreaker barge together as one, Seine looked at Wanless and said, "Stuart. You and me to the bow."

And they went.

Seine circled the old tool van, set dead center on the stern deck of *Odyssey*, not realizing that Irons had transferred it here. He felt strangely comforted to see it, as if some leftover limb of the camp barge remained with them to protect them. Seine and Wanless moved to the outboard and made a radio check. "Gotcha," Irons said, his voice crackling and barely audible through the handheld.

"The night effect," Seine said to Wanless. "Can't hear things in the transition from day to night. It's why radio is so touch-and-go up here. Lotta transition from day to night."

"Lemme know when you're clear of the snarl and we'll get under way again," Irons said, his voice breaking up slightly.

Wind funneled between gaps and made whistling and howling noises. Stacks of cargo lay at odd angles, pitched and leaning against each other in a state of precarious equilibrium.

As they picked their way forward, Wanless talked about nothing but Julia. "Come on, dude, tell me what you know about her. She's got this—I don't know—*sexual* thing about her. She been with a lotta guys?"

"I don't know, Stuart. Does it matter?"

"I don't know. I kinda like it if it's a lot. My girlfriend's such a *good girl*. It's getting *really* boring. On the other hand, what if Julia's been with like a thousand or something?"

"Yeah, what if."

"You just can't get the pictures out of your head if you've got a woman like that. They might, like, haunt you forever."

Seine took as deep a breath as cold lungs would allow and turned sideways to edge his way up the narrow side deck. Wanless stayed behind him, shuffle-stepping to keep up until a shipping container blocked the outboard path. It had shifted sideways with the last impact and now hung two feet over the edge, so Seine ducked inboard and crawled through a tunnel formed by toppled sacks of mud. Drill mud, a compound called barite, came in a heavy dry powder packed in large sacks that weighed two thousand pounds each. Mixed with water it formed a slurry that drillers pumped down the hole to provide a medium for drawing the drill cuttings upward and out. Barite and cut rock were the primary waste products in drilling an oil well, but now several bags had broken open, leaving the dry powder looking like metallic flour all over stacks of pipe. As he crawled, Seine imagined what it would feel like to have a bag of mud fall on him. A longshoreman he knew called it getting sacked.

Seine wanted to do whatever he could to avoid getting sacked, so he scaled fast upward, choosing his footing carefully, until he broke free to the top. He stepped just forward of the mud tanks, which rose like grain silos. The sky spread out clear for miles, lighted now by the vaguest of shimmerings to the east. "Look over there," Seine said. "Northern lights." Seine pointed to a strip of gauzy white light hanging lifeless in a band a few degrees above the horizon.

"It looks like a cloud at night," Wanless said.

"Yeah. Not a very good example, but that's it."

"I thought they were supposed to be, like, incredible up here," he said with evident disappointment.

They climbed forward to the flat roof of a shipping container, which gave a good view of the ice field that stretched before them and left them clear of potentially falling cargo. As they stood there in survey, Seine could have sworn he heard something out over the ice, the cries of something. Sound was known to travel great distances over the polar pack, but still he thought again he might be hallucinating these horrific cries, which came at him like the deaths of men.

Maybe he could hear the drill ship. Or maybe Moneymaker, on his eroding island of ice, screaming as the berg exploded and halved and rolled in its search for new equilibrium amid an ever-changing center of gravity. Seine and Wanless sat dangling their legs off the edge of the container, Seine clicking open his handheld radio to get Julia this time—"You have a lead two or three degrees off your port bow," he said. "You'll want to follow that for a few hundred yards."

"Coming two degrees port," Julia replied, and Seine heard the squeak of ice and a scraping sound resonating up from below—the underbelly. That's all the icebreaker was: thick plate steel on the bow and hollow cargo tanks laden with fuel for the drill ship. *Terror* shoved the barge into ice for a quarter mile, then came another degree to port. "Full ahead on two," Seine said. "You've got light ice to the next break."

"Roger that, Henry."

Stuart reeled. "God, don't you love her *voice?* She has the most amazing *voice!*" He looked around from their position on the bow. "You can't even hear the main engines! It's almost dead quiet out here! I love it!"

"Give it time," Seine said.

About two minutes as it turned out. It took that long before the tug reached full ahead on two. Icebreaker barges were designed to ride up onto floes and then settle down to break them from above, with a belly-rumble like thunder coming from five miles off.

"So you know Julia Lew pretty well then, I guess," Wanless said.

"Pretty well in some ways."

"And you think I'd have a chance—?"

Seine turned and glared. Wanless stopped.

Seine caught a glimpse of something over his shoulder. He quivered, a sudden head-and-shoulder shiver that made Wanless turn sharply to look. On the far end of the adjacent shipping container stood a gull, its sleek gray and white feathers unruffled in the wind, its eye a dead circle of black, its beak dished and curving to an aggressive hook, with a crimson streak like a bloodied lip. "*That* scared the shit out of me," Seine said, and quivered again.

"I didn't know they stayed up here this late in the year," said Wanless.

"Well, it's trapped now," Seine said. "It's gonna hang with us for food and warmth."

"Will it survive?"

"I don't know. Animals get trapped up here all the time. Like those narwhals trapped in that fjord. They won't make it out."

"Yeah, I read about that. They got an icebreaker over there to lead them out."

"And maybe it'll work and maybe next year it'll happen again and they won't even notice."

"Dude, you are so negative. Anybody ever tell you that?"

"Yeah. A few people. Thanks."

The spotlight flickered left and right, casting its tight beam far up ridges of ice, then sweeping out to the barely visible line of black water, like an ebony shore, out toward the Buff's mythic Rottingmule.

What looked a black shore was in fact open water, a polynya that stretched for fourteen miles, where ice sheared off her northern side. Polynyas were areas of persistent open water, found throughout the circumpolar arctic, places kept ice-free by currents and wind patterns. The edges fluctuated, ice tried to form, the north wind howled. As

Terror pushed up into the open seas, the choppy water rocked her, and the crew took the barge in tow to avoid the incessant bump and grind of the flat push knees against *Odyssey*'s stern.

A half hour after they'd made tow, Irons bounced down the stairs into the galley and stretched and yawned. "That broad can run a boat!" he announced.

"Sure," Seine said. "Julia's smooth."

"I bet you'd know," said the Buff.

"Not just smooth," Irons said. "She ain't afraid to put some balls into it. She can skipper in my fleet any day!"

The Wolf's highest compliment was only slightly diminished by the fact that he no longer had a fleet. He had a boat anyway, at least for now, and proceeded to devour two full plates of Julia's spicy Thai chicken with peanut sauce, the latter improvised from a jar of Skippy. Then he cried, "Jesus! She cooks like a goddamned gourmet! Top-drawer operation! I'm giving her a raise, by God!"

"I hear she gives good head too," said the Buff. "Whatta you say about *that*, Seine?"

"I say talk like that is uncool in a top-drawer operation," Seine said.

"Hypocrite!" said the Buff with a mouthful of food. "He don't mind fucking her, he just don't wanna talk about it."

The Buff was mostly eating, but he kept his eye on Seine the whole time. He ate with one arm curled around his plate, as if he'd learned to eat while doing three-to-five for armed robbery. In general it seemed that the cathartic effect of thumping Captain Fuck had passed, and the Buff was looking for another war to fight.

Seine just hoped it wouldn't be with him.

Before climbing topside, Seine pushed through the roar of the fiddley deck and checked the tow wire. The seas were ragged and short-capped, slamming the boat, spray popping over the bow with each wave and washing aft, a layer of ice glazing the deck. Wind speeds reached 50 knots, and ambient temperature dropped to 15 degrees F. Unlike the Gulf of Alaska, the main problem here was not huge waves, which in the shallow Beaufort Sea rarely rose above five feet. Here they faced short wave lengths, high winds, and subfreezing waters that hit the cold steel of the boat and caused rapid icing. Seine looked aft up the short towline to the bow of the breaker, which had already begun to form stalactites of ice like giant teeth along her shark-bow. He'd seen boats come in from routine ferry jobs looking like ice castles. Under bad conditions a vessel could build up four thousand pounds of ice in as little as an hour and get so top-heavy it could turn turtle without warning. Not unlike a crabber overloaded with crab pots, he thought.

Seine held to the spiraling handrail as he climbed the internal tower to the wheelhouse, where he saw Wanless standing next to Julia as she steered, the two rocking in time as if sharing a dance. Their feet were actually touching, wedged against each other, standing wide against the twisting, jerking motion of the boat.

They were talking in hushed tones, Wanless dipping his blond head toward her as he spoke, both of them so preoccupied they didn't see Seine right away.

"So what did he do, just like divorce the family?"

"Sort of," said Wanless. "He went to sea and never came back."

"I did that too. Of course, I had a stepfather who was trying to fuck me every night, so it was easy for me."

"Really?" Wanless looked stunned. "My God."

Seine stood there and watched, silently, as Wanless pulled out his wallet and photograph, showing it to Julia. "It's an old picture. He'd be thirty-five right now. That was taken when he was eighteen, I think."

"I see the resemblance," Julia said. "You're such a baby-faced boy, Stuart."

Wanless leaned toward her and whispered something, and Julia let out a laugh. "Younger, yes, just not one who's practically *illegal,*" she said.

"I'm legal! I am!" And he started shuffling through his wallet for his driver's license, in process catching sight of Seine standing there. "Henry!" he said, and stood upright and stiff.

Seine stepped up on the opposite side of Julia and checked the anemometer for wind speed and direction. "Have you seen this?" Julia asked, holding the picture.

"I've seen it," Seine said without even looking. "It's the Chemist."

Julia frowned at Seine. "You're kidding."

"You *know* him?" Wanless said.

"I knew him," Seine said.

"Dude, you sort of neglected to mention that one."

"Neglected isn't exactly the right word," Seine said. It was more a matter of denial. "He went by a different name. He called himself Auric, Bill Auric."

"Bill Auric? Who the hell is Bill Auric?"

"Why haven't you told him all this?" Julia asked.

"I was trying to find the right time."

"Tell me what? *What?*"

Julia turned forward and steered manually. She glanced at Seine. "If you don't, I will."

Seine said, "Stuart. Your brother is dead."

Wanless just frowned. He looked out the window, over the wind-swept blackness of the Beaufort Sea. His face turned even whiter than it was normally.

"How do you *know* this?" Wanless said.

"Because I was there. I was onboard."

"Onboard? It happened at sea? Bill—what? Auric?" Wanless's face was a swirl of incredulity, like a thousand points rotated through his brain.

"Last fall, the tug *Fearless* went down in the Gulf of Alaska. He was the skipper."

"My brother's not Auric. *Zach Wanless.*"

"It's him. People called him the Chemist. He studied chemistry at UW."

"That's right," Wanless said blankly. "He did. Are you sure he's *dead?*" He said the word as if trying to cement it in his mind.

"I'm sure."

Seine told him all of it—about *Fearless* and its hold-down, about False Pass and the DEW bars, and a mad dash to Seattle ahead of Julia Lew. The salvage job, faces behind the glass. When he'd finished, Seine felt like he'd lived it all over again, while Wanless looked like someone about to have a cerebrovascular accident. He said to Julia, looking at her as if seeing her for the first time, "So you and my brother were—?"

"No," said Julia, shaking her head. "We sailed together once."

Wanless turned to Seine, his face steeling over, and said matter-of-factly, "So it's true what the Big Man said. About people dying all around you."

Then Wanless slipped out the back and down the external ladder to the Texas deck below.

"Well," said Julia, staring forward. "That was fun. Good thing you waited for the right time."

Alpha Dog

I n the wheelhouse, Seine stood next to Julia and stared across a ten-mile stretch of open water to the drill ship *Alpha Dog,* the rig derrick slick and bright with wind barricades enclosing its sides, rising like an orange-shrouded Eiffel Tower out of the black ocean.

"I'm glad I told him. It's a shitty thing to hear, but at least I'm not holding it in anymore."

"It's not *what* you told him so much as *how,*" Julia said, standing on tiptoes to check for ice buildup on the bow. "Kind of abrupt, Henry."

"I wasn't trying to hurt him," he said.

"I know." She checked her instruments, adjusting subtly for set and drift and for the Coriolis force, the tendency of floating objects in the northern hemisphere to deflect to the right due to the earth's rotation. Then she reached up, clicked the radio, and did a channel check with the drill ship.

Seine looked up at the radios. He'd forgotten all about Moneymaker. "You hear anything from Flaw Island?"

"No, I've been monitoring the drill ship."

"Even by SSB? Don't you have VHF contact with the ship yet? You should keep the SSB on twenty-one eighty-two kilohertz."

"To be honest, Henry, I've been busy running a boat. Money-maker's *your* deal, right?"

Seine reached up and scanned the SSB channels but heard nothing at all from Moneymaker, not through two passes of the dial.

"Anyway, we can't do anything until we get rid of this cargo," Julia said. "Just hang tight."

He watched her short, shining black ponytail, reflecting the meager light from the console. But otherwise the wheelhouse was dark, like a pod somewhere in outer space. "We haven't even had a chance to talk."

"I know!" She turned, smiling. "We've been so busy. But things'll slow down. We'll have a chance."

"There's a lot I want to say."

She drew silent then. "Really? Like what?"

Julia stood with her legs wider, balancing against the twisting motion of the boat and the thudding thunder of spray over the exposed bow.

"The Buff accused me of something," Seine said. "I denied it, but the more I think about it—the more I think he was right."

"Uh-oh. When the Buff is right, watch out," she said, and let out a little laugh.

She tapped her fingers on the wheel, then came north a degree and settled into a face-on assault against a northwester. She checked aft, the bow rake of the *Odyssey* following them two hundred yards behind. They had three miles to go now, the drill ship rising like a lighted Christmas tree.

"He said the reason I didn't go with you—"

He stopped. The thought of actually admitting this overcame him then, and when he looked aft toward the trailing icebreaker, he saw that gull again, hunkered on the leeward side of the wheelhouse now, atop a flat white toolbox welded along the railing.

"Remember what I told you about my wife being there at Pier Nineteen to meet me? Well she wasn't. And the fact is, I knew she wouldn't be. She'd already filed for divorce by then. The Buff accused me of not going with you after the *Fearless* because of your reputation."

"My reputation? What reputation is that, Henry?"

"You know what I mean."

"I'm afraid I don't."

He tried to read her expression, but her eyes wouldn't let him in. Was it possible she was unaware of the stories told about her? Or was she just forcing Seine to say it aloud. "Shipboard stuff," he said. "Talk. The *Laurie A.*"

She frowned then, as if trying to figure something. "Ahh, the *Laurie A.* That story's really made its way around. So that's why you went back to your wife? The *Laurie A.*?"

"I never actually went back to her."

"Ohhh, I get it now. That's just what you *told* me. You were married, and I was a shipboard slut? So the Buff was right. You couldn't see yourself with a woman *like me. The horror.*"

For a moment he couldn't speak. Then he said, "I think he was only partly right."

"Well, it's no big fucking deal, Henry. If I were you, I'd just get over it. I mean, that whole I-love-you thing was just something to say anyway, right? It was for me."

Now his own face went dead. "Sure, I know that."

"You know something else?" she said, her voice acquiring an edge that cut through his chest. "I don't think I like the direction of this. My sex life isn't anybody's business but mine."

"It doesn't make me feel good about myself, you know. And I just wanted to say that—well, since Heather and I split—and this last winter—"

"Ahhhh. Somehow I thought you'd get around to you and *Heather* splitting."

"I mean to say that I've thought about it and I don't care about that anymore. I don't care what you did. Whatever you did."

She turned to him and he thought maybe she was about to slap him. Her voice crackled with irritation. "Well thanks *so* much for forgiving me, Henry. Tell you what, why don't you leave me alone. Go below and pull and lash deck lines along the port side so we don't have a lot of frozen lines to handle. When we approach the drill ship, we'll be taking the barge on our port hip. After you're finished with the lines, you should get some sleep. We'll be on cargo off-load in three hours."

Seine stood there, uncertain exactly how he had fucked that up but knowing for certain that he had. Out the wheelhouse window the gull huddled there, and then before he knew it there sat Marco Barn, next to the bird, turned away. He couldn't see his face, but he could feel it, right next to him then, like a black hole in a black night, drawing the life out of him.

The *Alpha Dog* sat in open sea winched tight on eight anchor wires like a giant spider. In order to slide in between the anchor wires without running them over, *Terror* would have to take the barge on the hip.

After breaking tow, Irons positioned the tugboat alongside the barge, three quarters of the way back, like a mother carrying an oversized baby on her hip. Seine hated hip-towing. Their ability to control the barge this way depended on tight lines, preferably winched tight with power capstans.

But *Terror* didn't have power capstans. Standing on the side deck of *Terror*, Seine watched tug and barge bounding up and down in opposite phase. One moment the barge was twenty feet above the tugboat, a sheer wall of black steel, the next the boat rose up as if she might set down right onto *Odyssey*'s back, high and dry.

They worked fast. Seine kept on the boat, with the Buff and Big Man topside on the barge, positioned to accept lines. They set the spring line first, on the boat's forward quarter. The Wolf powered forward to take up slack, Seine reeling in as he did, then snapping the line onto the bitt as fast as he could and standing out of the bight while Irons powered forward against the spring line.

Seine ran aft, coiled the heavy working line on one arm and threw a dead ringer onto the barge cleat, then gave the line a rolling flip and swung it behind the back of the cleat and took his wraps on the H-bitt. The head line came last. "OKAY, THERE WE GO," Irons said. "THREE LINES HARD AND FAST."

Not hard and fast enough for Seine's taste. Too much slack in the spring line made the boat bounce off the barge like a paddle ball on an elastic leash. But the drill ship had stopped drilling to wait for the cargo, and nobody would wait for Seine to be satisfied. They never had before.

He waited on the side deck, timing the insanely rough passage from boat to barge. The barge deck was above him, then below him, then right *there*—and he stepped across calmly, accepting the Big Man's hand.

"Mr. Balance Man! It is good to have you here," cried the Big Man against the wind. They stood on the narrow deck path along the starboard side of all that cargo, and the Big Man patted him on the back. A surge went through Seine, that after all this he'd never see these people again, that moments like this would evaporate, traceless, into his past.

Crane work was absurd drudgery. Seine hated stevedoring, especially in heavy seas, but with the Big Man and Buff he climbed and scampered and played slip-and-slide across ice-laden decks and shipping containers, attaching a four-way rigging onto the corners of each container and then guiding the cargo, away until little by little they emptied the icebreaker.

Seine felt a wild freedom as they chipped the cargo down, even though the job took eighteen hours and never did seem to include Stuart Wanless. Seine would have said something about that but thought maybe he'd said enough to Wanless of late, and besides, he didn't want to make any more trips back to the boat than he had to.

They worked through a windswept day and back into night again, and the winds flew brutally fast across the polar pack, a bitter north wind that gusted to sixty at times and made Seine wish for a warm bed and a bowl of hot soup. When they were left with one last bit of cargo, a ten-foot cylindrical tank of liquid nitrogen, they got the hail sign from the ship, and the deckhands far above them tossed the lines free, letting them flop into the frozen water.

"Those motherfuckers!" the Buff shouted, as they hauled saturated, freezing lines aboard. Even as they laid them flat they could see them start to solidify.

"Why the hell are we breaking off?" Seine asked.

"They say that they do not have room for the tank," said the Big Man. "We will have to pump it to them little by little."

"*Pump* it?" Seine said. "So we gotta stay here? Don't they *realize* what it's like down here?"

The Big Man shrugged.

Truth was, Seine had felt a lurking seasickness ever since they broke free of the push wires, when the boat felt the full force of the up-and-down seas. It had always been his weakness, from the time he was a boy. He knew the drill well: you worked no matter how many times you puked on your shoes. He kept on and wished for ice. Preferably lots of it.

Once *Terror* had motored away from the ship, free of her lines and from the risk of fouling her anchor wires, the flat frozen deck of the icebreaker held only the single tank of liquid nitrogen and a whole lot of accumulating deck ice. Seine noted that *Odyssey* was still holding her starboard list, down slightly by the bow. His first thought was they didn't have enough rock salt and ice bats to possibly get rid of it all.

They took the barge in tow, tethering it out behind them on the tow winch, and went into a holding pattern around the drill ship. They circled in the open windswept seas, while ambient temp dropped to minus 5 degrees F, maybe minus 45 degrees with wind chill. Then they went in for dinner—a hot dinner of vegetable barley soup and pot roast with roasted potatoes and gravy—and as he slid a forkful into his mouth Seine remembered carrying the frozen roasts aboard and then remembered the old woman.

Seine put his fork down and held his head. Seasickness not only made him feel like losing his lunch, it gave him a headache too. Everybody else seemed impervious. Julia worked over a hot stove, did the dishes, then went topside to run the boat. She was working eighteen-hour shifts regularly, making overtime like a madwoman, spelling Irons, cooking, doing the work of two. Seine hadn't a clue where her strength came from, he only knew he had to go to bed.

His last thought was a vague resentment of Wanless, wondering where he was, wondering whether he was doing any work at all. "So where the hell was Wanless through all that?" Seine wanted to know. "We could have used his help out there."

"Oh I'm sure he's one fine fucking stevedore!" laughed the Buff.

When Seine woke up it was the middle of the night and Julia Lew was curled in the bunk below him like a small animal. He watched her while he dressed, careful not to wake her but wanting nothing more than to crawl into bed with her and die there.

He felt no seasickness at all until he saw Stuart Wanless, who as it turned out had his brother's innate facility for enduring rough water. He not only didn't get sick, he was bouncing all over like he'd been re-born. "Great day, isn't it, Henry?"

"Where the hell you been?" Seine asked.

"Wolf didn't want me out there. He said stevedoring required sea-soned hands. I've been doing other things. What they call sanitary, which is just a nice word for cleaning toilets. And *this*—"

Wanless held up a wooden ice bat. He'd been clearing railings and tossing rock salt all over the place. He held the light baseball bat in one hand and looked stronger than Seine felt. "Now I'm off watch! Great day! I love it!"

Seine didn't see what made it so fucking great. For one thing it wasn't day, it was night—the start of a cold long night that wouldn't end until spring. He went topside and found the Wolf steering into the black seas, the forward windows taking sea spray that froze in sheets and now built up inexorably. "I'm in a goddamned igloo here," Irons said.

"I thought Wanless was on ice duty."

"He's been doing the decks. And *you've* been sleeping."

"Well excuse me for taking three hours. What the hell was he doing while we were out slinging pipe?"

"We all got our work, Seine," Irons said.

Jesus Christ, he thought. The image of hanging off the frozen wheel-house at night didn't exactly appeal to Seine's faded sense of adven-ture, but he knew there was no one else. Their watch schedules had been turned inside-out. People worked when work needed to be done, slept whenever they could, made overtime constantly. He went below, made his way into the room for his float suit, and found Julia and Wanless standing there in the middle of the room, separated by about five feet. Julia was sleepy-eyed, wearing only a tee shirt, and Wanless was in his socks and jeans, his hair down in an impressive cascade of golden locks. Seine had to shake his head—it was a surreal scene, not only for the way they stood but because he thought she had just been asleep, that Wanless had been out on deck. He felt lost in time.

"Excuse me," Seine said. "Sorry to disturb. I'm on ice duty."

Wanless glanced at Seine and bit his lower lip. "Can you excuse us, please?"

"I just said excuse me," Seine said. And the way the two stood there—awkward, interrupted, somehow intimate despite standing five feet apart—made everything fall into clear relief. His face burning, Seine reached for his float suit, past Wanless with his bare smooth chest, his long hair, his soft frown looking like it might curl into a sob, his grand mood gone.

Seine shut the door behind him, went out to the galley, and started pulling the float suit on over his boots, which was a big pain in the ass. The float suit was a bulky set of coveralls, lined internally with foam insulation and designed to extend your life overboard by ten or fifteen minutes. Unlike a survival suit, it had no built-in feet but was used for work floatation in extreme cold weather. Finally Seine grew so frustrated by trying to get it on, he just took his boots off and started over, and by then Julia had come out, dressed, and put on a pot of coffee.

"He's been in such a fucking great mood, I guess it makes sense."

"He's not in such a great mood now," she said.

"I noticed. You ought to avoid pity fucks."

She stood over the coffeemaker, which started to drip steaming coffee. "You know something?" she said, as if talking to the coffee. "I suppose I've done some things that a lot of people would judge as bad, but I never felt really bad about them until I met you."

"What do I do, Julia?"

"You're so goddamned transparent. You can't hold back a look, or an edge in your voice, to spare anybody anything. And for some reason I can't understand, I care about what you think."

He zipped the float suit up in front and just sat there. "I'm sorry," he said, not entirely sure what he was apologizing for.

But lurking somewhere under the surface he sensed he did know, even if he couldn't allow himself to put words to reasons. Something deep and old in himself that wouldn't let him or anybody else off the hook, wouldn't leave him no matter how fast he ran or how hard he worked. He had killed a man, he thought, had killed many men, and guilt hovered over him like the fogged vision of judgment.

He grabbed a lineman's belt from the boatswain's locker and climbed topside from the outside now, up that long horrible ladder that seemed to stretch to the sky. The whole way up, one rung at a time, he thought of *Fearless*. He edged his way around the wheelhouse, strapped to the railing. He held an ice bat in one hand and his life in the other, his feet wedged onto the narrow deck—it was more of a lip—that ran all the way around the house. He felt dangled over the ragged windblown stretch of open sea. The bow raised high, then slammed down into the chop, left his stomach in his chest, and nearly knocked him off his perch until he got into the rhythm of it. The lineman's belt gave him some security, but he had no desire to test it. He proceeded to whale on the ice built up on the steel window frame until he broke the bat in half and had to go below for another one. He looked down to see that even at slow ahead they were taking a steady rain of sea spray over their bow. Sheets of subfreezing seawater washed the bow and side decks, and already the layers were starting to form, freezing seas that made walking on deck the crew's primary hazard.

In the boatswain's locker, he not only grabbed another ice bat but checked the supply of rock salt. He rummaged through the various shelves and storage bins but found only a single bag—maybe they had some in the forepeak. When he turned to check there, Julia was standing before him.

"There's something you don't know," she said.

"You don't owe me any explanation."

"For a year after our little affair down the Inside Passage I didn't sleep with anybody."

He searched her eyes, waiting for the shutter to go down. "Why is that?"

"I don't know. I just didn't want to."

"Then why Wanless? Why now?" he asked. To push him away, he thought, to do the one thing that would trouble Seine and to do it right under his nose.

She dipped her head, as if searching the deck for the answer. "He told me he loved me. And he seems so innocent. It seems like the truth."

Seine felt mute and foolish. He remembered the I-love-you game, a sex game on one level, but even at the time he had known there was more to it. Maybe that was all she had ever wanted from anybody—the truth about *I love you*. He felt a rush of affection and would have pulled her close and held her if the Buff hadn't appeared behind her with a worried look on his face, and since Seine had never seen the Buff concerned, much less worried, it got his attention.

"Seine, fast, I need some help in the basement." And then he was gone.

EIGHTEEN

Overboard

There, check it out." The Buff pointed.

They had crawled down into the loud engine room, where they needed to shout to be heard, and in the aft section, back in the depth of the wheel well, where the propeller shafts ran out of the engines and through the hull to the outside, Seine saw the broken weld. "Is that the one Mr. Hanson repaired?"

"Yeah. Which bugs me. Cause I know if Mr. Hanson repaired it, it's gonna be stronger. So that tells me we got an underlying problem. Rudder strut split, and the torque on it running through all this ice is putting a bad stress on that steel hull. But I think there's more. I think it's the shaft. The shaft we didn't change. I think it was bent by that walrus episode."

"I told you it was."

"Yeah, I know, but I didn't figure this kinda pressure on it."

"This is no ice boat, Buff," Seine said.

"It's no *anything* boat! It's a hybrid mongrel piece of shit!" the Buff shouted.

Seine traced the splitting steel, which brought a seepage of water into the bilges not fast, but something they didn't want to leave untended. "It's going to be okay, isn't it? You can weld it?"

"From the inside. But the split's on the outside. I maybe can hold it for as long as we need. But there's the shaft. It's vibrating like a motherfucker, so the stress that's causing the problem is still there."

"I'll string leads," Seine said, and moved forward, pulling the cables off the arc welder, dragging them aft, sweating his ass off inside the float suit. He lit off the welding machine, which made no audible sound over the din of the main engines. Then he left the Buff to weld the splits, and went topside, hot as hell, and stripped off his float suit. He threw on dry coveralls and his Carhartt jacket, with a work vest over that, and went out into the morning light to off-load the damned nitro tank.

Alpha Dog had finally cleared some deck space, and now they wanted the whole tank. Seine kept focusing on his job, saying *the job, my job* over and over as if some sanity would come of it. As they broke tow and took the *Odyssey* back on the hip, Seine peered out the long flat deck to the liquid nitrogen tank. The whole idea of pushing into the frozen Arctic Ocean in order to deliver cargo that hovered at minus 230 degrees F would have struck Seine as funny if it hadn't been so absurdly treacherous. He timed his jump with skill—feeling in his bones what would happen if he fell between barge and boat.

The only thing left on deck besides the nitro tank and the tool van was ten tons of accumulated sea ice along the entirety of the outboard edge. Inboard, mid-deck, lay a thin layer of gravel from the year before, when they'd used the *Odyssey* as the base for the clamshell cranes in the construction of Muktuk Island.

Just as he timed his jump, he heard Stuart Wanless behind him. "Wolf said I should help you off-load this tank," he said.

"Sure you can handle it?"

Stuart didn't reply; he just stared bitterly, bearing his loss openly, so Seine just waved for him to follow onto the empty deck and gave him a hand to grab as he jumped across, the barge coming up hard and slamming him to his knees. On deck they waited for ten minutes before the drill ship's crane swung into position. But the operator just sat up there in his heated cab, shrugging toward them every so often to signal that *something* wasn't ready. "Ain't my fault," he mouthed, and Seine could read his lips perfectly.

The wind howled dry and cold out of the north, and Wanless was back to bouncing up and down, while Seine lifted his arms in a prolonged gesture of question. *"What's going on?"* he called, as if anybody could hear him. Someone shouted down from the deck of the drill ship, something Seine couldn't hear. He cupped his ear toward them and heard a rig worker say, "Pussies!" and then laugh.

Seine heard the loudhailer crackle from the tugboat and ran aft toward the ice-laden form of the tug, leaving Wanless by the nitrogen tank, until he was close enough to hear the Wolf tell him the ship wouldn't swing the crane over until the barge crew had hard hats on.

"Hard hats?" Seine yelled. "We off-loaded for eighteen hours without fucking hard hats! They didn't say anything then!"

"Different shift foreman or something," the Wolf said, with evident fatigue. "OSHA regs, Seine. Anyway, you gotta get hard hats."

OSHA! Now *that* was funny. This whole *operation* was a violation of occupational safety and health. Seine shook his head and stood on the edge, watching the alternating up-and-down motion. He jumped to the foredeck of the tugboat, the motion popping him twenty feet in the air and then dropping with a hard thump that brought impact pain up through both feet and legs and hips and back, in a causal chain of pain.

"Fuck!" He grabbed his ankle. He'd felt it twist, the sharp pain angling from ligaments he could only hope he hadn't torn. He stood up on the icy deck and promptly slipped and fell to his tailbone. "God *damn* it!"

Then Julia was there, extending her hand. "You all right?"

"I'm okay." She helped him to his feet. "Can you salt this deck while I get hard hats?"

"Umm, I could, but we had a little misstep."

"Oh, *great*. What now?"

"Stuart got a little overzealous last night. We're down to one sack of rock salt."

"Shit!" Seine brushed past her, nearly knocking her over before he caught himself and then her. "Sorry. I'm sorry."

"It's okay. I'm all right."

He held her shoulders an instant and felt the frustration ease a bit, watching the dark pools of her eyes, thinking he could climb right inside them, enter an alternate reality, find everything he'd been missing.

Then he went inside the boatswain's locker for hard hats.

"Get one for me too," she called after him. "I'll give you guys a hand."

Five minutes later, carrying a hard hat in each hand and one on his head, he made his way forward to where Julia and Wanless now stood on the open barge deck, hiding downwind of the nitro tank. Last time he'd been in the wheelhouse the anemometer had been bouncing all over, tracking gusts between 40 and 60.

Seine jammed his own hat down onto his head and snapped the liner into place to keep it from blowing off. He gave Julia one, then Stuart. Stuart fumbled with the orange plastic hat. "How's it work?" Wanless said. "I've never worn one of these." Seine noticed he had no gloves on, and his fingers showed blue on their tips.

Seine had little patience for Wanless about then; in fact, given his choice in an amoral universe, he might have just shoved him overboard and let him sink into the ice water between the barge and the drill ship. He hated him for many reasons now: the rock salt, and Julia, and being related to that fucker the Chemist, and looking like a girl, and for being innocent and friendly and for not knowing how to put on a goddamned hard hat.

Wanless finally got the hard hat on, but ineptly; it tilted to one side and he couldn't seem to get the liner buttoned. Even as the crane hoisted the tank into the air, he was still fiddling with the thing. They had three tag lines tied to the tank, to steady it in the gusting winds, and just as the crane operator swung the tank toward the edge, Wanless let go of his line to grab his hat. The hard hat caught air and sailed fifteen feet straight up, then dived and slammed to the deck and skidded off toward the edge. "Leave it!" Seine yelled, but Wanless was already gone, scrambling after it, leaving his end of the tank to swing hard right.

Seine yelled again, but Wanless just kept on running, and it looked to Seine that he was about to hit the icy deck and slide right on overboard. So he too dropped his tag line and took off after Wanless, while on the windward side, Julia held tight to her tag line, not seeing what was happening, leaning way back on flat feet trying to hold the tank steady, yelling, "What are you *doing*? *Help* me, goddamnit—!"

The crane operator, trying to do just that, dropped the tank abruptly from five feet off the deck, slamming it onto a barge cleat that popped the tank open on a seam. Liquid nitrogen spewed from the split, sending vapors billowing in a frozen fog downwind of Julia.

Wanless finally got to his hat. He grabbed it, stood upright, and turned to look in triumph at Seine, who was himself trying like hell to stop and finding nothing beneath his feet but ice. He went down hard, his momentum carrying him past Wanless, arms flailing for Wanless's leg before he realized he'd drag Wanless overboard too. So he passed that chance by and managed to rotate onto his belly while sliding fast, and went over the side like a slippery fish.

Both hands clawed for a hold on the edge, and for a moment he thought he could hold himself there, hang like Jimmy Stewart in *Vertigo*, but the edge was gone in an instant and he saw a flash of black hull and then he was under water in a rush.

Seawater surrounded him—subfreezing but still liquid. He surfaced—but without a float suit, barely. The small work vest rode up around his ears. Still he felt no sensation of cold, which surprised him, and he became aware then of the weight of his steel-toed boots. He thought of getting free of them, but cast it off as too time-consuming. He scanned the barge hull for a quick way out. He heard a voice call out from the ship, which rose forty feet above him in a straight wall of orange steel.

Two deckhands craned their heads over and started lowering a line. Julia yelled, *"All stop! All stop!"* up to the ship in an effort to keep Seine from being sucked into their wheels.

But the ship's propellers didn't worry Seine. He knew the real danger was both more immediate and much further out of anybody's control—the simple reality of cold water. Julia poked her head over the side, and then the face of a sheepish Stuart Wanless appeared next to her. Seine reached his hand for a line lowered over the side of the ship, saw then that it was crooked, a frozen deck line that carried an immense curving S within its bight, and it hung there five feet out of reach, with the deckhands above holding it by the bitter end.

"Henry, swim back to the rung ladder, swim back along the barge," Julia called down to him.

"I'm waiting for this line," he said, but somehow his voice had no power to lift itself up and out of the narrow space between the two vessels. He felt like he was swimming between two skyscrapers, had never felt so goddamned small except maybe during that night he'd spent floating in the Gulf of Alaska.

The seas pitched him between the side shells, subfreezing water lifting him, dropping him, yet oddly carrying no chill. He licked his lip and tasted salt water. He watched as the drill ship deckhands tied another line to the first, and then they lowered the line all the way to him. He hooked his arm through the frozen eye and then promptly pulled the line right out of their hands. It fell in a frozen heap, rattling and crashing the water all around him and on top of his head, that old line about hard hats running through his mind, the one Anchorage longshoremen liked so much, that wearing a hard hat didn't do any good if you really got *sacked;* it was only good for a handy way to scoop you up afterward.

But the Anchorage longshoremen were wrong—the hat saved his life, even though he was battered senseless in the process. He floated for a few seconds, and now Julia was above him, screaming at him, while Seine thought, *I'm okay, I'm okay, I'm just resting.*

"Henry Seine, get your ass astern!" she shouted. *"Right now! Now!"*

"I'm just resting," he said, and only when he tried to speak aloud did he realize that his face lay in the water.

"I said right fucking now!" Julia screamed. *"Time's up! Time to get out of that water!"*

He lifted his head, saw her face up there, so small and tiny and worried, and so he took a stroke backward, floating on his back, his head dizzy, his ears ringing. He took another stroke, and saw the Big Man appear next to Julia carrying a fire ax, and he started chopping at a coil of barge line that had frozen to the deck five days before.

Seine paddled back still farther.

"There. There!" Julia yelled, and he looked up at the barge and saw the rung ladder, set into the side shell. He reached a slippery gloved hand up to it, and marveled at the way the seawater solidified on contact with the frozen air. He saw his own breath erupt in clouds of hanging fog, felt ice freezing his eyes shut, and then he pulled himself out.

Or tried to. He realized how bad his wrists and hands were when he couldn't feel his hands to pull, then realized that it wasn't his carpal tunnel but his entire body. He had no strength to pull himself out. And he promptly fell back into the water and just bobbed there. He reached up and hooked his elbow through the first rung, still up to his chest in frigid water.

"Can you pull yourself up?" Julia asked.

"No. But I can hang here until hell freezes over."

"I think it's already done that," Julia said with a sharp sardonic laugh, and then she was scampering down the ladder with a line looped around her shoulder, trailing back up the barge.

She put her arms around him to tie a quick-and-dirty French bowline under his butt, dipping her soft arms into the cold water. She ran the second eye up under his armpits, adjusted it for tension, and then Seine felt himself flying, bounding past her and leaving her there on the ladder, falling away below him.

Flying.

Thank God for Julia, he thought; *thank God she's saved me again,* and he looked up to see the Big Man's arms working, pulling him hand over hand, hoisting him into the gray sky. Thank God for the Big Man, thank God for his shipmates. Everything moved fast then. The Big Man lifted him to the deck and dragged him to his feet, two hands under his armpits. He stood Seine up like a mason righting a fallen statue, and then released him and grabbed at him as he fell over. "I can't feel my legs."

"What *can* you feel, Mr. Seine?" asked the Big Man, holding him up.

"Fear," Seine said.

He had been overboard for a little over five minutes, and he was still not out of danger. His lips curled blue as he spoke. "I shoulda had my float suit on," he said, only forming half of each word. His head spun,

his vision went spotted like a snow flurry and then washed over completely.

Julia hauled herself up over the barge side and barked at the Big
Man. "Get him under his arms, we'll take his legs," and Wanless joined
in. They moved him fifteen feet taking shuffling baby steps, when the
Big Man set him down and said, "Step back. There is an easier way,"
and he grabbed Seine by an arm and threw him over his shoulders in
a fireman's carry, groaning the entire way. He carried Seine to the end
of the boat, where he made one long lone step down to the side deck
of *Terror*. "Ohhhhhh," he groaned as he moved in long strides down
the side deck and into the passage before the main deck head, where
he crumpled and held his back, crying out, "I have blown my back
out—ohhhh!" as he dropped Seine to the deck in a heap.

Seine experienced the impact as a vague vibration in his bones and
the sound of his own body hitting the deck like a pair of wet jeans
flopping on concrete. Then he heard a scraping as Julia and the Buff
dragged him like a limp cold carcass into the main deck shower.

"Keep it cold," Julia said, reaching in to feel the water spray. "Bring
it up slowly."

Seine slumped to the shower floor, saw out the door to where Stuart Wanless stood peeking in like a little boy. Seine felt the water strike
his face and his body with a distant sensation of spray. Julia stood over
him, getting wet from the spattering shower, herding the others out of
the bathroom and closing the door on Wanless. "Shit, Henry. Shit!"
she said, turning.

"I'm okay. I think I'm okay."

And she inched the shower to warm. And then toward hot, until
steam rose all around him, and he watched her sit back on the toilet
seat and hold her head while his skin turned pink from the shower
spray. She took a deep breath and visibly quaked, as if her nerves were

shaking off excess energy. "That's twice," she said, looking directly at him.

Then she locked the door, and he watched in stunned ecstasy while she unsnapped the shoulder straps of her denim overalls and let them fall to the floor. A moment later, she stepped into the shower with him, drawing him to his feet as if he were light as air. Then she engulfed him in her warm, wet body, and felt the cold drain out of him. "Two bodies are warmer than one," she said, and shivered against his skin. And then they kissed. Her mouth was warm, he thought, warmer than melted butter.

Hot Soup

An hour later Julia fed him hot soup and hot chocolate and then leaned over and kissed him again. Her touch made him delirious, pumping adrenaline until his fingertips tingled. "You're just doing that to keep me from freezing," he said.

"Yes." She smiled. "That's exactly what I'm doing."

He sat on the edge of her bunk drinking beef broth and letting the electric wall heater glow orange a solid twenty minutes, and still he felt a chill. An hour had passed since they'd hauled him out, and when Julia came in with a thermometer she'd dug out of the middle-deck first-aid kit, his temperature was still only 95.5. "I think you're out of the woods," she said. "But you're gonna feel like you ran a marathon when you wake up."

"I feel like I ran one right now."

"Let's get more food in you. Little at a time."

So she sat next to him, her hair still damp from the shower, her clothes changed, and she draped a wool blanket from her bunk over his shoulders. The blanket smelled like her, and he let his nose fall to her shoulder to breathe in her scent. He swirled with associations—rum down the Inside Passage, sex in a hail of I-love-yous. His mind raced backward and forward in time like a runner in a psychological trench war.

"Lie back and rest, Henry."

As she stood up, he reached for her, felt the hard curve of her hip-bone and the soft turn of her waist. He pulled her to his lap, his arms enfolding her. "I have dreams about you. We're floating in the Great Salt Lake, in warm salt water."

When she kissed him, her mouth relaxed, lips opening, tasting him. She drew his tongue into her mouth and suckled it, a circle of sensation that sent a bolt down his spine, where it exploded at his groin.

"Let me go now," she said, and stood up. But he didn't want to let her go now. He finally had her before him and he wanted to taste every inch of her—for pleasure, for purpose, like food.

"Not yet," she said, as if reading his mind, and then eased his head back to the pillow. "Later."

He felt the chill of his still-wet hair against his own scalp, and a shiver ran down through him. He looked up to see her, but instead there was Cliff the Cook. *Ya got yourself a clear conscience, Henry Seine? Ya need a clear conscience if ya expect to sleep good.*

"I don't know," he mumbled, and then he was out.

He awakened sometime later, he didn't know how long, to a nudge on his shoulder, and a steaming bowl of spaghetti with meat sauce, sprinkled with parmesan cheese, and Julia sat next to him on a chair while he devoured it with a warm mug of broth as a chaser. She just watched him eat. He could hear the voices of the crew, muffled by the closed door. Her face was as warm as the food. And then he was out again.

He wasn't sure if he dreamed it or if he awakened slightly, but he was sure that night had fallen when he heard the shaft brakes squeak and begin their job, the working rumble of main engines, and the work calls from out on deck, the footfalls of the Buff and Big Man, and the pattering steps of Stuart Wanless trying to catch up. And then the shaft brakes ended, and there was only the dull monotonous roar of the mains, the persistent vibration of that bum shaft, the grinding of ice, the rumble of far-off thunder.

Sometime late in the night she came to bed, crawled next to him in the single bunk too small for two. She curled on the wall side, wedged herself there, her small, muscular body clinging to his, and slept. Just when he awakened to her touch, he couldn't have said, nor did he care. Time had no meaning now. Her skin was at once smooth as polished stone and soft as summer sand. His eyes barely opened, his body responded to the warmth and the wetness of her mouth surrounding him, drawing him into her in a long ecstatic slide. "Julia, Julia—" he said, his brain rising out of ice fog.

TWENTY

Iceteroids

The renewed squeal of the shaft brakes awakened him while it was still dark outside. His entire body felt stiff, every muscle as if he'd exercised it to exhaustion the day before. As he hauled himself out of bed, he heard shouts and the crackle of the loudhailer, the Wolf's voice amplified and blaring into distortion. "MAKE HER FAST MAKE HER FAST!"

Seine pulled aching joints up the dimly lit tower, spiraling topside, the stiffness in his legs and hips easing as his blood began to flow. He entered the wheelhouse to find it dead black save for the tiny lamp over the chart table, the glowing faces of radios and controls, and Irons himself.

"We got ice shear all along the north side of the drill ship. We gotta fend her off. Man the spot."

Seine tracked the spotlight up the starboard side, through a thickening snowstorm that blew out of the darkness and slashed across them at a horizontal. One moment Seine could see the figures of Wanless and Julia, huddled a football field away on the bow of *Odyssey;* the next moment they disappeared behind a wall of white.

"Where's the Buff?"

"Basement. Got a little *leak* problem, he finally informs me." Irons pointed north by east toward a wall of ice. "Now *that!*"

Irons jammed both engines forward.

"Iceteroids!" Julia yelled over the radio, and Seine could hear the smile in her voice. She liked it here, he could tell; she was more like the Wolf than she would ever admit. She liked iceteroids and icebreaker barges and the rush of everything urgent and necessary.

Like the old video game Asteroids, iceteroids involved protecting the mother ship against methodical attack.

They anchored the *Odyssey* a half mile off in the open water and ran around light, *Terror* alone maneuvering into position and shoving ice off the drill ship.

The blowing snow eased off then, and like a shutter flying open Seine caught a glimpse into the blackness, a craggy array of ice floes and pressure ridges, stacked up against each other, riding atop one another in slabs of flat ice that were now setting down on the north side of *Alpha Dog.* Over the radio they heard Julia cry, "Watch that one!" and Irons bellowed, "Good God!" before shoving full ahead around the north side of the ship, shoving ice away from its pointed bow.

The ship's radioman came over VHF, warning Irons they had two miles of drill pipe shoved into the ground at that moment, and *Terror* had better keep the ice off them.

Irons picked up the microphone, barked, "Roger that!" and tossed the mike aside.

Through shifting visibility, Seine again caught sight of Wanless and Julia. They had moved to the boat, were now crouching behind the bow railing of *Terror,* almost directly below him. Wanless wore sunglasses to protect his eyes from blowing snow, and with a wool scarf wrapped around his face, the tail whipping downwind, he looked like the Invisible Man. Seine laughed inside himself until he heard Julia Lew say, *"Oh, God, all stop! Back on two, back on two!"*

And there before them it looked as if somebody had parked the White Cliffs of Dover off their starboard bow.

"Iceberg," Julia said into the radio. "Big one."

"We don't get icebergs in these waters, Lew."

But there was no mistaking it. Tabular icebergs were the monstrosities of the polar seas, and this one looked to be a pretty good specimen, appearing magically out of a false horizon, five hundred feet off the drill ship's forward anchor wires.

Irons powered full blast toward it, the impotence of his scream of *"Goddamnit!"* striking Seine as hard as they themselves struck the iceberg.

The push knees of *Terror* made a blunt hit on the berg's east side and bounced off, one knee crumping from the pressure, as Irons applied full power into the iceberg's side for five minutes, the wheels of *Terror* sucking chunks of ice and grinding them up, vibration rattling through them as if the boat would come flying apart all at once. Turbochargers sang out in a whine that rose above the roar of the main engines.

Seine directed the fluttering spotlight straight across at the berg's side, a gnarled, craggy palisade of white ice. In the wheelhouse, ceramic coffee cups jumped and bounded across the console. Irons shoved full ahead until the Buff came over the intercom, yelling, "Let off or you're gonna smoke my mains!"

But Irons just clicked the intercom off to shut him up and then punched forward on the throttle levers even though they were both pegged. Still the berg shoved them backward toward the drill ship. Swinging the spotlight back behind them, Seine saw the collision coming. "We got a problem," he said, nodding toward the ship.

Irons turned. They were fifty feet from being shoved into the forward anchor wires—and maybe a minute from being slammed against the ship itself.

"Wolf, you gotta back outa here," Seine said.

He reached for the radio to warn the drill ship.

"Goddamnit, don't touch that!" Irons snapped.

"We're gonna get pinched here. Back out!"

"*Motherfucker!*" Irons screamed, realizing Seine was right. He jammed both engines to neutral, then straight back hard on two, the tug responding sluggishly at first, then gaining momentum she powered her way out of the jam. They floated there, all stop, and stared like failures at the great white face of the tabular berg. It was a testament to human impotence that the *Terror* pushing or not pushing seemed to make no difference at all.

The berg moved inexorably until it was afoul of the anchor wires. When the first wire snapped it went like a guitar string, the two-inch steel cable quivering faster and faster until it oscillated at a thousand cycles a second and then just flew apart, one end flailing over the ice water toward *Terror*. Seine and Irons ducked instinctively as the wire slapped at the deckhouse below them like a horsetail flog, gouging half-inch troughs in the steel bulkhead.

"For the love of Pete!"

They lay sideways to the ship, parallel and downwind of it now, inside a snow-shadow, affording better visibility. Seine peered down and saw Julia and Wanless flat on their bellies behind the bow railing, then watched out the side window as the tabular berg fouled the ship's remaining anchor wires, bending them inward, drawing the entire drill ship downward as if it might just lever it underwater and walk right over it. The second anchor wire gave way with an explosive crack, and then the third—and then the ship seemed to leap from the water like a toy in a very cold bathtub.

The ship settled back into the water, with shouts coming from all along her decks as the crew peered tentatively from the bulwarks, the massive slab of ice pressing into them. One man stuck his arms out and pushed while his shipmates shook their heads and laughed at the futility of it.

They still had five anchor wires out, and the berg leaned into the ship and shoved her over. The hull raised out of the water, then listed horribly to port, and Seine heard shouting and screaming from all along the high hull, and no one joked about pushing the berg away; they were too busy running for their lives.

Just as it seemed the ship would capsize, Seine saw the remaining five anchor wires fall to the water as the crew above jettisoned them with maybe a second to spare.

Anchorless, the ship bounced off the tabular berg, heeled, then settled into the water and sat there like a stunned boxer taking a standing eight-count. Her work lights illuminated the ship from stem to stern. Without anchors, she couldn't drill anymore. If *this* was any indication of the difficulties in drilling for oil this far out, Seine thought, he for one would just start riding a bike everywhere he went.

The drill supervisor had thought fast, though, and activated the emergency shear mechanism set on the ocean floor. This shut down the flow of oil and the drill string—the length of drill pipe from ship's bottom to ocean floor—dropped, a long limp sacrifice that avoided a blowout.

After ten minutes cartwheeling against the constantly shifting ice, *Alpha Dog* radioed *Terror* and informed them of what *Terror* already knew. The operation was finished. The drill ship powered up and swung south, sliding like a freight train out of a railyard, except that it was gone so fast it made Seine's eyes hurt trying to track it. Within five minutes it had receded into the night blizzard and disappeared.

Irons sat at his stool, *Terror* floating adrift while the tabular berg ground past their port beam. Smaller ice swirled all around, knocking against their hull, turning them slowly, their rotation tracked by the slow movement of the spotlight as it panned across the icebound night.

"Jesus Christ," Irons said. "About shot my wad on that one." He spoke deliberately, showing no haste whatever.

Everything moved in slow motion but the wind.

"You hear anything from that Moneymaker guy?" Irons asked.

"No," Seine said. He reached up to the radio and spun the dial to seek.

Irons looked wholly unsatisfied, as if he'd only managed to fuck things up even more than they were before he took the boat away from Captain Fuck. He let the ice bounce them around while he stared into the night and Seine tuned the sideband.

Irons finally turned and hunched over a nautical chart, using parallels and a compass to inscribe circles on a white expanse of chart representing unknown details in a frozen ocean.

A limpness spread through Seine's body, but his mind was clear and alert as he spied the radios and listened for Moneymaker. "Where are we?" Seine asked.

"My last position fix is there." Irons pointed to the chart table, where calculations had been scrawled in a hurried pencil. "They correspond to our SatNav—so far."

"What now?"

"Well, we see if we can contact your guy again. All this excitement I haven't paid any attention."

Seine couldn't stop the flow of warm thoughts, floating fantasies in the Great Salt Lake. In this way he started to doubt the entire enterprise, especially since he hadn't seen the Shade of Marco Barn in more than three days. Nothing like an insane situation to bring out a sane reaction, he thought.

He tuned the single-sideband to 2182 kHz but heard nothing, so he scanned to pick up what he could of Moneymaker and got nothing but white noise with occasional disruptive static. "He's gone. I can't raise him."

Irons stepped over and played with the sideband for a minute, grimacing and snorting. His face was drawn and pale, and he looked every bit of his sixty years. "Could be in a skip zone."

"Or he could be right next to us. The fact is, we have no idea *where* he is."

Seine stood before the Wolf, pondering whether to say what was spinning through his head, that they should maybe reconsider about Moneymaker, give him up as lost and head south like the drill ship. And all at once the truth about himself and those moments with his father and with the Chemist and the Indonesian stevedores came clear. His conscience would take him only so far, and then he would find himself in this position, now just as then. *Time to back off. This is where you always back off—you come close and say the right things and do the right things and then back off and that's why people die.*

He didn't know whose voice it was inside him; it sounded like his own now, but the words were those of his father, the Chemist, Marco Barn. Maybe it was little more than the voice of logic descending: *If the Canadian Coast Guard doesn't know where he is, what makes you think you do?*

The difference was that this time he couldn't step off the dock and wave good-bye to his father or take the survival suit and go overboard into the Gulf. There were other people involved, people he'd stirred to an emotional action, people braver and crazier than he was, and they wouldn't back down now—not Irons, he knew.

That's because he's willing to die here, said the voice.

Irons sneezed then, and gave himself a nosebleed. "Aw, for chris-sakes!" and he pulled a handkerchief from his pocket and held it against his face.

"What do you think about this anyway? This Moneymaker thing?" Seine said.

The Wolf eyed him, holding the nose as he talked. In a nasal, wolfy murmur, he asked, "What, you getting cold feet?"

"Cold body," Seine said, and tried a weak laugh.

Irons didn't share the humor. "That's bullshit. You of all people, Seine. You know what it's like—I seen you. Mid-Gulf salvaging that towboat last year. And now, goddamnit, running after Wanless to save his faggot ass—you didn't think about it, you just *did* it."

"To be honest with you, it's thinking that's usually saved my bacon."

"Well then maybe there's more important things."

"I know. I just don't know what they are."

"Well I do! The thing made Julia run her cute little tush down that rung ladder with a line to save your ugly butt! Or the Big Man busting his back hauling you out. That's the thing! That's why this place is better than any safe goddamned office. Now lookit here."

Irons nodded toward the chart table, refusing to wait for any kind of protest, maybe because he knew he'd won and maybe because he knew he hadn't.

"We both know radio signals are all over the map up here. So I plotted this: a circle of uncertainty with a twenty-mile radius. I figure based on your two RDF readings, plus set and drift over these past few days, we got an eighty-percent chance he's somewhere in there. So we're gonna drive ourselves through ice right up the gut of this circle, and when we're out of this skip zone we're gonna take new readings off the RDF and adjust our course as necessary. And we're gonna find this Moneymaker character if I have to chase Flaw Island to the fricking North Pole!" he shouted.

Blood sprayed out his nose, but he didn't seem to notice. He seemed to notice Seine instead, as if for the first time. He stopped shouting and seemed to calm instantly.

"Now you buck up."

"I'm all right. I'll be all right."

"Good! You had whatcha call momentary fantods!" Irons laughed. "It's this fricking boat. It's got doom written all over it. But we're gonna beat that. Gonna rewrite it like bad graffiti on a bathroom wall, by God!"

Seine didn't know how to fight Irons—he was doing it all over again, getting himself deeper into a spot; he could feel the jam coming but couldn't seem to stop it. Just as he did something positive to purge the ghosts, they came out in legions, running up stairways, chirping on radios, dancing in midair to taunt him with his own stupidity, voices squeaky on sideband: *You're gonna die, fucker; you're gonna die, fool!*

He saw a thousand things wrong with Irons's plan. For one thing, the RDF lines were now three and four days old. For another, the set and drift Irons was talking about was completely unreliable, given ice shear and shifting weather.

As Seine turned to the chart table and surveyed the scattered array of notes Irons had made, he decided he'd learned nothing in his life. He traced parallels out to the center of the circle, then spun back to look forward. "Heading zero-zero-two," he said. "That's our first course. Let's take it for five minutes, then take another reading."

"All right!" Irons bellowed, and slapped him on the back. "Now let's go hump some bergy bits."

Seine only hoped the bergy bits didn't hump them.

They retrieved the *Odyssey,* wired up behind her, and broke ice for five hours into the purple dawn, rising to gray skies, sliding up leads and slamming flat sections, the bow of the breaker riding onto the sea ice and sinking down to break through in a rolling thunderous rhythm that got them five miles in less than an hour, and out of the radio blackout of the skip zone. The ionosphere was kind to them then—they heard Moneymaker for the first time in three days.

TWENTY-ONE

The Night Effect

S eine was stooping over the chart table, drawing a new circle, when Moneymaker faded in over sideband as if he hadn't stopped talking all that time:

"*. . . we were taking core samples from the center of the ice island when we noticed the fissure running through it, and every day we went back to that spot and measured its progress until it became apparent it was going to break in half. But none of us were prepared for the catastrophic nature of it, explosion after explosion. First it split in half and began to roll; two men were killed instantly, crushed by half a berg flipping over to find a new state of balance—a rushing grinding explosion of bergs calving bergs. On the eighteenth of September before a westerly gale, grinding past more pack ice, ice island NP-32 disintegrated to a tenth of its original size. No mistake, it's still gargantuan, but by the minute it melts out from under me while I freeze to death on its surface.*"

The Wolf manned the wheel with about ten inches of toilet paper shoved up one nostril. He picked up the mike. "Flaw Island, this is tug *Terror*, over."

"TUG *TERROR*! WHOOOOOOOOO! TUG *TERROR*!" Moneymaker screamed, his voice distorting through the scratchy speakers. "You're the first person I've heard in two weeks. Two weeks! My satellite navigation equipment is out; my radio is barely functional; my position is unknown, repeat unknown—"

"You just hold onto your shorts there, all right? We're making our way toward you. We got a little night effect that gets in the way of radio transmissions, so we lost you there for a bit."

When Irons looked at him, Seine was already on the RDF, jotting the bearing on a pad of paper. But the RDF was bouncing like the digital readout on a pinball machine.

"We got an RDF line on you like right now," the Wolf said. "Long as you keep talking we can adjust for any error."

"I got nothing solid," Seine said. "It's swinging all over."

"Take an average and redraw the circle," Irons said.

As Seine went to the chart table, the Buff burst into the wheelhouse. "We got one fuck of a problem downstairs."

Nobody paid any attention. Seine was manipulating triangles and compass, while Irons was trying to get Moneymaker to buck up. "You're gonna be A-okay, friend, you're gonna be A-okay."

"If you don't mind an observation, that's one hell of an easy thing for you to say," Moneymaker said.

"Who's that? That him? Lemme talk to him!" the Buff said, and picked up the mike. "Yo, Moneymaker! You got a first name?"

"Louis."

"Okay, Louis. This here is Buff Errol. Here's the deal. Keep your sorry ass talking. Say anything you fucking want, we don't give a shit, only don't expect us to talk back and hold your goddamned hand. Tell us your whole miserable life story—and make it good or we won't come save your skinny ass!"

"I have a Ph.D. in geology, you know. I'm not some idiot out here."

The Buff laughed. "You hear this guy? Guy like this oughta stick to a college campus." He clicked open the mike. "Don't you get it? Anybody lost in the arctic's an idiot by definition!"

Seine went back to the RDF to take a new reading, found the digital readout showing a completely new bearing, and wondered if they hadn't changed direction radically since his last. Radio direction finders expressed a bearing to any radio signal they were tuned to, but the bearing was relative to the heading of the vessel, so maybe they'd rotated since the last readout. "Looks to me like he's east now," Seine said to Irons. "Swinging east."

"East?" Irons said. He checked his gyrocompass—070, but swinging in 10-degree increments. Gyros lost considerable reliability above about 72 degrees north. "How far east?" Irons wanted to know.

"One-two-five degrees. Tell Wanless to look for leads there."

"We pass right by him or what? How the hell could he be east? We were barely into the circle."

"Last reading says east by south."

Meantime, Irons used his rudders only to make a broad sweeping circle, keeping full ahead on both engines, moaning the entire time how goddamned sluggish the steering on this tub of shit was. Then he adjusted their heading east and again they were pounding ice, shoving whole sections ahead of them at slow ahead, then finding a lead and sprinting at full power until the Buff finally told him that the sluggish steering was why he'd come up to begin with. He was almost sure that they'd lost the starboard rudder.

"Lost a rudder! You gotta be shitting me! No wonder this thing's handling like a station wagon."

"I'm having a hell of a time keeping this sucker from springing leaks, Bob."

"Leaks? What the hell's *that* about?"

"Same deal. It's all related. I'm talking about a weld split right down the line of that rudder strut that won't seal to save my ass. I've welded it three times and it keeps breaking past the weld. It's split from the outside, and I'm patching it from the inside. Like puttin' a Band-Aid on a stab wound."

"You better seal it to save your ass! And if you won't do that, then seal it to save *my* ass!"

And the Buff ran downstairs again.

"Jesus, what kinda shit is that?" Irons said to himself, and was surprised to hear Julia.

"The bad kind?" She stood at the top of the stairs, looking wrung out. "I heard. Let me help."

"You should sleep more. You ain't slept in three days, near as I can tell."

"Hey, a solid two hours. I'm like brand-new."

Irons smirked at her with more affection than Seine had ever seen him express to anybody. "All right. Then talk to Wanless. See what he sees out there. I can't see shit."

Wanless could evidently hear Julia, but nobody could hear Wanless, whose voice came in a garbled flood of howling wind.

"Seine," Irons barked, "I need you out there. Take another radio and you two take up positions on either side of the bow, and tell the kid to get his radio mike inside his shirt so I can hear him."

So Seine nodded and pulled another handheld radio from the drawer under the chart table and then briefly put his hand to Julia's back, where she stood over the chart. She glanced up only after he moved for the spiral stairs, going down to gear up.

"All right, Lew," he heard Irons say. "Take another RDF reading."

Then the fuzz of Moneymaker came and went.

"We're in a skip zone again," Julia said.

"For the love of *God*!"

* * *

On the pointed bow of the icebreaker barge, Seine and Wanless settled on opposite sides, facing away from each other. In his float suit Seine hunkered and stared east by south, the wind raking sideways across his eyeballs. Even with a pair of safety goggles he'd retrieved from the tool van and a ski mask he'd found in the boatswain's locker, tears formed in his eyes and froze before they got to his eyelids, and before long he couldn't even blink.

Seine did a radio check with Wanless, who said, "I thought it wasn't supposed to be this goddamned cold when it snows!"

"This isn't falling snow—it's ground blizzard."

Wanless didn't reply, just clicked his mike open and closed, indicating he didn't want to talk. Even though the kid was only fifty feet away across the barge deck, Seine could barely make him out, but by the way he held himself Seine could tell he'd entered survival mode now. Seine leaned against the anchor winch to shield himself from the blow and looked forward, heard the Wolf's voice: "Hang on for a minute, Seine, we're still in a skip zone."

Blackout. Whiteout. Another skip zone gave Seine the idea that they were actually too close to hear him, and it gave him the idea to check for Moneymaker on the the short-range VHF. He reached down and peeled his glove off and switched his handheld to emergency channel 16, and there, crisp as a northern dawn, came the frost-weakened voice of Louis Moneymaker, saying, "MAYDAY, MAYDAY, MAYDAY, this is research station NP-32 Flaw Island, NP-32 Flaw Island—"

"I got him! I got him on VHF!" Seine shouted, but Wanless didn't react. He clicked open the mike and repeated, "Flaw Island, Flaw Island, this is tug *Terror,* over."

Seine waited. No answer. He felt a tingle of anticipation, then repeated, "Flaw Island, Flaw Island, this is tug *Terror,* over."

But he got no reply. He curled into a tuck position to conserve heat and pulled one glove off to change back to their working channel, but in his haste he felt the wind grab the glove and send it fifty feet aft, scattering along the deck and then blowing overboard. He watched it go with longing, with neither the time nor the ability to go after it. "Wolf, I got him! Channel sixteen, VHF. He can't hear me, but I can hear him."

"That's good! If you heard him on a handheld he can't be more than a couple of miles."

Seine went over to Wanless and shouted over the blow, *"We made contact with him! Why don't you go in?"*

"Don't think I can hack it out here?" Wanless stared at Seine with pain in his eyes, a petulant anger that made Seine bristle.

"Wise up! You see where you are here?"

"Not exactly a tourist destination!"

"Fine. Whatever you want, Stuart."

Seine peered out toward the gray offing that swirled in blowing snow, a horizontal slash of hard snow that peppered him and forced him to duck his eyes to see. The horizon light appeared and disappeared, formed and re-formed until he felt like everything he saw had to be a hallucination. He felt the vessel swing again. He looked over the side and there, five feet down from the barge edge, was the ocean. Five feet of freeboard? God! A bolt of fear stabbed through him. He clicked open his mike. "Look, Wolf, we gotta do something about this list. We're *way* down by the bow, a good eight feet, I'd say. You can't tell from the wheelhouse cause you can't see anything but blowing snow, but this sucker is down to starboard by a good eight feet."

All at once it seemed the *Odyssey* was sinking.

Somehow Moneymaker sounded worse over the short-range high-frequency radio, if only because the transmission was clearer and revealed in his voice a ragged weakness. "I got a problem," he croaked.

"What's your problem?" Julia asked.

"I can't see now. I been staring at ice. I haven't eaten in three days."

"Jesus Christ," Irons said. He reached for the SSB to radio the Canadian outfit in Tuk, but he got no reply. He had no idea if the message found its way to anybody, or if the radio waves just bounded out into space. He tried the drill ship *Alpha Dog* then, found her cruising into port at Barrow. "We'll relay a message," they told him. "Doubtful any air rescue can be mounted in this weather, but there may be commercial breakers in your vicinity, over."

Frankly, they were getting blown out; he had no idea of the direction or velocity of their set and drift, only that it was significant—maybe huge.

Julia paused in her talk with Moneymaker and turned to check the SatNav, swinging the readout to where Irons could see it glowing. "No way!" Irons said.

Julia shrugged.

"Listen," Irons said into the sideband. "Our SatNav is reading out at sixty-two degrees thirteen minutes north and"—Irons paused, barely able to say it because he couldn't believe it—"and one hundred seventy-nine degrees forty-two minutes *east!*" He closed off his mike and looked at Julia. "The eastern fucking hemisphere? You think we've blown six hundred miles in the twelve hours since we left the drill ship?"

"I don't know. Seems unlikely."

"Do you have a satellite navigation fix, over?"

"Yeah!" Irons said. "SatNav's got us eighteen miles inland running due south into central Siberia, but all I see is ice!"

Irons scanned what did for the horizon, which was no horizon at all—not even a false one. His visibility was maybe two hundred feet.

Julia took up the VHF and said, "You just hang tight, now, Louis, just hang tight. The fact that we're talking right now over VHF means we're close, real close. We just need to find you through this weather."

"I've had nothing *but* weather," Moneymaker said.

Irons was left to jockey and push, ease off and swing around toward the south, watching his gyrocompass start a slow spin—

"He's east of us now. East-southeast," Julia said.

"Don't give me that shit. He can't be. What's he got, a hovercraft, for chrissakes?"

"There's bears around," Moneymaker said over the VHF. "White ones!"

TWENTY-TWO

Great Circles

Through the gray day, everything around Seine came in a rake of driving snow squall and swirling ice. Cut off from Moneymaker, cut off from navigation and sideband and RDF, he felt a brooding isolation sweep over him, realizing in all his sensory deprivation just how Far Out they were. Electronics had failed them, celestial navigation was impossible without something to take a fix off, and the barge was listing, down another foot by Seine's estimation. He wanted the Buff to take a look at the internal tank to see if they hadn't punched a hole in it, so he ran aft on a gale that blew him onto the ice-laden boat.

Snow and ice had built up to a solid six inches along the bulwarks of the side deck, Seine squeezing, slipping along on his feet to swing around the stack housing into the winch room, where the snow and ice dissipated from the engine-room heat. There over the open freezer, in the midst of a cloud of mosquitoes hovering in the heat, stood the Buff, gazing down at the old woman. "What's up, man?"

"Just thinking," the Buff said. "About my mother. She was Eskimo. She died in some flu epidemic when I was four."

"Listen, I'm sorry to interrupt this, but I need you to look at the barge. See if she's got a leak."

The Buff looked dazed. "I been welding this fucker nonstop. I don't know. I got it stopped for now, but that shaft is vibrating the whole stern end apart."

The Buff's face was as close to gaunt as a bowling-ball face could be, his eyes drawn with fatigue. They'd all been running on an extreme lack of sleep. The Buff stroked his frozen Fu Manchu, then swatted at a mosquito that landed on his neck. He wore only thin coveralls, without insulation, and in the heat of working below he'd unzipped them to midway down his chest.

The way he held his body, the Buff looked defeated, staring at the woman's face, the frosted face like a rubberized death mask. "You know who she is? I wish the fuck I knew who she was," he said.

"Come look at the barge," Seine said, pulling him gently by the arm, coaxing him to focus on something practical. There on the melted snow of the afterdeck stood the gull, pecking at a plastic bag of garbage. "*Hah!*" the Buff called, and the bird flew off in a circle and was swept away downwind.

They stepped around the stack housing and up the icebound side deck where a fire ax was mounted on the deckhouse. Seine grabbed that, then continued on up the push knees, which barely reached the barge deck now. "See that? See how far she's down by the bow? It's levering the stern up. Our push knees are barely reaching. Maybe he can't steer cause of that. Maybe it's not the rudder."

"Maybe." The Buff grimaced and ducked his head as they climbed up the knee and crawled onto the barge deck ten feet before they tried standing up and leaning into the blow. Wind raked their faces. When they finally made the bow, the Buff stood with wind tearing through his hair, blowing it straight back, his eyes squinting at the minimal freeboard. He seemed to Seine to be impervious to cold, even as he took his tools. "No way to know if there's a hole unless we check," he said, and began loosening the bolts that sealed the hatch that led below into the bow tanks.

Buff and Seine climbed below into the primer-coated interior of the forward tank. The ladder led down to the base, where six inches of water had pooled—not a lot, but sign of a possible leak. While the Buff checked the starboard side, Seine scanned with his flashlight up the port framework. Angle iron and cross struts ran out from the center-line in wide sweeping semicircles that flexed and thundered through each collision with the ice, and again Irons was running hard, the impact quaking up through Seine's body, forcing him to take a hand-hold to keep from falling. He scanned with the flashlight along each weld line and saw some bent girders but no breaks. Working inside the forward rake tank of an icebreaker was about like working inside a gong, and neither the Buff nor Seine could get out fast enough.

Topside, they traded the bellowing of the tanks for the shrieking wind. "I didn't see a goddamned thing wrong," said the Buff. "It's ice buildup. Get going with them axes and try to clear as much as you can."

Julia had come up to join in the ax work and took about four chops for every one of Wanless's. Seine had just started helping the Buff collect his tools when they heard twin explosions in rapid succession—which from the bow of the breaker sounded like a vague *pop-pop.* "What the hell was that?" Seine asked.

He thought he might be hearing things again out over the ice, but when he looked back he saw the tug rise upward and spin sideways, heeling away from the stern of the barge—and he knew. "Shock cords are gone!" he yelled, and started running.

The Buff took off running aft with Seine, the handheld radio crackling with Irons's voice, as close to panic as it ever got, yelling, *"Wires parted, wires parted! I need a line to the barge NOW!"*

Irons backed hard on one engine and full ahead on the other to twin-screw the *Terror* in a circle—but nothing happened. The wind shoved *Terror* sideways, and as she drifted out from behind the shadow of the barge, the wind caught the flat side of the deckhouse like a sail and blew the boat twenty feet off. Irons powered forward on his port engine, but the boat responded sluggishly, and the wind drove him off another fifty feet.

By the time the barge crew reached the stern, the wind had blown *Terror* a full three hundred feet away, and Irons was fighting thick slabs of ice trying to make his way back. "What the hell's the matter with this boat, damnit?" he barked over the radio.

The Buff watched Irons spin a wide circle trying to swing and approach from the port side, in the process doing what on a sailboat would have been a jibe, a downwind turn that blew him *another* hundred yards off. "What the hell is he doing?" the Buff yelled at Seine.

"He says something's wrong with the boat. Here, talk to him!"

The Buff took the mike. "Yeah, Wolf, what's up?"

"I got nothing from the port side. Nothing. My port engine is running full power and I got no port-wheel wash!"

The Buff squeezed his eyes shut and tipped his head skyward. "Fuck." Then he turned to Seine. "Wheel's gone. He lost his port wheel. *Jesus Christ!*"

Seine just stared, as Julia and Stuart Wanless arrived from the bow. The four of them stood to the leeward of the tool van, shaded from wind and blowing snow, and watched Irons continue his clockwise swing around the barge. "You need to call in a Mayday right now," Buff said. "Right now."

"Yeah, roger that," Irons said.

They tracked him, through the gray day traced his circular course around the barge just as the barge and the boat traced a circular

course around the pole. But somehow *Terror* never did manage to get
upwind of them. They were all spinning, Seine thought, like twin
planets around a frozen sun.

"I can't *believe* I'm not on that boat. The engineer and I'm not even
on the boat."

"You and me both," Julia said, staring at the vessel. "You and me
both."

More ice swirled between them, and Irons must have known he
couldn't fight it out of the way. He seemed to roll with the one-two
punch of wind and ice shear and dipped still farther downwind, trying
to circle.

"How's the Big Man's back?" Seine asked.

"Shot. He can barely stand upright."

"This is bad," Wanless said, and all three turned toward him methodically.

"No shit, Stuart," said Seine.

"He has to get upwind of us," Julia said. "Let her drift into us."

"He can't get there."

"He's not really circling us. We're spinning upwind of him."

And the ice between them made closing the gap all but impossible,
at least for *Terror,* limping as she was. The four tracked the wide swing
of the boat up the starboard side of the barge, walking along with it.

Then Irons found a lead and they could hear him press ahead on
one, moving toward them now.

"That's it!" Julia pointed. "There's his lead."

But when Irons tried to turn upwind to approach the barge, wind
and ice together shoved him off again and he hadn't the power to
come within fifty yards. They could see the Big Man on deck, walking
awkwardly, bent from the knees to protect his back, holding a heaving
line looped in his right hand. But his back couldn't withstand the
twist necessary to get into the throw. Dead into the wind, the mon-

key's fist arched high into the air and fluttered, dying at its apex—and then fell amid the ice. "Jesus Christ what kinda throw was that? You can just tell he grew up playing some fucking commie sport like soccer," said the Buff.

"We could try to go for them," Wanless said.

"In case you didn't notice, Stuart, this is a barge. It has no power of its own."

"I meant on foot!" Wanless cried. "Jesus!"

"You wouldn't make it twenty yards," Seine said.

But the Buff eyed Wanless steadily, then looked at the boat and nodded his head. He didn't move from his position off the starboard beam. Even when the wind seemed to pick up, blowing more snow at them, and Seine said quietly, "I'm going to check out the tool van, see what's there"—even then, the Buff refused to move.

The tool van stretched the length of a shipping container, maybe twenty foot long, with wooden cubbyhole shelves built along the inside walls. There, the three (minus the Buff) leaned against the shelves, waiting and pondering realities. Outside, Errol pondered nothing at all but simply watched the boat. He refused to hide out inside while *Terror* still motored, crippled, in the offing. He stood out there in the subfreeze wearing only those thin coveralls, his black hair raked sideways by wind.

Inside, without a generator, the tool van had no heat, only its insulated walls from its days as a reefer van and the single air duct off one side leading to the motor. "It just figures that we'd end up trying to stay warm in the arctic by hiding in a goddamned refrigerator," Seine said.

They scrounged through the van for an inventory of supplies. In addition to three chain saws, four sets of combination wrenches, hammers, saws, and brooms, they found nine flotation vests, two flashlights, and a ragged old float coat. Stuffed up on the top shelf was a hundred-yard spool of half-inch poly line, a first-aid kit, and a host of other completely useless items. But the find of the hour was Julia's: a flare-gun kit and an unopened case of military-issue Meals Ready to Eat, along with a case of canned water.

Seine snatched the mike from a wall-mounted VHF radio, powered it up, and clicked to channel 16, where the incessant drone of Money-maker came at them uninterrupted. *"The bear came from nowhere, and so I shot at it with my flare gun. That scared it off awhile, but then it came back and so I shot at it again. And now I have no more flares. . . ."*

Seine couldn't break in on Moneymaker, who was transmitting without pause now, so he flipped to the working channel and raised Irons, who was battling his own problems, trying to swing a hobbled tugboat in a sweeping circle that would bring him back to the ice-breaker. Was there any word from the Coast Guard or anyone? Affir-mative, they had made broken contact with the Canadians, who were sending an icebreaking tug in their direction, but they were still two or three days' sail to the east. The Big Man ran the spotlight and kept their channel open, transmitting continuously over 2182 kHz so they might find and maintain an RDF fix, only to realize after a half hour that they'd lost contact.

Daylight dimmed as Julia slipped outside for a look around and then ducked back and said, "Henry. Check it out. That iceberg."

Peering out the door, Seine saw the rising flat-topped mountain of the tabular berg and the tiny form of the tug *Terror* swinging in front of it. They were both about a half mile off. Slowly, the tabular berg was turning, a gentle counterclockwise motion. At the awesome sight of the boat against the white berg, Julia reached for and found Seine's hand and clasped it hard, and when Seine turned he caught Wanless looking at them.

Inside, Wanless sat back in a heap and crossed his arms. "An iceberg! Jesus, can't we get away from that thing? What is that? Huh? It's like that gull—haunting us or something. I don't like shit like that."

They were all bundled up in their outside gear. "Okay, try to relax," Julia said. "Irons will get the boat back here. We're going to be fine."

Then she moved to the rear of the van, slid the case of MREs forward, and took one for each of them. She opened the canned water with her Buck knife. "Help me out here, Stuart," she said, and together they poured the canned water into the cooking bags, the chemical strips bringing the water to a boil, steam rising in the dry cold air. Seine smelled spaghetti with meat sauce, beef stew, and beef chili.

"I gotta go out. I can't let the Buff stand out there all by himself," Seine said.

Seine stepped to the door, opened it, and felt the resistance of wind pushing directly at them. He shoved hard to get it open a foot, slipped out, and felt himself blown sideways. When he found the Buff, he noticed nightfall making its inevitable slide. How long had they been here? He didn't know. He wore no watch; the watch he'd once owned had frozen a long time back—in May, he thought.

"Whatta you want?" the Buff said.

"We got food in the van."

"I ain't going in there."

"Why not? Don't be stupid."

"You don't get it, you never did get it. That's why people always die around you, Seine."

"Oh? Why's that?"

"Because you *let 'em!*"

"You don't know anything about it."

"I know enough."

"You're going to freeze to death out here."

"Good. I got it coming."

"*That's* why everybody always dies around me!"

And Seine left him out there.

Back inside, Seine ate beef stew and they sat in the darkening van, listening to the barge do its methodical pirouettes in the wind, shoved by ice and currents into a gentle spin westward.

"Do we have any idea where we are?" Seine asked.

Julia shrugged. "All our electronics were giving us strange readouts. Even the gyro was spinning like crazy. We're pretty far north now, I know that."

Seine moved to the far end of the unit, thinking they didn't know where they were any more than Moneymaker did, and no matter how close they were, they were now both lost. The Lemming Effect. He had the sensation of flying through space. He looked up at the grated duct that led to the reefer motor. Then he looked out the door again, where *Terror* was coming into view, and it was obvious she was down badly by the stern. "Night's coming," Seine said. "We really should try to get the Buff inside."

"I'll go," Julia said. "Let me give it a try."

She geared up and went. She was gone for five minutes, and when she returned the Buff was right behind her, looking glum and blue in the lips. He hoisted himself to the workbench that ran along the first third of the van, set against one wall. He started playing with the vice mounted there, cranking it down on his fingers, pinching them until they were white and almost flat.

"Keep doing that and you're going to lose your fingers, Maxwell," Julia said.

"Do this instead," Seine said, and set a bag of hot military food in front of him.

Errol took the thick plastic bag and looked at Seine, then at Julia.

"Nobody calls me Maxwell. Not even my mother. Course, she's dead." He stopped with the vice and ate. Then he belched. "Not bad. Better than my day in the navy."

He stood up. His circular scar had turned purple in the cold.

"I'm thinking I should make a run for the boat, like Wanlow here said. They got no hope without somebody tending to that engine room."

"You won't make it," Seine said.

"I might. It's in my blood. That old lady—you know, the one in the freezer? I can't let her just stay there like that, right?"

"What's that have to do with it? She's dead, you're not."

"I know, but see, I don't know. I keep thinking about that Rotting-mule thing. I know, you know it's bullshit, but it's not, too. I ain't ready for that giving-up shit. I ain't walking off like some old tooth-less Skeemo, know what I'm saying? And then there's my old maw, you know. She was Eskimo even if I never did know her."

Seine said, "What the hell are you talking about?"

Julia smiled and pushed her fist gently into the Buff's shoulder. "You talk so tough."

"I know it. I am tough too." And he smiled. "I'll like chant or some-thing, say 'Hoo-nah, hah-nah, hah-nah, hah-nah,' like a Indian, get in touch with my Skeemo half and then go floe-hopping to save the Old Woman of Nunivak."

A long moment passed between Seine and Julia: they both knew it was a bad idea, and they both knew there was nothing they could do to stop him.

"Stay in here and warm up, get your energy back," Julia said.

"And put on my float suit," Seine said.

"Now you people are talking sanity!" said the Buff. "I like it. I like it a lot. Life sucks without a mission, Seine. Now I got me a *mission*."

The Buff got up and checked for the tugboat. It had swung almost dead abeam of the barge by then, lingering a half mile off, its lone engine grinding. "Damn, would you look at that! He ain't got the horses, one-legged like he is."

"We don't belong here," Wanless said.

"No shit, Stuart. You have a talent for the obvious, don't you?"

"We should be down south, our toes in the sand. Mexico."

"Mexico, hell," Seine said. "I'd settle for a shack in Kaktovik."

With food to warm their insides, they slept curled together on the van deck, until through the Plexiglas window in the door they noticed a rising light, and the Buff rose to check the boat again, pressing his face against the square window. "Mile off, I guess. Gimme another one of them rations," he said, and when he'd finished boiling a bag of food, and downing it in a hot slide, the Buff pulled out a tin of tobacco and passed it around. "Can't believe there ain't no coffee in them MREs," he said.

"You're going to do that?" Wanless asked, when he saw Julia accept the tobacco tin from Buffy Errol.

"Sure. I never did; seems like a good time to try something new."

"That's just too . . . I don't know. It's gross."

"Get over it, Stuart." And Julia loaded a pinch of Copenhagen into her lip. "It's not that bad," she said, and worked it around with her tongue and laughed.

"Gross!" Wanless said. "Look at your teeth!"

The kid scowled disgustedly, scrutinizing each of them in turn, as if he'd only now noticed the people he was stranded with, and that he couldn't believe, somehow, that he'd die with these people, and that he'd never see another normal person again. The whole thing pissed him off. He said to the Buff, "So how *did* you get that scar?"

"My Buff scar?" said the Buff, fingering the nub of tissue. "You wanna be a Buff?"

"I don't know," Wanless said, incredulous. "Probably not. What do you have to do?"

"First you take a rosebud. You know what that is?"

"A sled?" Wanless said.

"A sled? Fuck no—a sled?"

"Never mind."

"It's a heating tip for a torch. You heat it up till it's practically white hot and then you blow it out and you press it into your chest, like that." He mimed the motion. "Hold it there long as you can. Then you'll be a Buff."

"Uhh—I don't think so," said Wanless.

"There's a shock! Wanlow no Buff."

"That's *really* how you got that scar?"

The Buff sat there and looked around. He saw Julia smiling at him and he finally said, "Naw, what really happened is I got shot in the neck once in the Mekong and my teammate give me a tracheotomy."

"I thought you did it to yourself," Seine said.

"I did! Stuck my neck out too far and got it shot!"

The three laughed as if they were at a party in a safe spot, Seattle or somewhere, reminiscing about close calls. But through their laughter, which left Wanless staring blankly at them, they noticed with vigilance the real daylight now, a rising gray out the lone window, and how the wind battered their tin can of civilization.

Wanless frowned at Julia again, saying, "I can't believe you're chewing tobacco. I never met a girl who chews tobacco."

"That's cause she ain't a *girl*," the Buff said. "She's a *woman*, and real women chew muck. Muck it up!"

"I'll do anything once," she said. "Twice if I like it."

"Yeah, I think you probably proved that to everybody the world over," Wanless said, and glared at her, then faced the stares of all three. "Oh, never mind!" And he just hunkered in a ball on the deck.

"Don't let jealousy make you a madman, Wanlow!" the Buff said, spitting tobacco into a cup and standing up to stretch. "Jealousy is evil. For one thing, we got bigger fish to fry."

"You can say that again," Seine said.

"For another thing it makes you stupid. I been so jealous I was blind. Insane blind. I mean it, like nothing you ever saw from anybody, that's for sure."

"I don't think I'd want to see that," Julia said.

"I got a confession, but you all can't tell nobody."

"I'm not a priest," Wanless said.

"Then shut your ears, cause I ain't Catholic. Well, my old man was, but I don't think he ever went to church. Anyway, I never told nobody this."

"I can't wait," Julia said.

Seine figured something bad was coming, and to make it worse, the Buff looked right at him when he spoke, as if *he* was the confessor. "When my girlfriend cheated on me while I was away in the navy, I come back and I found the guy she done it with. He worked on a crabber out of Homer. We was living in the Kenai then, so I drove down there one night and I killed him."

"Jesus," said Seine. "Don't be telling us shit like that, Buff. We don't want to know shit like that."

"Sorry, I had to tell somebody."

"Then go to church or something. Don't tell me shit like that. I don't wanna know."

"That's cause you don't believe in confession."

Seine felt a sinking feeling, a pit in his stomach like a snowball melting in his belly and sliding down his legs. When he looked up, there sat Marco Barn on the bench by the Buff, with blood seeping down out of his hairline. Seine just stared at him, even as Marco got up, walked toward him, and put his mouth right up into his face to where Seine could feel his beard tickle his lips. Blood seeped from his ears. "No," Seine said aloud. "Don't."

"You *are* aware," Julia said to the Buff, "that the statute of limitations never runs out on murder, right? So you can still go to prison for it."

"Yeah, but you won't tell nobody. I know you. I trust you. You people here are maybe the only ones I trust. Even you, Wanless. You three and Irons and the Big Man are the only ones. My shipmates. I can trust you all, right?"

"Sure," Seine said, but inside he was brushing away the mouth of the Shade, turning his head away involuntarily and grimacing at the tobacco breath and wishing the Buff didn't trust him so much.

"Good," the Buff said. "Cause I need to tell you something else."

"This is *so* sick," said Wanless.

"How I did it is I snuck on board his crab boat and busted his neck and then used the deck crane to drop a crab pot on his head. Then I dumped him in Cook Inlet on a wicked ebb tide. Swept him right into the Shelikof Strait or maybe out into the Gulf. That's how I got rid of the body. They found him finally. Ruled it accidental."

Wanless had both hands covering his face. "Great! That's just great," he said, his voice muffled into his palms. "Who am I? Why am I here? Is that gull still out there? Where in the hell *do* the gulls go when everything freezes, huh? Can anybody tell me? No. You telling me they just live up here? *I doubt it!*"

Everybody frowned at Wanless. The Buff moved to the Plexiglas window and looked out for *Terror*. She was a quarter mile off then, down by the stern, with her running lights glowing even though skies had broken to a slate-colored gray. No sun that they could see, but the dim light of dawn in a grayscape. Adrift in an endless ocean of ice.

"Close as she's gonna get," the Buff said.

Julia eyed him. "I still don't think it's a good idea."

"Me either," Seine said. "Skies are breaking maybe. We're too far for a chopper, but a C-130 might at least locate us."

"This ain't about sitting around waiting for someone else to come get us. I got nothing left to do now. I confessed my sins. It's about that boat. When I was on board I was welding like a maniac just to keep up with that sucker. Without me there, they ain't got a chance, I'm telling you. Now maybe you three wanna sit back and die in each other's arms, but I got a little problem with that. First off, I ain't *got* anybody's arms to die in except Wanlow's, and I ain't gonna let his faggot ass touch me."

"I'm not gay, goddamnit!" Wanless yelled.

"Yeah, okay, whatever you say. Anyway, second off, I'm a man of *action*. Damn few left." He cackled in a macho way; then he winked.

"All my life!" Wanless yelled. "I am so *tired* of being called a fag!"

"Hush up, Stuart," said Julia.

The Buff refused to take Seine's float suit because the ten minutes gained if submerged in the water wasn't good enough for the Buff, not as a tradeoff against the extra bulk. "Fat guy like me needs to stay light," he said, and grabbed a ragged old float coat, slipping it on over his coveralls, finally covering his chest. Seine saw then that the name BLAKE was stenciled on the coat. "Good ol' Blake!" Seine said. "Wonder where he is."

The Buff shook his head. "Don't know. I know where I wish he was. *Here*, instead of me!" He looked out the Plexiglas door. "All right, man, I'm gonna do it, you'll see," said the Buff. "This is it."

Outside, the Buff moved to the edge and started to lower himself over the side to the rung ladder, his round face shining out from the hood of the float coat. Seine stopped him, still with the invisible face of the Shade of Marco Barn breathing into his mouth.

"I got a confession too."

"What's that?"

He didn't know why, but instinct told him to say something now, to clear things with the Buff, because the man was about to die maybe, and he wanted to clear it somehow. "It's about Marco. I never told anybody. Maybe I didn't even want to admit it to myself—goddamn I feel shitty about it, Buff. But I did toss that padeye down the hole. I was just trying to scare him. I got so sick of him taking chances, being so cocky about it like nothing would happen to him. I looked down and I swear he wasn't there when I tossed it. And when I heard the crack, I knew—Jesus, it makes me sick."

Buff eyed him, and for an instant Seine felt the weight of judgment. Then the Buff nodded. "Yeah, well, he always figured so."

"I was just trying to scare him. I'm not saying it's an excuse but he pissed me off, being careless. My fucking old man was the same way. Nobody could convince him to be safe. He was a macho fuck just like Marco. I wanted him to feel it."

"He did!" Buff let out a dark laugh.

Seine said nothing. He took a deep cold breath.

"Hey, man, look. We all got ghosts. Put 'em on the garbage barge, ship 'em south, Henry."

Seine didn't want to cry for fear he'd freeze his eyeballs shut. He just closed his eyes and felt the wind and breathed in slow even breaths.

"Hey, fuck it, it's over. In a way you were right and he was wrong. He paid for it, that's it. You do the best you can. Sometimes you fuck up. Everybody does. Now stay here and keep Wanless from diving overboard looking for ducks or something, and I'll bring that goddamned boat back if it's the last thing I do."

"Think we ought to drop anchor?"

"Ice'll just shear it off. Might as well go with the flow. That's what I'm planning."

Seine watched the Buff climb down in the gale and snow and hop from one floe to the next, going nimbly, clinging like a bulky Spider-Man to the flattest parts of the floes he could find. *Move right,* Seine urged inside, *now left, now right—that's it.* . . .

The Buff had made it a third of the way to *Terror* when Julia came out and stood next to Seine, and they watched him, as if exposing themselves to the cold knife-edge of the wind somehow paid homage to the Buff's effort. The wind tore at him at fifty yards off, and he hopped awkwardly then, as shifting ice bogged him down and the wind nearly blew him over. He disappeared from their view as gusts of ground blizzard blew past. When he reappeared, a lead had opened, shoving him southeast. Seine squinted through his safety goggles, watching as the Buff tried to leap across the narrow fissure, his foot slipping, his body sliding, hands and feet scrambling as he slipped down a hillock of slick ice into the frigid water between. He struggled to haul himself back out, looking like an dying walrus, and within a minute or two he was pinned between floes the size of baseball diamonds, his cries flying off the other way, barely audible, like some distant recording of an animal being put to death.

They listened helplessly for what seemed hours, though in fact it was less than ten minutes before Seine said, "Fuck it. I'm going to get him."

"Henry," Julia said, "don't do it. Don't. You'll end up in the same boat."

"Pardon the pun, but we're already in the same boat," Seine said.

"Lemmings to the sea," Julia said.

"We're all lemmings to the sea! Moneymaker! He's lost, and now we're lost too!"

Seine had been haunted so long he barely knew what it felt like to be free of his own guilt, to breathe fully into the lightness of his own chest. Now he couldn't bear not doing everything possible to hold onto it. This and the thought of being haunted by the Buff was enough to drive him to heroism.

Julia paused as if to size him up, to see if he could be argued out of it. "Wait here," she said, and ran inside to where Wanless sat back against the rear wall of the tool van, wearing a frozen look. She unspooled an entire lot of half-inch poly line, said, "The Buff's down. Henry's going after him," and ran out.

"Shit," Wanless said, and came to life, rising to follow.

She threw a bowline around Seine's waist and tethered it out as he climbed down the rung ladder to the ice. He stepped out gingerly, gained his footing, and moved from floe to floe. He bounced, kept moving with a practiced agility; he staggered, fought the wind, and felt himself blown over, sitting abruptly onto his butt, looking back to see Julia and Wanless on the barge. Julia had taken two turns around the aft barge cleat, and let the line slip through her gloved hands as Seine moved farther off. The lifeline ran between them, and little by little he closed on the Buff until he sat down next to him.

"Seine, Seine. Goddamnit, this is what I get, I swear to Christ, for not being a better Eskimo."

"Obviously there's a trick to floe hopping that you never learned," Seine said, and the Buff tried to laugh. If he felt any fear, he didn't show it.

Seine scanned for the tugboat, at first not catching it at all, and then seeing the smudge of the black hull. It had spun a half mile off, drifting dark now. He wasn't sure, but he thought maybe the wind had let up some.

The Buff's arms were propped up, the floes squeezing him at the chest. He puffed air, blew it hard out of his mouth and sucked harder to draw some meager amount inside. "I'm freezing my fucking lungs!"

The wind and snow raked at Seine, and he shielded the Buff by working upwind of him. Underneath, the Buff shoved, working his legs, grunting and wheezing trying to force the floes apart. But he was fighting a thousand tons of old ice. "My one leg's pinned behind me, dammit. If I could just get that fucking leg in front of me I could get some goddamned leverage—"

Seine reached down and grabbed him under the armpits, pulled as hard as he could, but the Buff didn't budge. "Don't do that no more. That fucking hurts."

"And your legs?"

"They don't hurt, not like that."

Only because they were freezing, Seine thought; he knew that feeling. He sat on one floe and wedged himself as low as he could and tried to push with his legs. It was like pushing against a concrete wall.

He pushed and imagined some movement, but the Buff only grimaced in pain. "Ahhhhhh—Jesus, Jeeeeeeezus!"

Seine stood upright, felt the wind take his float suit and topple him over, falling nearly on top of the Buff, and then going over himself, off the back end of the floe. He felt the line go tight, enough to keep him up. He pulled on it, looked up the long line of yellow connecting him to the barge, sitting high in the water, tipped down by the icy bow, with the two gray outlines of Julia and Wanless on deck.

"Just leave me here, just leave me here. It's okay."

"It's not okay, Buff. It's really not okay."

"It don't matter now, man. It just don't fucking matter. Retirement, death, it's all the fucking same. You can have my house, man. It's been empty for about a year. Unlike you, I own it outright!" And he let out a gasping laugh.

Seine hunkered a moment. "These floes have *got* to shift, Buff, and when they do we'll pull you out. I'll use the capstan on the anchor winch. It's all timing."

"*Bad* timing, near as I can tell. They're shifting now—ahhhhhhhhhhhh, god*daaamnit*!" and he lost his breath. His lips had gone blue, spreading toward his nose, and now his eyes bulged.

Seine reached around the Buff's armpits, tied a bowline around his chest, and then didn't know what to do. He put his hand on the Buff's head and just sat there. That the Buff didn't protest the touch made Seine realize how far gone he was already. The line went taut, pressure from the barge to the floe, and Seine realized then that the lifeline was now part of the problem, not the solution. The barge and the Buff were now engaged in a frozen tug-of-war that the Buff was sure to lose. Seine moved to untie the line from under his arms, when the Buff said, "*No!* Just leave—" and in the exertion of talking, passed out.

"Ah shit, Buff," Seine said, then let out a sudden sharp yell, thought he saw a faint glowing from above, then caught a granule of snow in the eye. He ducked his head and sat there with his arm on the Buff, keeping him company to the end.

Later, he had no idea how long, Seine left the line tied around the Buff's armpits, cinched it tight, and double-looped it so they wouldn't lose him. And then he walked back, following the tight line until it got too high to reach, and then he took his chances for the last thirty feet, climbed the rung ladder, and slumped to the deck. He watched Julia, who tied a series of clove hitches around the cleat, and then turned to him, her face anguished—for him, he thought; she felt bad for him. She put her hand to his shoulder and took his arm to help him up.

Wanless just stood there, still wearing the hard hat he'd been wearing ever since the drill ship fiasco, cocked sideways and back on his head, its felt liner finally buttoned under his chin. A faint wisp of beard grew there, Seine noticed. He could tell because frost had started to form on it.

Seine let his head fall back and looked straight up, through blowing snow and wind and clouds, to a patch of sky above him, clear. "Please break," he said.

"Yeah, please," said Wanless, as if the severity of their predicament had finally dawned on him.

Back inside, Wanless prepared an MRE for Seine while Seine and Julia leaned into each other with their float suits zipped tight, hoods on to conserve heat. They said nothing now, until Wanless brought the bag of food over for Henry and then moved for the door. "Don't you think we should go get him?" he said.

"We've done everything we can," Julia said.

"My goddamned brother died in a place like this and nobody went to get him!"

"We tried," Julia said. "It just didn't work out."

"Well, this could work out. Isn't that like some thing of the marines: You don't leave a man out there?"

"We aren't in the marines, Stuart."

"Merchant marines or whatever—same thing!"

Wanless's hard hat had fallen back on his head and sort of hung there. "We're going to freeze here! Can you eat fast enough to keep from freezing? Can you? Nobody's going to find us. We need a sideband radio, we need—"

"Stuart," Julia said. "Sit down. Don't panic."

"I think I've been pretty fucking calm! Don't you think it's about time we *did* something?"

And they just watched him. There wasn't a thing to say to that except to agree. Moneymaker came on then, talking about circles. He had a thing about randomness, chaos, and circles. He reminded Seine of the Chemist. "We're spinning," he said. "We are, the ice all around us is, it's all spinning without direction or control. . . ."

TWENTY-THREE

Frozen Tug

Seine rolled Al George's quarter along his fingers and watched through the Plexiglas. Daylight came dominated by the white of shifting ground blizzard, and with it the threat of live burial. Night came with blackened sky and hopeful glimmers of starlight, or moonlight, or the glittering array of the Northern Lights, tantalizing and despairing all at once.

Inside, he lay there feeling Julia's measured breath as she rested her head on his lap, and he sat back, reclining his head against the workbench. He drifted off listening to the monotone of Moneymaker, grown scratchy over the handheld VHF, telling the geologic history of ice islands, of which Flaw was one.

"They are calved like any berg, but in the north from the ice shelves off Ellesmere Island. Flaw Island was once four miles long. I have no idea how long it is now. The numb takes you," Moneymaker said. *"Staring at ice makes the mind numb. Counting bergy bits and growlers not to mention the ice island itself. Along its broken middle old striations of ice, older than anything, white as Dover. Shaped like the tabular bergs of Antarctica. . . ."*

Seine's eyes fluttered. Something reached out, needled him in the temple. *Wake up. Wake up. Hear that? Hear that?* But he did not awaken; he slept instead and dreamed that he was on the barge but out on the open deck, lying flat on his back as the steel hull was squeezed by icebergs on all sides, towering spires of ice, green and blue, with ancient striations and thaw years, telling the whole history of human exploratory stupidity, like the rings inside a giant redwood, while overhead the aurora borealis danced in desperate celebration. Then he was a bird, an arctic tern, flying up and up, weaving in and out of the beadlight of the aurora. The icebreaker hull buckled and whined below him, under the squeeze of the polar pack, pressure ridges formed from beneath, lifting him up, lifting the entire barge up until he bathed in the aurora, shimmering reds and violets glowing through him, and then—nothing.

The black overtook him. The circles spun through his head, and he was no longer a bird or a man. He drifted away, felt the dissipation.

When he awoke he laughed, remembering that the Buff had given him his house. Now he had a house, but still no home; now he had walls, but still no door; now he had a ceiling, but still no roof. And he leaned down and whispered in Julia's ear, "Come live with me."

While Moneymaker droned on.

"—you wonder what makes sense, what's predictable in the uneven flow of the ice, it meanders like some river down a long slope, and you can stand at the top and watch the first drop of water run into a rill, and not predict in a million years where the rill will turn right or left over this or that pebble, pick up a partner and become a runnel, flow farther over stones and boulders, merge with others to become a rivulet—and you can't stand there at the top of that slope and tell where the river will find the sea—you'll die long before you can predict the spot—so now the question is, Where will I be dying . . . ?"

Besides Moneymaker's despair, all Seine heard was the quivering van, the rattling cage that separated them from the darkest place he had ever seen, darker than the Gulf, darker than Cross Island on a

midwinter drill rig working for the Big Man, darker than Bainbridge
Island through a rain-bound winter. And as he continued on, Seine
was no longer sure if the voice was Moneymaker's or his own, mur-
muring inside, chanting in a death-dream; he was no longer sure if he
stood or walked or talked.

The van rattled. Showered by gravel and ice. His hand reached out.
The door opened easily and then snapped out of his hand and flew
open, battering its own hinges in the gale. When he tried to close it, he
saw the hinges had hyperextended, and now groaned against his attempt to close the door again. A six-inch gap of howling wind and
blowing snow.

Outside, Seine and Julia hunkered in the gloom of morning and
watched the tug appear as a black smudge. Ice clogged the path between barge and boat. Irons had been trying for two days to limp a
counterclockwise spiral around and toward them. The tactic would
have worked if *Terror* had had enough power, but now as she turned
against ice shear, they saw not only how far down the stern sat, but, as
the silhouette grew larger and more defined along its edges, they saw
it had no power: no deck lights, no running lights, no stack smoke.
"The engine room is flooded," Seine said.

Color came to him, the dim paint against the gray dawn, the vague
multishaded blue of company colors, and the Biller logo on the stack
housing. The bow reached high now, showing discolored steel below
the normal waterline—a kind of lurid exposure he recognized only too
well. On the afterdeck, the waterline rose toward the house at a foot
every minute, and there in the last warm hollow of the winch room,
the gull stood perched on the tow winch.

"They're dead in the water," Seine said.

Julia ran back to the van, returned with a handheld air horn, and blew it three times, shrieking over the wind, but if the two men heard they made no indication of it. "Surely he can see us," Julia said. "He's a half mile off. Surely he can see us!"

Seine watched out as the two figures of the Wolf and the Big Man moved up the side deck, carrying the orange-colored, beer-barrel-shaped canister that contained the Switlik. The Big Man, who wore a bright orange survival suit, lifted it to his chest and heaved it over-board, hanging to the static release. As the orange barrel hit the ice it halved open like a coconut and out boiled an orange raft, tented, whipping in the gale, and the raft blew off, jerking the tether out of the Big Man's grasp, and he could only watch as the raft rolled out over the pack ice like a tumbleweed over a frozen prairie, trailing its blue flashing beacon.

And *Terror* slipped a foot or two farther down—a consistent move-ment now, visible.

"Oh, shit," Julia said. "Is Irons even wearing a survival suit?"

Seine didn't think so; the Big Man was so clearly orange in the suit that Irons looked like a gray smudge by comparison. "The boat's going," Seine said.

But the two men stood on the side deck as if no urgency moved them, while the boat tilted backward, the wheelhouse angling back like a horse falling, its head writhing, its neck arching backward in death. Then the Big Man made a move. Slowly he straddled the bul-wark, climbed over, and lowered himself to the ice. Holding his back, he scrambled away from the sinking boat.

Suddenly and inexplicably, Irons went the opposite direction. The boat slipped farther down, slush reaching the middle of the house, ice shoving in all around them. Seine thought maybe if he had to go he might have a better run than the Buff did, since ice seemed to have packed more tightly now.

Irons moved down into the ice water and around to the winch room. What in hell was he doing? Seine couldn't tell; it seemed senseless until Irons emerged a moment later, carrying the body of the Old Woman of Nunivak.

"Oh, God—why is he—? That's just nuts—"

The boat slid faster backward; Irons held the woman close as if cradling a curled infant, teetered once, then slipped and went under. The Old Woman floated there in the slush water, ice floes pinching in to shove her against the house as Irons flailed to haul himself out onto a piece of ice, his arms reaching for something to grab hold of, slipping, grabbing at the woman. She turned over as he grabbed for her, and he slid down.

The boat slipped another yard downward, the Wolf's mouth reaching for the sky as if to gobble breath, the boat slipping still farther, the stackhouse shoving down on top of him, the sliding now beyond anything Seine had ever witnessed, worse somehow than *Fearless* if only because of the terrible slowness of its slide, 45 degrees, bow reaching upward, stern sliding downward onto the Wolf, and accelerating in a sternward rush, the boat disappeared. The gull fluttered up in the sky, flew away in a tight semicircle, and landed on the ice.

Julia put her hand to her mouth. Her face flooded with tears that froze. Seine felt a burning at his eyeballs, his own tears trapped in their ducts and freezing there in swollen pain.

Meanwhile the Big Man was scrambling, looking backward in wide-eyed fear, crawling from floe to floe with a nightmarish impotence. His injured back left him a shell of himself. He stood up, disappeared behind ground blizzard, stumbled, and wandered north in the wrong direction.

Julia blew the air horn three times, crisp and sharp, the sound blowing off downwind. The Big Man kept going, not quickly, but steadily, dragging himself toward a confused death. Rottingmule, Seine thought; floe hopping, stepping, flying like a seabird to the Buff's Rottingmule. Seine couldn't process it all. He scrambled down the rung ladder and hung there, while Julia again let off three bursts from the air horn.

There were thousands of Moneymakers in his life, in the lives of everyone, lemming-like attempts at going out there to help someone else only to find it was he himself who needed help all along. The dilemma rattled back and forth inside him—to go or not to go. He hung to the ladder, watching the Big Man move away from him, a dark figure through the blow. He stepped awkwardly in the Gumby suit, wide-legged with boots stuffed inside, and bareheaded, the suit so small it couldn't reach over the top to seal him.

Wandering meat. Seine stepped off the rung ladder to the ice below. Polar bears fatting themselves for the winter. He felt them out there. He heard them mumble and talk. Move east. Move west. Lunching on a cast-off shipmate. A maroon on an icebound sea. In fact the sea seemed more icebound now than ever, the floes more tightly packed. Where *Terror* had gone down the ice had squeezed back in to cover the spot over, and all around Seine sensed he could move more easily now than earlier.

This was one of those times; this was the time for positive action. So armed with a knife and a length of polyester line, Seine stepped off the barge and began stepping from floe to floe in the direction of the Big Man.

As he stepped out he realized that the tightness of the floes was partly illusory. Snow had blown in from some distant storm, tailing on a three-day ground blizzard to drift up behind pressure ridges and tall floes, giving the ice a surreal look of solid rubble, like the surface of a whited moon. But there was nothing uniform or solid about it; the ice shifted, swirled constantly, and left him drifting with currents

and the Coriolis force in directions he couldn't perceive. He heard
Julia say something from above, but the wind at his ears prevented his
understanding it. He stepped forward, slipped, and came out from behind the barge to feel the wind shove his face. As he started moving he
realized how remote he was from any fixed geographic reality. The
only truth was the barge, and the Big Man, now a lone figure receding
to the north, a darkening smudge of directionless motion. Why didn't
he look back? He must be delusional, confused. Seine hadn't any idea,
but perhaps it was all a false horizon, all the arctic mirage. Sun dogs.
False suns. Ice blink.

Wind gusted, and with it the ground blizzard intensified, flooding
Seine in a torrent of snow-grit and ice granules. When he looked back
he couldn't see the barge, and then the panic rose in his chest. The
world lay within the two-foot radius around his feet. Traction was
everything.

He walked, continued walking, meandering now, fighting the sense
of dread and isolation and panic that came from having no idea where
he was or where he was going. He touched the coin in his pocket. He
took one step after another, imagining them all as swirling in random circles around each other, that their only hope now lay in some
chaotic moment where they might intersect by little more than blind
luck. He stopped. Should he turn around? Go back? He called out for
the Big Man, his voice blown straight back into his face before flying
downwind.

His own physical pain—sore knees, numbed hands, the stigmatic
knife to the palm—these were all a memory. He moved and gained
rhythm, and found a source somewhere inside to push past doubt and
keep moving because a stationary target would be struck down. He
bounced and hopped and moved, calling toward the Big Man, hearing
nothing of Julia's air horn now, nothing of his own voice even.

He walked and stepped and persevered into the blow, until a form came to him, a black form that grew wider like a black cliff, like an ebony shore, and deeper as he approached, and looking up through goggles fogged and frozen he saw the icebreaker barge *Odyssey* looming like a listing slab of steel. "Oh, my God," Seine sighed, exhausted. He had walked in a giant circle and ended just where he'd begun.

The Cold Core

B ack in the tool van, the radio went silent without ceremony. Batteries and light-emitting diodes faded and died, taking the voice of Moneymaker with them. His rambling treatise on arctic devolution slipped away to nothing. Seine's purpose slipped away with it. He was haunted then by the image of the Big Man, stumbling and wandering off across the ice like some kind of Gothic monster, unable to make a straight line. Somehow the loss of Moneymaker seemed pale by comparison.

The tool van door was ajar, and no amount of beating with a sledgehammer would make it close, so Seine finally tied it with a length of line and figured they'd live with the six-inch gap. The wind shrieked into the van, blowing bits of granulated snow and gravel with it, so they moved into the back as far as they could and hunkered into their float suits.

"Is there any food left? Maybe we should eat some more. I'm cold."

"We're all cold, it's cold. Food's the only heat we have."

"How long will it last?"

Julia checked the boxes and found eight MREs and twelve cans of military water left.

They listened only to the steady beating of the door against the line Seine had tied it with, and snow sliding in and swirling in eddies on the van deck.

"You never know how it's going to end, do you?" Julia said.

They were the first words of pessimism that Seine had ever heard Julia Lew say, and they settled into the pit of his stomach and froze there.

They all fell silent then, for a long time, and Seine didn't experience a flashing of his life as he had expected and maybe hoped, but more like a prolonged freezer burn. He was conscious every minute, through the burning extremities and the numbness and the giddy euphoric lovely memories, and during that time he thought of every moment of every year he had been coming north, and of the way it drew him to his own death like an alluring but diseased lover. He thought of that moment of recognition with the Buff, hearing his confession, offering his own dark truth about himself, and strangely enough he felt guiltless for the first time in a long while, felt no hint of shades or ghosts or hallucinations, or whatever they were.

But you brought them here, he thought. *You brought them here and they died.*

They brought themselves here. They brought themselves into the same circle. They chose.

He had borne enough guilt. Now, as he neared the end, he felt none. And a kind of odd relief came in the simple truth that he would die with Julia.

He thought they might be blowing south now, blowing home like geese for the winter; they'd make Mexico, warm their feet in sunbaked sand, and laugh about how close they had come.

She moved close to him, and then they fell together in an embrace made awkward by bulky clothing, allowing only their cold faces to press together. Kissing her lips made him warm for an instant;

they kissed again and again and then just lay flat and held each other.

Midnight might have passed. The van froze over inside, icicles hanging from above, hoarfrost sprouting from the deck and the walls. They ceased looking out the Plexiglas porthole.

The van spun around his body because he had no body left. His mind floated free, wondering how he might stand in such a state, but he felt certain he was standing, or maybe flying now, a bird in a dream, or floating like an eider duck. He found himself lying back in a deep warm pool of water with rain falling on his head and then looked downward into the glassy water to see himself in this van lying with Julia, and thought, Maybe this is it, this is death.

He stumbled outside into the blow. The wind hadn't dropped a single knot, he thought, and he spun against its force, let it take him, thinking there were worse ways to die than to be blown overboard. Maybe it would sweep him skyward, make him fly as in dreams. Tremors moved through his body in irregular fashion, his body sacrificing the heat of the extremities for the heat of the core, a sacrifice that would lead to the loss of limbs. They were all a single limb of a way of life that couldn't last, he thought; the dirty little secret remained the illusion of infinite growth in a finite system. Go farther north, punch more holes, extract more oil, suck more air. When it's all finished we can fly to fucking Mars.

The ocean flattened into a moonscape, a rubbled white terrain against a vaguely rising moonlight, awash in colors of the aurora. Ice surrounded them. The tabular berg loomed off their starboard side. It spun with them, caught in the same gravitational back eddy. He didn't know what he dreamed or what he knew to be real, whether he was inside or outside, whether he was north or south, east or west, blowing farther on or running in place.

A gull hovered over his head, wings fixed, stationary against the blow. All around came the old ice, slow-moving as the millennium, spiraling deeply poleward like a glacial maelstrom.

Back inside for twenty minutes, trying not to sleep, nudging the other two continually, saying, "Don't sleep! Wanless, wake up! *Wake up or you're dead.*"

Wanless groaned and lifted his face, and Seine saw his lips were blue. Then he himself looked up and saw a hand reach inside the van, and he felt a shiver run through him. The only one standing, Seine fully expected the Chemist to walk in—or, worse, the Buff. He would have called out to the hand, except that he wasn't convinced there was anything real to call out to. But then Julia saw the hand too and let out a little yelp.

And the hand grasped for the door, unhooking the length of rope that held it partially closed, and the door swung open hard, and into the doorway stepped a man none of them had ever seen before. The form confused Seine, and his mind worked slowly to process the image of the man, gaunt and looking even weaker than he himself felt.

"It's Dr. Moneymaker," Julia said.

And the man smiled a weak smile. "Thank God," he said, and stumbled inside. "You're here to save me!"

"Actually," Seine said, "we were hoping *you* were here to save *us.*"

And with that, Moneymaker fell over like a frozen corpse.

They pulled him away from the door and back into the makeshift cubbyhole shielded by the stacked flotation vests, and Seine went to close the door. "How in the hell did you get here?" he asked.

"I flew," said Moneymaker.

"Wise guy," said Seine. "I was gonna say you don't look up for a trek on the polar pack."

"Trek? My only battery ran out of juice and I couldn't broadcast anymore, so I just sat there in the wind until I heard something grinding across the island. And when I looked out I saw your barge. Right there! Like you'd come to pick me up. I walked across twenty feet of ice and climbed the ladder."

"Twenty feet?" Seine said. He looked out the door and saw the tabular berg looming like a flat-topped mountain. "*That's* Flaw Island? You've been right next to us all along!" His head spun, cloudy. He relived the moments pushing hard against the tabular berg. They had come full circle, out and back in a frozen dream, their goal right next to them the entire time. Seine didn't know whether to laugh or cry.

"There are twenty chunks of it floating around. The polar pack is melting, ladies and gentlemen."

Seine shook his head and started to laugh. Why not laugh? The realization swam between his ears, even as he reached out for the door and pulled it closed against the wind. He was about to retie his length of line when he looked out over the ice and noticed the night had cleared, though the wind still blew. Overhead, he caught sight of the moon, full and bright, and out over the ice it cast its eerie, craggy light. He saw a shape move, way out—maybe not so far out, two hundred yards or so. He wiped at the frost on his safety glasses, looked again and saw a polar bear, directly downwind of them and sniffing the air, making a zigzag toward them. "Polar bear," he said. He tied the line again, and moved for the flare gun.

Julia rolled Moneymaker over. He was still conscious but said nothing at first, then: "I've been chasing them off for two weeks!"

Moneymaker, Seine thought shaking his head, this is goddamned *Moneymaker.* He kept staring at him, a red-bearded, blond-haired tossle of a man, about Seine's height and build. He looked thinner, maybe . . . like he'd been out here longer.

Seine checked the shells for the flare gun, jammed one into the gun and closed the breech, and peered out the gap in the door. The bear had shambled off out of view, and Seine moved back into the van while Moneymaker ate an MRE.

"Maybe it's gone after the Buff," Seine said.

"Better him than us," Wanless said.

Seine slumped to the deck and held his head. Suddenly he let out a chuckle, and then a rising laugh that he couldn't put a lid on. "After all the hides he was running, it figures the Buff would end up as polar-bear food," Seine said.

And all three of them laughed. The meat cycle was complete.

Moneymaker fed himself slowly, his beard frosted, the tip of his nose smudged charcoal black from frostbite. "Careful you don't lose that nose or you'll end up like Wolf Irons," Seine said.

Moneymaker stopped chewing. "Who?"

"Robert Irons. We called him the Wolf."

"He skippered our boat out here. To come get you."

"Oh!" And Moneymaker nodded. "Where is he now?"

"He went down," Seine said. "About a mile off."

"Oh." Moneymaker's eyes cast about—gray eyes searching—as if he finally understood something about their sacrifice but was entirely too fatigued to dig for details.

"He looks like you, Seine," Wanless said.

"What?"

"Yeah, I was going to say something about that," Julia said. "He does."

"Like me?" Seine looked at the guy stuffing a shaking spoon of food into his mouth. "I look like that?"

"Well, not the starvation part," Julia said. "The eyes. Those hang-dog eyes."

"Hangdog? Geez."

Seine had just turned from Moneymaker to the door when the

black nose of a polar bear stuck through the gap in the van door and brought everybody leaping to their feet.

"Bear! Bear!" Wanless yelled, pointing and trying to scramble backward even though he was already as far back into the van as he could go.

Seine pointed the flare gun directly at the bear's snout and fired. The flare ricocheted off the edge of the door and bounded back into the van. They ducked and screamed as the pink-hot flare streaked around the van, burrowed into a box of bolts, and fizzled out. The smoke was noxious, and they all covered their faces in whatever clothing they could, but the flare at least frightened the bear off.

Seine threw the door open wide, the wind whipping through the van to clear the smoke. "Jesus Christ, Henry!" Julia said. "Be careful!"

"I guess I'm no marksman," he said.

"Guess he didn't want the Buff after all," Wanless said. "He's frozen, we're fresh!" and laughter rippled through the van, even Moneymaker.

"Meals Ready to Eat!" Moneymaker said.

And they laughed even harder, too hard, before their paroxysms faded away into the truth of the moment.

Julia pulled the box down and stepped into it with her small boot, crushing out the last of the flare. "How about safety first, Seine."

"A bear is sticking its nose in here, I think scaring it off *is* safety first."

"Just don't light us on fire, 'kay?"

And that made Seine think about being lit on fire. He imagined how it would feel and in his flawed and frozen judgment thought burning would come as welcome relief. He looked up at the three chain saws sitting on the top shelf of the van, above the screws and nuts and pipe fittings, and all at once it hit him. He didn't know why he hadn't thought of it sooner except that he guessed he was running scared from ghosts, chasing Moneymaker and those like him. And there were a hundred just like him, and despite the real one sitting curled in a fetal ball ten feet away, Seine knew now that they were in fact all stacked up inside his own brain.

But inspiration came from odd places. He reached up, took the first chain saw, then grabbed a pickaroon from the corner and moved for the door. "What are you doing?" Julia asked, as if he'd lost it completely. It struck him how crazy he must have looked.

"I'm going do what I should have done two days ago. I'm going to burn the barge deck."

And they all looked at him as if he were a genius.

They left Moneymaker in the van, and Julia and Wanless backed Seine up, as they stepped outside carefully, spying around the van to check if the bear still lurked. Seine carried the chain saw at the ready, lighting it off just as soon as he stood on open deck. Julia held the flare gun two-handed, like a cop pointing a pistol, and scanned a three-sixty while Seine and Wanless stabbed with pickaroons and lifted a deck timber from its slot. Seine lopped off the end with the chain saw.

They cut blocks of Douglas fir until they had a good pile, set middeck amid the open sweep of the *Odyssey*. Wanless worked hard and without complaint. When the pile was big enough to light, Seine took the spare fuel can, doused the wood with the two-stroke fuel mixture, and torched it.

Wanless kept cutting wood while Seine retrieved Moneymaker from the van, and they sat warming themselves as the fire grew. They added more blocks of cut deck timbers, and finally Seine just dragged whole lengths of four-by-twelves onto the flames, until they had a bonfire that hissed and rippled and bent downwind.

They stayed on bear watch the entire time, but soon the fire was so large they just stood back, awed by its sound and the way the wind tried to kill the flames only to feed them instead. Flaw Island hovered there like a wall of white, and they warmed themselves, rubbing their hands together, until they heard overhead the sound of a C-130. "Coast Guard," Seine said. "No power for the radios."

And they sank into a gloom.

As Flaw Island rotated, they saw Moneymaker's camp, nestled against an ice ridge, curled with a radio antenna and a generator silent and dead, flickering in the firelight. They could see a torn and rumpled tent on the edge, where the island had broken apart. "We used to be up top," Moneymaker said, "up there, but when the crack split us in half I barely made it to the one side. I salvaged the radios and one battery. That's why I couldn't transmit constantly. It was hit or miss." His colleagues hadn't been so lucky. They were lost over the side when the island broke. "The bears started coming around," Moneymaker said. "Those who made it out didn't make it far."

Seine pulled up a block of wood and sat down on it, made a bench three blocks high and ten feet long, and all four of them—Moneymaker too—sat out there as if they'd come to roast marshmallows.

"This was a great idea," Wanless said.

They had a three-hundred-foot barge full of deck timbers to burn. Through the night, they burned maybe a quarter of it, and the next day broke clear and still, with a layer of ice fog, what trawlermen called white frost, stretching as far as they could see in all directions. It reached only to their waists, and they waded in it as if floating by their lower halves on an earthly cloud. The sun was a pale white disk, streaking along the horizon, and Seine had just begun to wonder if maybe they wouldn't have to go eat the Buff after all when he smelled diesel exhaust in the air. He stood up and, like the bear that probably still roamed somewhere in the fog, he sniffed the sky. "Diesel. You smell it?"

"I smell it!" Wanless screeched. "I do!"

And before long they heard the rumbling noise of diesel engines, and then a vessel's wheelhouse, swimming toward them through a pillowy white. No ghost ship this time, just work engines and an icebreaker—a big one, impressive, modern, dwarfing the *Odyssey*. The crew stood on the forward railing wearing float suits, shouting to them in gibberish that before long became Russian.

Seine ran toward the barge edge before he realized that he didn't know quite where the barge edge was. He stopped and waved his arms over his head. "Ahoy! *Do svidaniya! Iz venychie!*"

"You know Russian?" Julia asked Seine.

"Only those two phrases. I think they mean *good-bye* and *I'm doing fine.*" He laughed and looked back toward the ship, which swung along their port beam. "*Bruten yash pupadeanya schneaky!*" Seine yelled.

"Bruten, what? What's that mean?"

"Actually, that's from a commercial. For Brute cologne. It means *That Brute is sneaky stuff!*" and he laughed so hard he thought he'd cry.

Julia laughed too. "Seine. You're funny when you're happy. I've never seen you happy."

"I've never been happy!" he said, and laughed again.

Julia kissed him. Wanless jumped up and down and clapped, then flung himself onto them both, the crackle of Russian loudhailers moving through them like electricity.

TWENTY-FIVE

South by East

The Russian icebreaking tug *Vrangelya* had received the MAYDAY transmissions of Wolf Irons's last hours and broke ice for two days in their direction. She wound up a hearse too, worse than *Terror* had ever been. The skipper zigzagged through the blanket of white frost, picking blindly for three and a half hours until the fog layer finally broke and they saw the orange humped form of the Big Man out toward the north, and the Buff down below them, so close they'd almost run him over, his eyes frozen shut, his mouth frozen open.

To Seine's surprise he felt no superstition in hauling their bodies up and off the ice to the afterdeck. All the stories and the lore of sailors evaporated before the simple sadness, and a vague anger at Moneymaker that was both unreasonable and unsustainable.

Moneymaker felt responsible. He paced the afterdeck as they worked, saying, "Jesus! Jesus my God!" and holding his head. "What have I done? What have I done? I feel like hell about this. I can't tell you how absolutely horrible I feel about this." He looked with wide questioning eyes for forgiveness.

Seine understood the feeling and knew there wasn't a word he could say to remove it. They wrapped the frozen bodies in canvas and laid them out respectfully on the boat deck, where they would stay frozen for the trip to Barrow. After everybody else went inside, Seine stayed on the boat deck, sitting between the covered bodies of Buffy and the Big Man, and he patted the no-skid deck paint with his hand. Then finally he steeled himself and pulled the canvas back.

The Buff's face was frozen, eyes frosted closed, skin as white as the ice floes that had killed him. Seine reached into the Buff's pocket and pulled out a jangle of keys: house keys to the house that overlooked Lake Washington in green Seattle. He wanted to go home. He wanted to go home with Julia—and with Wanless too. He slid the keys into the pocket of his work jeans and felt Al George's quarter, which had worn a pale circle on the outside of his denim pocket.

He sat hugging his knees, eyes only peeking out to where the ice surrounded *Vrangelya,* stretching in all directions, spreading out in varying degrees of thickness and craggy as the surface of some alien planet. Ice screamed and exploded ahead of the tug and merged in a broken uniform wake of slush. The sky shone white, streaking east. Irons and the Old Woman rode bottom currents then; Seine knew from others lost overboard in the north how long it took for a body to decay in the cold and float up; by then they'd rise to the underside of some ice floe and merge with the ice.

In the offing, a polar bear stood on all fours, flat-footed, and watched the tug grind past. Then, as if fleeing the sound and terror of machinery, the white bear shambled west and north, bounding from floe to floe with a lumbering sort of grace.

Inside a guest cabin, they slept in separate bunks, all four of them snoring through a day and a night. When Seine awakened he would hear the squeal of ice work, of the slamming home, and he simply lay there listening, knowing it would soon pass.

In the galley, Seine and Julia and Wanless ate warm stew in a close huddle and afterward toured the boat with the captain himself, who spoke a convoluted English that made Seine think of the Big Man. He showed them around his vessel with garrulous pride. "She is new! Note it? Top navigation systems. Not like tug *Terror!*"

They stood three across in the wheelhouse as the tug broke its way on a southerly course, getting into a rhythm of rising and falling and rising and falling, the rumble of ice on the hull filtering up from below.

Seine gazed out and about the wheelhouse in a kind of ceaseless wonder. He felt resurrected. He wanted to clutch the feeling close to his skin, hold it in his mouth, click his teeth against it, make rebirth a part of himself forever. The captain laughed the hearty laugh of simplicity, of teeth and great eyes, and said, "You like frozen vodka? Ah?"

They didn't know what to do besides nod. What the hell else did you do with the person who had just saved your life? You celebrate, Seine thought. You hoist a frozen punctuation mark. The captain ducked out the side door to a box with holes in it like some kind of birdhouse, and out of it he produced a screw-top bottle of frozen Stolichnaya. In the wheelhouse itself the three hoisted heavy shot glasses of frozen vodka. The skipper cried, "To survival here! Bottom up!" and they shot the frozen liquid back to freeze their throats and set their bellies on fire.

"Where's Moneymaker?" Wanless wanted to know.

"He's in his bunk. He's feeling bad, I think, about the others. Responsible."

"What was he supposed to do?" Julia said. "He was lost, he needed help, so he called for help."

"Let me go get him," Seine said.

Seine scampered down the stairs, for reasons he couldn't define wanting Moneymaker there with them. It seemed only right, natural, necessary that they'd commune with the object of their mission, however failed or turned on its head it ended up being. He found him at the writing desk, wearing a pair of glasses that had been battered and scratched and bent. They looked just like the Chemist's before he'd lost them, except that Seine was suddenly taken by how much Moneymaker did look like himself. He saw the resemblance now. It was in the eyes. He recognized the lost stare, the worry, the burden of memory.

"Come topside," Seine said. "We're having a survival toast."

"Well, it sounds exquisite, but I'm not sure I'm up to it," Moneymaker said. "I'm trying to write this all down. I'm going to have one hell of a lot of explaining to do." He looked out the porthole at the passing pack ice. "For four months, all I've seen is ice. I feel so weak. A toast would finish me."

"Probably do the same to me. Just come on up. For one drink. He's Russian. He'll be insulted if you don't."

"If he's Russian he'll probably be glad—there's more left for him." He squinted at Seine, took off his glasses, and finally said, "Well, I suppose." Then he smiled. "I gather we have a few items to be grateful for, don't we, Henry. You don't mind if I call you Henry, do you?" And he let out a squirrelly laugh that made Seine smile and imagine him at faculty parties, wearing tweed jackets with elbow patches. Dr. Moneymaker.

"Not at all, Louis."

In the wheelhouse they stood around in a circle and the captain poured the frozen vodka. "Bottom up!"

"*Nastrovia,*" said Moneymaker, and belted it back.

They drank two more before the captain showed them the tug's billiard room, ignoring completely the absurdity of playing pool on a constantly shifting surface, piling all the balls on the center of the table, and watching as they clicked and rolled around in irregular circles influenced by the movement of the vessel. "Look! Look at them dance!" the skipper cried. "Like ballet of chance!"

They laughed as the balls bounced and disappeared into the pockets, finally, until there was only one left and it took that last ball a long time of meandering around until it finally found a pocket to settle in. Seine wondered if it was a Russian thing to have a pool table on an icebreaker. "How do you get an even surface?"

"No even surface! No such thing on boat! No such thing anywhere!"

"It's all chaos when you look at it," said Moneymaker, gazing at the pool balls as if at the starkness of human tragedy.

TWENTY-SIX

Warm Rain

S eine had always looked forward to the trip south, the closing of
the circle: hush of airline jets, forced air, the Anchor Town bar.
Moneymaker flew from Anchorage to Vancouver, B.C., disappearing
down the metal airline chute with not one but three backward glances
and nods, an unknown quantity of frozen vodka glowing inside him.
After that, Seine held tight to his shipmates, his last shipmates. They
craved things as a threesome, craved earth and rain, craved each other
in ways that none of them could name.

Seattle rose to meet them, reached up like a mom and plucked
them from the airliner and held them inside the canned noise and
kerosene exhaust of Sea-Tac Airport. For reasons none of them understood they went to yet another airport bar, a little alcove drinking center, not because they liked airports, not because they needed another
drink certainly, but because, without knowing it, they each wanted to
hold on to the image of their own survival. They wanted to see normal
people, business travelers, families of five come to see Dad mount the
gangway, arms open. They wanted to see lovers part in tears and re-
unite seconds later in still more tears. You could find it all in an airport, Seine thought. If you sat there long enough you saw the whole
world cycle past.

But doing it together meant they held the secret between them; together they were survivors, could reach a hand out to a nearby witness and say, You are alive, I am breathing, and our mutual witnessing of the fact makes it real. He knew the feeling; it was always the same in Seattle, except that now he had no home. He patted the keys in his pocket and remembered the Buff.

"What should we do?" Wanless asked.

"Go home, I guess," said Julia, distantly.

"Seems like not enough somehow," said Wanless.

"I have no home," Seine said. "So to me it sounds like either too much or not enough, I'm not sure which."

Julia laughed. "Seine, you're funny. How come I never knew that?"

"Mostly because we didn't talk much that first time."

"True."

"We could go buy a bottle of Stoli and go over to my apartment," Wanless said. "I got a freezer. My roommate probably thinks I'm lost at sea by now. It'll be like returning from the dead."

"I have a better idea," Seine said.

In reality, it was nothing so abstract as an idea or so concrete as a plan of action, but a ragged claw lifting itself inch by inch up the inside of his chest since Anchorage, born partly of the wonderment of the home he didn't have and partly of the need to remember. He couldn't get the Buff out of his mind, and he didn't want these two to leave him yet. He had no idea where he would go when they did.

He felt a push on his shoulder. Julia. Seattle. Wanless. The Buff: the aching terrible crushing death of a man he'd often disliked and almost always feared. Now he felt a strange affection, an aching loss.

"So what's your idea, Henry?" Julia asked.

He said nothing, just held up the keys.

*   *   *

Outside Sea-Tac, the world was all green hillsides and buses that sent him on a diesel flashback to the smell of a towboat afterdeck cruising on clear water. Seine missed the bleak arctic already, unable to bear the beauty of Seattle. The fir trees and the cedar scent and the long low shadows of northern autumn pierced his heart.

He smiled though his eyes burned, laughed in a way that sounded like crying, and then breathed in, filling his entire body with fresh air. "Have you ever tasted air like this in your life?" he said.

Julia shook her head. "Never," she said. "Never like this, and I've lived here since I was three."

Stuart Wanless looked too stunned to reply. He just stared around as if seeing earth for the first time. "It's warm," he said. "It's warm."

And moist. The air held them close, like home.

North up I-5, Rainier loomed in the rearview, clouds beckoned but did not threaten. Seine drove a rental car, zigged and zagged and looped uphill toward the Buff's house. "He wouldn't mind," Seine said. "He'd like it we hoisted a few to his memory, you know."

"Yeah, he would," Julia said, smiling. "I keep thinking of him in that tool van there on the *Odyssey* before he went over. Damn." She shook her head, as if searching for a way to describe or make sense of the Buff. "He was such a pig," she said, "but—"

She fell silent, shrugging, what the hell.

"You mean he was such a pig, but . . . or such a pig butt?" Seine wondered.

Julia let out a bursting laugh. "Both!"

They stopped for some beer at a 7-Eleven, and drove uphill again. Built in the forties, Buffy Errol's house rose two stories on a split-level lot, with steep concrete stairs up the front and a wide concrete porch where Halloween decorations from last year still hung from the rafters: a black widow amid a cluster of fake cobwebs, a jack-o'-lantern that looked eerily like the Buff himself.

Inside, the house smelled a pleasant kind of musty, just as Seine's childhood home had after a two-week vacation. Seine loved those vacations. They were the only time all year he wasn't on the water. They'd drive inland, see dust and dry air, stay at a different motel every night, and return home to open the windows and let the moist ocean air inside.

They did that now. Seine felt like a trespasser in the Buff's life, didn't want to look too long at anything. Didn't want to judge anybody anymore, even himself. The cool air of pre-storm Seattle drifted into the second story.

Out the back spread Lake Washington, like a giant liquid emerald. Seine decided then on the rightness of not finding Irons, of leaving him to Rottingmule. The company could divest themselves of Arctic Ops, but Irons couldn't.

The three of them stood in the Buff's backyard, before a circular wading pool, ten feet in diameter and two-feet deep—but empty.

"I don't know," said Julia. "It seems kind of . . . like robbing the dead, you know."

"I know. What the fuck. We can always just leave it there."

"Oh, yeah, right," said Wanless. "We'll leave it there and let the estate attorneys take it as their commission for selling the house."

"It's my house. He gave it to me."

"Yeah, like that'll hold up in court."

They slid the hard plastic wading pool from its position on the back lawn, revealing circular patches of glowing yellow grass. "You think it's down there?" Julia said.

"I don't know. You never know. Look at Muktuk Island. Nothing was down there."

Seine spiked the circles of turf with a gardening tool, and pulled the grass up. The smell of turf brought to mind high school football, Friday nights bursting with exuberant hope.

Beneath the circles of sod lay the lids of coffee cans. And when they opened them up, there was nothing there at all, just empty rusted coffee cans. The three stood upright and shook their heads, staring at one another with smiles twisting their mouths.

"Look! A hundred thousand dollars!" Seine shouted.

And they all laughed.

"The earth ate his money," Julia said.

"I'm glad it's not there. I'd feel like way too guilty and then I'd hate myself for giving it back."

Without a word they slid the wading pool back into position, and with a hose connected to the nearby laundry room they filled it with hot water. Seine called it a Buffy Errol hot tub, and then they were naked, sliding themselves into the warmth of the wading pool, sinking until they were submerged to their chins, feet meeting at the pool's middle, sitting under rain that misted out of Seattle skies; and out to the east the luster of Lake Washington lay still like a gray-green mirror. And Julia's hand slipped into Seine's, the outline of her mouth reflected back on itself as she kissed the water's surface. She closed her eyes and murmured softly. "It's warm," she said.

"Dude! It is like *so* warm right now!" Wanless said, and Seine laughed so hard he thought he might pee in the pool.

They all three giggled with eyes closed, soft laughter rolling like waves to a sandy shore. Their shoulders bounced quietly, quivers passing through their bodies and rippling the rain-speckled water. Seine traced his toe up the soft slippery leg of Julia Lew. He tipped his head backward, opened his mouth to let out the boiling unstoppable joy, and felt the warm Washington rain tapping his tongue.

ACKNOWLEDGMENTS

I am indebted to so many people whose lives and careers and stories contributed to the crafting of this book, that it is fairly impossible to list them all. First my own gone shipmates, dead and alive; those I wish could have lived to see this book: Roy Sjogren, Jim Jerome, Beverly Charles, Chris Reault, Joseph Masiel; and cohorts from Alaskan waters, better men than I. Swan, Schmarr, Iles, Baron, Z, Rommie, Jim Bowman, Mr. Ooey, Jeff Salenjus, Tom Eddy, Darold Anderson, and last but not least, Bill Payne—for putting up with me and teaching me more than they ever realized.

My parents, Richard and Valerie Masiel, for their unyielding sense of ethics—work and otherwise—and for nurturing dreams just enough to give me a sense of optimism in the face of all evidence to the contrary.

My wife, Dawn Yackzan, for her superhuman patience and loyalty and hard work that enabled me to carve out the time from teaching high school English to write this book; her countless readings of early drafts and portions of the manuscript were invaluable, as always.

My children, Emily and Jackson, who in their love and trust and vulnerability have, without knowing it, taught me about fundamental realities.

Morwenna Robinson Yackzan, the best mother-in-law anyone could hope for, and the reason I eschew mother-in-law jokes.

My high school English teacher, Ed Hewitson, who once told me that only fools became writers, and who probably doesn't even remember who I am, much less that he told me that.

To all my faculty colleagues and former students at Sacramento Country Day School, who in their lofty expectations and constant intellectual searching conspired to give me the gift of a literary education.

My friend Robert Clark Young for his refusal to allow me to give up on myself as a novelist, and his insistence that I listen to no one but him when it came to the opening scene.

To my friend Scott Phillips I owe a debt of incalculable gratitude for his faith in this book and his tireless help in finding others who might share that faith.

To my editors, Courtney Hodell and Tim Farrell at Random House, for pressing the pursuit of the best possible *2182*; for their insightful readings, questions, and commentaries.

And finally to my agent, Nicole Aragi, without whose passion and brilliance and stubbornness I would still be circulating loose-leaf manuscripts to friends instead of insisting that they buy this book.

DAVID MASIEL was born in Oakland, California, and grew up in Richmond, where he used to sit at an old Formica-topped table and listen to his grandfather's stories of rogues, riverboats, sailors, and the sea. He has worked as a golf instructor, a maintenance man, an English teacher, and an oilfield laborer. For ten years he worked as a merchant seaman on oceangoing tugboats and icebreakers from Seattle to Barter Island, Alaska. During that time he earned an M.A. in creative writing from the University of California at Davis. He now lives in Davis, California, with his wife and their two children.